Voices from the Dead

Also by Tony Bassett

DETECTIVES ROY AND ROSCOE
Book 1: Murder on Oxford Lane
Book 2: The Crossbow Stalker
Book 3: Murder of a Doctor
Book 4: Out for Revenge
Book 5: Heir to Murder
Book 6: It Never Rains
Book 7: Not My Valentine
Book 8: Voices from the Dead

STANDALONE
Seat 97

VOICES FROM THE DEAD

Detectives Roy and Roscoe Book 8

Tony Bassett

THE BOOK FOLKS

The Books Folks
A Joffe Books Company
www.thebookfolks.com

First published in Great Britain in 2025

ISBN: 978-1-80462-360-2

Scitote quoniam peccatum vestrum adprehendet vos
Be sure your sin will find you out (Numbers 32:23)

Chapter 1

Cynthia Ecclestone had always considered herself an outgoing and convivial party animal.

But after two hours at her great-nephew's celebration, she felt sure the description no longer suited her.

At the age of seventy-six, she was glad to have been invited to help mark his thirtieth birthday at the modern, town centre hotel. She would have been annoyed if her name had been omitted from the invitation list sent out two months earlier. But she could feel a migraine on the way and could not stand any more of the electronic sounds and heavy bass that young people regarded as music these days. She was also finding it increasingly difficult to hold a conversation with the other guests.

So she waited until the lad had blown out the candles on his cake – nearly singeing his eyebrows in the process – before making excuses to her niece.

'I think I'm going to go up to my room now, Angela,' she said.

'You're not leaving already, are you? You've come all this way,' her niece replied.

'I'm sorry. It's been lovely catching up with everyone,' said Cynthia, brushing cake crumbs from her pale-green dress, 'but I can feel one of my headaches coming on.'

'All right,' said Angela. 'But don't forget you and Mum are coming over to our place tonight.'

'I'm looking forward to it,' said Cynthia, trying her best to sound sincere. 'I've already got the taxi booked to pick me up here at eight o'clock.'

She kissed her niece on the cheek before making her way out of the function room with its high ceilings, soft lighting and luxurious furnishings.

The retired nurse, who was short and slightly overweight despite her best efforts to diet, heaved a sigh of relief as she approached the hotel's main reception area. The sounds of the raucous revellers and deafening music were fading into the distance.

'My party animal must have gone into permanent hibernation,' she muttered while waiting for a lift to arrive.

She quickly forgot the boisterous behaviour of the younger family members as she unlocked her room just after four o'clock. She stepped inside and slumped down onto her bed with its Egyptian cotton sheets and blankets.

Exhausted and replete after the three-course meal she ate earlier, she felt completely relaxed. She was looking forward to a quieter evening with Angela and her husband, and perhaps watching an ABBA concert on television.

The couple had invited her for drinks and a light meal at their cottage in the nearby village of Norton Prior. This would be her first serious opportunity to catch up with all the latest news and gossip in the McEwan family. Why was Simon, the birthday boy, still single as he entered his thirtieth year? How was Simon's sister, Leanne, enjoying married life? How was Angela coping since her husband, Andrew, had confessed to having a mistress and made a firm commitment to give up the woman?

It was past six o'clock when Cynthia stirred from her bed and glanced at her watch, which she had earlier taken off and placed on her bedside table beside her grey clutch bag.

'I must have fallen asleep,' she muttered.

She sat up and looked around. 'Something must have woken me,' she decided.

Perhaps a noise from somewhere had roused her from her slumber in the plush, four-star hotel. Maybe it was a shout or a peel of laughter from the courtyard below.

'It's just as well,' she told herself, glancing at her watch. 'I must get ready for tonight.'

But, before going to the wardrobe to find her outfit, she strolled to the patio door and tugged it open. It had been a glorious May afternoon. She ventured outside where she was greeted by a gentle breeze. For several minutes, she stood there, enjoying the warmth of the evening, closing her eyes and imagining for a moment she was basking in the sun's rays on a beach in the south of France.

The balcony provided breathtaking views across the Warwickshire town of Queensbridge. She gazed out across the tiled and slated roofs of the shops and houses. She could even make out some hills in the distance, which resembled folds or creases in a vast verdant blanket.

Then she leaned over the small balcony and peered down. To confirm her suspicions about her awakening, a crowd of customers were huddled round outdoor tables in the courtyard, chatting and laughing beneath giant, fawn-coloured umbrellas.

She turned towards the left, where a modern, three-storey extension jutted out from the side of the seventeenth-century building.

It was only then that she noticed the couple. They were standing together in the third window along, which was level with her balcony and only a few metres away. She peered at them.

The woman, in her late twenties, seemed to have a svelte figure. It was hard to tell. She had long, blonde, flowing hair and was wearing a white crop top with a revealing, bright-red flared pants suit. There was a defiant, truculent expression on her attractive face.

The man was wearing a check shirt. His hair was dark, but she could not judge his age as she was unable to see his face. He constantly had his back to her and was partly hidden by the curtain.

At first, they appeared to be arguing. The woman bore a fierce expression and was evidently shouting.

The man slunk away from the woman briefly then, unexpectedly, as Cynthia watched in horror, his arms reached out from behind the left curtain. He thrust the young woman against the wall and, in the next moment, had a twisted towel in his hands. He pushed her into the far corner by the window and wrapped it tightly round her neck.

Cynthia's heart was pounding and her breath coming in short gasps. Her hands were shaking. She was consumed by an overwhelming sense of fear. But she continued to watch, transfixed, as if beguiled by a witch's spell.

Surely the man must realise he can be seen, thought Cynthia. He was standing so close to the window. For all she knew, other hotel guests might have been watching the attack from their rooms as well. Perhaps the brute was so absorbed by his actions, she supposed, that he had no fear of being observed.

The attacker clamped the towel round his victim's throat for several more seconds until the ashen-faced woman seemed to pass out and slipped from view.

Cynthia rushed to her bedside table and dialled the concierge desk on her room phone.

'Come on. Come on,' she pleaded as precious seconds ticked by.

At last, the receptionist answered.

'This is Mrs Ecclestone,' she said. She was so overwrought that she was struggling to think of the right words to say. 'I'm in Room 203. Please call the police quickly. I think a woman's being murdered.'

Chapter 2

The hotel receptionist in a navy-blue suit gave a gentle smile as Sunita Roy approached his desk.

'I wanted to check what time breakfast is served in the morning,' she said.

He raised his right finger as a signal for her to wait a moment while he picked up his desk phone.

'Reception. Can I help?' he asked the caller.

Sunita was joined at the counter by her partner, Tom Vickers.

'Come on, Sunita,' he urged her. 'We can find out the breakfast times later.'

'Don't be so impatient,' she replied, glancing towards him and cleaning some dust off her pale-pink sari. 'This should only take a second.'

She turned her attention back to the ginger-haired man at the desk who was still speaking on his handset.

'Please try and calm down, madam,' he was saying. 'You say you were on your balcony and saw someone being attacked. When did this happen? … A minute ago? … Yes, madam. I'll call the police in a moment. I think that perhaps I ought to come up to your room and talk to you first.'

He shook his head. He bore the look of a man reaching the end of a long shift and eager to get home.

'You're in Room 203 – is that right? … Stay right there and I'll be with you.'

After hanging up the phone, he looked up at Sunita, a slim woman of thirty-one with silky, black, flowing hair and striking dark eyes.

'Sorry, madam,' he said, hoisting himself up from his stool. 'I've got an emergency.'

'I couldn't help overhearing that call,' said Sunita. 'We're actually off-duty police officers.'

She produced her warrant card from her handbag to show the man, who was wearing a lapel badge saying, 'Justin Hemming – Assistant Manager'.

He nodded. 'Just at the right time,' he remarked.

After alerting a colleague in a back room to monitor the desk, he accompanied the two detectives to the second floor.

'You're with the wedding party, aren't you?' he asked as the lift began to ascend.

'That's right,' she replied.

'I thought so,' he said. The lift shuddered to a halt and they got out.

Hemming turned right on the landing before revealing that Room 203 was in the old, original part of the hotel building. It was the second one on the left along the corridor. A grey-haired lady was standing by the open door.

'Mrs Ecclestone?' Hemming asked her.

'Yes,' said Cynthia, who was shaking her head and looking agitated. 'I was just standing on my balcony and saw a woman being strangled with a white towel. If you're quick, you may be in time to save her. I'm a retired nurse. I know how vital speed can be in matters like this.'

'Where was the woman?'

'She was standing by the third window along in the new part of the building,' said Cynthia. 'If you come over here, I'll show you the window.'

'Are you sure the man hadn't just passed her the towel so she could take a shower?' said Hemming. 'People often put towels round their shoulders before going to wash.'

'I know what I saw, and I saw a man strangling the woman,' Cynthia insisted.

'All right. Show us the window. This couple are police officers, by the way, who happen to be staying in the hotel,' he quickly explained.

The visitors followed Cynthia past the en suite bathroom into the classic room with its king-size bed, wall tapestries and period furniture.

'Here you are,' she said, stepping across the parquet floor and opening the patio door.

Hemming joined her on the balcony as she pointed out the third window.

'I'm pretty sure that's Room 224,' he said.

'I'm DS Roy from Heart of England Police,' Sunita told Cynthia. 'This is DI Vickers. When did this happen?'

'Three minutes ago. Please hurry,' she replied. 'There might be time to save the poor woman.'

Hemming and the two detectives retraced their steps to the lift and then the duty manager led them across the landing into the hotel's new extension. They stopped in the corridor outside the third door on the right.

'This is it. Room 224,' he said, tapping on the door. After a few seconds, he removed a keycard from his pocket and opened it.

The room, which was light, airy and decorated in a more contemporary style than Cynthia's, was strangely quiet.

'Hello,' Hemming called. 'Anyone here?'

Nothing stirred.

'Do you want to go in?' he asked his companions. 'Looks like the room's empty, but you never know.'

Tom Vickers, an amiable detective inspector who was slightly overweight with short, brown hair, stepped gingerly inside, glancing to the left and right as he proceeded.

'There's no one here,' he remarked, venturing as far as the foot of the king-size bed, which was strewn with women's clothing. He glanced across to the double-glazed picture window, where a closed suitcase stood. A soft drink can and a glass tumbler could be seen in the centre of the low-level sideboard.

'Oh God. What a waste of time,' Hemming complained. 'These old biddies with their vivid imaginations. I could have done without this. I'm due off at seven.'

The assistant manager took out his mobile phone and dialled a number as the detectives gazed round the room. He stood quietly, his head bowed. Sunita thought he resembled a priest about to hear a confession. Then a woman's voice answered.

'Eileen, who's booked into Room 224?' he asked. 'Can you have a look?'

After a brief pause, a buzzing noise signalled that Hemming's colleague had given her reply.

'How many nights were they booked in for?' he asked.

He listened to her response and then hung up.

'It's a couple and we've got the surname Goodhope. They were booked in for last night and tonight,' he told them.

'So where are they?' said Vickers. 'I imagine you've got both their mobile numbers?'

Hemming nodded his head.

'Yes, we'll have them down at reception. I think Mrs Ecclestone's imagination's run away with her. She probably saw Mrs Goodhope holding up various outfits by the window and falsely assumed she was being assaulted. That's all I can think.'

'So has the woman got changed and gone out again?' Vickers asked.

'Probably. Yes, I imagine she's out enjoying herself, which is what that lady in Room 203 should be doing – instead of cooking up wild stories we have to deal with.' He paused for a moment.

'Candy Goodhope,' Hemming continued. 'Now I come to think of it, I do seem to remember a rather pretty woman with long, wavy hair who arrived last night. She said she was from Gloucester and had come to Queensbridge to meet someone. Eileen was dealing with her. I don't remember seeing the husband.'

'Maybe he was parking their car,' Sunita suggested. 'She didn't say why they were in the town?'

'Just to visit friends, I think,' he said. 'People stay here for a wide variety of reasons. For weddings, hen parties, birthdays – all sorts of events. How was the wedding today?'

'Absolutely fine,' said Sunita.

'I was best man,' said Vickers. 'I'm pleased to say my speech went down very well earlier on.'

'The bride and groom are holding a dance in the ballroom this evening, aren't they?' said Hemming.

'Yes, that reminds me,' said Vickers, 'we'd better get down there. Gary and Selena will be wondering where we are.'

'Better just check the room thoroughly,' said Sunita. 'We haven't tried the en suite.'

'I'll do that,' said Vickers, spinning round and poking his head inside the marble bathroom.

Sunita stepped past Hemming and made her way to the window. Nothing seemed out of the ordinary. A little light dust had settled on the window ledge and a brown circular mark was visible where a cup had been placed. The beige curtains hung neatly from either side of the window.

Then she turned round and gasped in horror. Blonde tresses of hair were protruding from beneath the bed.

Chapter 3

Tom Vickers wasted no time in taking charge of the situation. He explained to Justin Hemming it was imperative that the corpse should not be disturbed for fear of destroying any evidence. However, so they could make an initial assessment, he asked them both to help him lift the bed away from the body.

Sunita gazed down at the motionless form stretched out on the timber floor. The victim's face was feminine and attractive. Her hazel eyes were open and lifeless.

A tangled white towel was curled around her upper torso, but Sunita could clearly see a horizontal ligature mark encircling the neck. The skin round her throat was bruised and speckled with blood.

The blonde-haired woman was wearing a white, cotton top with a full-length pair of red flared pants.

'That's her,' Hemming shouted in amazement. 'That's the woman from Gloucester. I recognise her hair.'

They stood close to the body, peering down.

'It doesn't matter how many times we see a dead body in our work, Tom,' said Sunita, 'it doesn't get any easier.'

'No, it doesn't,' he agreed.

'I need to get out,' she said, brushing past the two men.

Vickers was concerned to see his partner in distress. He ushered the assistant manager out into the corridor, closing the door behind them. Then he attended to Sunita, who was crouching on the carpet, visibly upset.

'Are you all right?' he asked.

Highly embarrassed, she raised her head and nodded.

'Yes. It was just a bit stuffy in there,' she replied.

He turned his attention away from her.

'Justin, could you go back to reception and stop anyone from leaving or entering the building for the moment? We'll also need a keycard for this room, which must be kept locked until officers get here.'

As Hemming took the lift downstairs, Vickers slipped his phone from his pocket and called his force control.

'So Mrs Ecclestone was right,' said Sunita after he ended his call. She hauled herself up from the floor, deeply regretting that the sight of the corpse had left her queasy.

'Yes,' Vickers said. 'We'll have to take a full statement from her. I'll also let the DCI know.'

* * *

Less than an hour later, the hotel was swarming with police and scenes-of-crime staff. The irate general manager of the hotel, notified by Hemming, confronted Vickers, claiming all the restrictions on guests coming and going was disrupting his business.

But the inspector quickly pointed out the importance of maintaining the integrity of the scene. A suspected murder investigation was under way. If he wished to make an official complaint, he should raise the matter with his boss, Detective Chief Inspector Gavin Roscoe, who was head of CID and due to arrive imminently.

Half an hour passed in which hordes of chattering guests were questioned and asked to provide personal details to police. Then, just before a quarter past seven, the chief inspector arrived.

'Tom!' said Roscoe as he weaved his way past groups of guests and greeted his colleague near the reception desk. 'I'd forgotten about your friend's wedding. You look very smart.'

'Thanks, guv,' said Vickers as the chief inspector ruffled the orange flower in his lapel.

'So, what do we know about this woman who was attacked?'

'Not a great deal at present,' said Vickers. 'Her name's Candy Goodhope and she lives in Gloucester. She runs a chain of beauty salons.'

'Was she staying in the hotel on her own?' asked Roscoe.

'No, guv. She's listed on the register as staying here with her husband, but he hasn't been around since we found the body under the bed.'

'It's urgent we find him.'

Roscoe, a tall, stout, genial man, said he had been informed about a sharp-eyed lady called Cynthia Ecclestone.

'That's right, guv. Mrs Ecclestone was round the corner from Room 203 and saw the attack take place.'

Roscoe frowned. He remained stoically composed. By good luck, an eyewitness had unexpectedly been on hand. This might be of great benefit to them.

'No description of the attacker, I suppose?' he said.

'Not much detail to go on, guv.'

'There never is,' he said cynically. 'And where's DS Roy right now?'

'She's with Mrs Ecclestone at the moment, trying to get as much information as she can,' Vickers replied. 'By the way, guv, up until now, we've stopped guests from leaving the premises. But I believe we've got all the names and addresses now. PC Underhill and his colleagues have been round, so…'

'Yes. There's no necessity to hold everyone up. Let them all go, if they wish. I hear it's been quite hectic here today.'

'Yes, guv. What with the wedding of my pal Gary and somebody's thirtieth birthday party. It's been manic.'

'Tom, we ought to have a word with the hotel manager and get hold of their CCTV footage.'

'No problem, guv. That's all in hand.'

'I must say it's very handy that you and DS Roy were here on the spot as it happened,' said Roscoe. 'We need a statement from the assistant manager – Justin someone, wasn't it?'

'That's right, guv. Justin Hemming.'

'I'll get DC Dawson to do that when he gets here.'

'Hemming is desperate to go home, guv,' Vickers pointed out.

'I'm sure he is,' said Roscoe, 'but the investigation comes first. The main priority now is to find the husband. Any idea of his full name?'

Vickers shook his head.

'I'll get it from the hotel register, guv.'

'We need to treat him with kid gloves, obviously,' said Roscoe. 'He's just lost his missus in a savage and brutal way and we can expect he's going to be devastated – or, at least, react as though he's devastated. By the same token, a witness has seen a man attacking the victim inside her room. So, as far as we're concerned, until we've spoken to him and been able to eliminate him, he's bound to be one of our principal suspects.'

Chapter 4

Now fully recovered after the unsettling episode of discovering Candy Goodhope's body, Sunita Roy knocked on Cynthia Ecclestone's door.

'Oh, it's you,' said Cynthia as she greeted her visitor. 'DS Roy, isn't it?'

'That's right,' said Sunita. 'I need to ask you more about what you saw.'

'You'd better come in,' said Cynthia, looking elegant after changing into a blue cardigan and grey pleated skirt. 'Did you find the poor woman?'

'Yes. Sadly, we weren't in time.'

'Oh my God. You mean she's dead?' said Cynthia. 'That's terrible. I'll have to sit down.'

The detective cast her eyes around as she followed Cynthia inside. A women's magazine and some knitting lay on the low-level sideboard. A kettle was boiling in the corner.

Cynthia sat down on her bed and reached for a tissue from a box on a bedside cabinet. She wiped away a tear that had formed in one of her eyes while the sergeant sat down in the room's single armchair. The kettle, now boiled, switched itself off with a click.

'I suppose you can't tell me who the woman was?' she asked.

Sunita shook her head.

'I'm sorry, no. To be honest, the family haven't been informed yet, and the body will have to be identified officially before we can release a name anyway.'

'You know, I came here for the weekend expecting a relaxing break, meeting the family and enjoying my time in one of the leading hotels in Queensbridge,' said Cynthia. 'I had to make my excuses after my great-nephew's party got out of hand, and then here I am witnessing a murder. I'm due to visit some of my relatives in an hour's time, but I don't know if I'm going to be up to it.'

Sunita leaned forward in her chair and nodded sympathetically.

'Seeing that lady being attacked clearly came as a great shock to you,' she said. 'I completely understand. I've been upset myself over what happened.'

'Where are my manners?' said Cynthia, suddenly perking up. 'I was just in the process of making some tea. Would you like some?'

Sunita nodded.

'That's nice of you. No milk and no sugar,' she replied.

'So you found the woman?' said Cynthia while using two mugs to make the hot drinks.

'Yes.'

'And what about the man?'

'There was no one else in the room when we got there,' said Sunita. 'Mrs Ecclestone, I'm afraid we're going to have to ask you about what you saw. We're going to need every little detail.'

'Oh dear,' said Cynthia. 'I've really been trying to erase the memory.'

She handed her visitor a mug of tea, placed her own mug on the sideboard and resumed her place on the bed.

'What caused you to go out onto your balcony this evening?' asked Sunita, slipping a small notebook from her pocket.

'To be honest, I'd had a couple of small glasses of wine at the birthday party in the function room,' Cynthia explained, briefly breaking into a smile. 'That, coupled with my long journey down from Leeds, must have contributed to my feeling tired. I came up here and had a little nap. Then some noise from the courtyard woke me up at a few minutes past six.'

'You're sure of the time?'

'Yes. I looked at my watch. I wandered outside and glanced down at all the people drinking in the courtyard. Then I gazed around and happened to notice the woman in the window.'

'So what time would this have been?'

'About ten past six,' said Cynthia.

'Can you describe exactly what you saw?' asked Sunita, taking a sip of her tea.

'Yes. I'll never forget her face.'

She paused fleetingly while the horrifying memory of the attack played out in her mind, like a clip from a horror film.

'She was in her twenties,' the old lady continued. 'She had long blonde hair. She had a white top and red trousers. She was talking to a man with short, dark hair and looked extremely annoyed with him. I thought she might have been shouting.'

'Can you tell me more about the man?'

'I didn't see much of him. A curtain was in the way part of the time, but he was a white man. Caucasian, they call it, don't they? About the same height as the woman. He had a check shirt.'

'Short-sleeved?'

'Yes.'

'Any idea of his age?'

Cynthia shook her head.

‘What actually happened?’ asked Sunita after taking another sip of her steaming drink.

‘The man knocked the woman against the wall by the window. It must have been so painful for her. Then he suddenly produced a white towel. I watched as he wrapped this tangled towel round the woman’s throat and began to choke her. Oh my God. It was terrible. She had such a look of horror on her face. I’ll never forget it as long as I live.’

‘What do you remember next?’

‘Well, the woman vanished from view. I’m guessing she collapsed on the floor.’

‘Did you see the man after that?’

‘No.’

‘This might seem a strange question,’ said Sunita, ‘but do you have any idea who the couple were?’

‘No.’

‘I mean, you hadn’t seen the woman around the hotel? At the birthday party? Hanging around in reception?’

‘No. I’d never seen her before. I certainly hope I don’t ever come across that man, I can tell you. He was so brazen. How can you behave like that when you’re standing in a window? He didn’t seem bothered at all that there was a risk of being seen. I wouldn’t be surprised if a guest from another room witnessed what happened, or someone from the courtyard.’

Sunita shrugged her shoulders.

‘The people in the courtyard probably couldn’t have seen anything because of those giant umbrellas screening them from the sun,’ she told Cynthia. ‘But I suppose it’s possible another guest in one of the bedrooms might have seen something. Listen, we’re mostly concerned now about the man you saw.’

‘Yes, well, that’s the problem,’ said Cynthia. ‘He was behind the curtain.’

She paused for a moment before clasping her hands to her face.

'Oh my God! A terrible thought's just occurred to me,' she said. 'If the man gets to know I had a ringside view of the attack, maybe he'll come after me.'

Sunita shook her head. She reached across to Cynthia and patted her arm.

'No, that's not going to happen,' she assured her. 'Everything you've told us is totally confidential. You haven't told anyone, have you? About what you saw?'

'Only my niece, Angela,' she replied.

'If it's not too late, best to tell her to keep mum about that.'

'Yes, but if and when you catch that man, it's all going to come out, anyway.'

'Don't worry. We'll do our utmost to protect you,' said Sunita, although she was aware Cynthia's anonymity might become an issue at some point in the future.

Eager to steer the conversation away from the witness's worries, Sunita asked, 'Do you remember anything else about the man? The slightest thing might help us. How would you describe the way his hair was styled at the back? Was it a classic taper, an ears-level fade, a blocked style, a rounded taper, an undercut fade or a low taper?'

'Good Lord. I hadn't realised there were so many different styles.'

'I'm studying for a police exam and spent a couple of days last week studying hairstyles.'

'Well,' said Cynthia, 'as I say, I only caught a couple of quick glimpses. I really couldn't describe the back of the man's head.'

'Did he have any distinguishing marks?' asked Sunita. 'Any tattoos? Any signs of wearing glasses? Prominent ears? A missing finger?'

'My word. You have to think of everything in your job, don't you?' said Cynthia, sipping her tea. 'No. I don't recall anything like that.'

'What about a mole, birthmark or scar?'

The old lady shook her head.

'No. I wasn't close enough to see. But one thing that stood out for me was he had rather large hands – well, larger than the woman's anyway. And he had a gold ring on one of the fingers on his right hand.'

Chapter 5

Having parked his black Tesla Model 3 in the hotel car park, Jack Bayliss walked round to the front of the hotel and was surprised to see four police vehicles outside in the blue-and-yellow livery of Heart of England Police.

He was about to push his way through the revolving doors when one of three officers on duty stopped him in his tracks.

'Not so fast, chum,' said the stern-faced young policeman. 'We're checking everyone who's going in. Got any ID?'

The fair-haired journalist took his press card from his pocket and presented it.

'What's happened?' he asked.

'That's fine,' said the constable after studying the card. 'There's been an incident inside the hotel.'

'What sort of incident?'

'You know the rules. You'd better speak to our media office.'

The puzzled hotel guest proceeded through the doors and headed for the reception desk. Two broad-shouldered men in suits that he assumed might be detectives were holding a conversation at the end of the counter.

'I've been away for a few hours,' he explained to the dark-haired woman behind the desk. 'I was wondering what's happened.'

'There's been a serious incident,' the woman said. 'I can't say more than that. What room are you in?'

'I think it's 224. I left the keycard with my partner,' he said.

The receptionist stiffened.

'I think you need to speak to these gentlemen, sir,' she suggested. 'They're the police.'

'Oh my God,' said Bayliss. 'You don't mean something's happened to Candy?'

Gavin Roscoe, who was with Tom Vickers, overheard the last part of the conversation.

'Are you Mr Goodhope, by any chance?' he said.

'No,' said the journalist. 'My name's Bayliss – Jack Bayliss – but I've been staying here with Candy Goodhope. Has something happened to her?'

The woman behind the desk, whose name tag bore the name 'Eileen', said, 'Mr Roscoe, would you like to use the manager's office? It's free at the moment.'

'Good idea,' said Roscoe. 'Mr Bayliss, would you like to come with us? And I'll explain what's happened.'

Just then, the constable who'd spoken to Bayliss at the door approached Roscoe. He stepped back from the desk while the officer whispered a few words to him. The chief inspector then rejoined his colleague.

Eileen opened a hatch in the counter and led the three men into a small, cluttered office, which contained a writing bureau and three chairs.

'Mr Bayliss, I'm DCI Roscoe. This is my colleague DI Vickers,' said the chief inspector with a frown. 'I've just been informed you're a journalist. Is that correct?'

'Yes,' said Bayliss, 'but I'm not on a job at the moment.'

'You've been staying at the hotel in Room 224 with Candy Goodhope, is that right?' said Roscoe as they all sat down.

The anxious man nodded. 'Yes. Is she OK?'

'No easy way to say this,' said Roscoe. 'She's been found dead.'

'Oh, for Christ's sake. I was with her only a few hours ago,' said Bayliss, becoming pale. He stepped round in a circle, shaking his head repeatedly, while the detectives sat down. 'How the hell did this happen?'

'Before we go any further, what's your relationship with Mrs Goodhope?' asked Roscoe.

Briefly, the man appeared embarrassed.

'I'm Candy's boyfriend,' he said.

Roscoe stroked his chin. Bayliss noticed the confusion in his eyes.

'I know she's married. I'm not proud,' Bayliss admitted, slumping down into a chair.

'All right,' said Roscoe. 'You came away with her for a weekend together. And perhaps you could explain where you've been this afternoon?'

'My car developed a puncture and we knew we'd have to get it fixed before we drove back. So I've been out getting a new tyre. You've no idea how hard it is to find a tyre place open on a Saturday afternoon.'

Vickers leaned forward in his chair beside the writing bureau.

'Can we see the receipt for the tyre?' he asked.

Bayliss fumbled in one of the pockets of his jeans and drew out a paper receipt.

'Here you are,' he said, handing it to Vickers.

The inspector glanced at the receipt before passing it back. 'Yes, it's all right, guv,' he told his colleague. 'It shows he was at Queensbridge Tyres at half past five.'

'It's getting on towards seven now,' said Vickers. 'Can I ask where you've been since five thirty?'

'I had to get some money out for tonight. Then it took an age to find a charging point for the car,' said Bayliss. 'Right. I've answered your questions. Can you tell me what's happened to Candy, for God's sake?'

Roscoe frowned. 'I'm afraid someone was inside Room 224 with her late in the afternoon and she was strangled.'

Bayliss leaned forward and buried his head in his hands.

'How terrible,' he said. A few seconds passed before he continued, 'She was such a lovely girl. Are you sure it was her?'

'Long, blonde hair, five feet eight inches tall, white top and red pants suit,' said Vickers.

'Oh my God,' said Bayliss, who was now shaking his head and staring at the carpet. 'This is unreal.'

Roscoe patted him on the back. 'I can get you a paramedic if you want,' he said.

'I'll be all right,' he insisted. 'What about my gear? My luggage is up in the room.'

'You won't be able to go in the room for the moment,' the chief inspector explained. 'The pathologist is up there. But, if you give us your number, we'll give you a call later and let you know when you'll be able to collect your personal effects. Anyway, are you up to answering some questions?'

'I'll try and help,' said Bayliss.

'Before we go any further, guv,' said Vickers, 'I'd like to know why Mr Bayliss came in through the main door just now. The car park is at the back of the building. If he's got a car and parked in the hotel car park, I'd have expected him to come in through the back entrance.'

'We only had one keycard for the room, so I left it with Candy,' Bayliss explained. 'You need a keycard to get through the rear door.'

'Can you tell us a little about Mrs Goodhope?' said Roscoe. 'Where she lived, her job, her husband's name?'

'Yes, sure. Candy runs beauty salons in Gloucester and Bristol. She's a make-up artist, YouTuber and Instagram star. She's also a celebrity blogger with more than three million followers, giving tips on hair and beauty. She was filming in a beautician's around the corner from here this morning, along with two assistants, Roxanne and Tiffany.'

'What's her business called?' asked Vickers.

'It's called Sweet Candy Kisses Beauty World.'

'Her address?' asked Vickers, removing a notebook from his pocket.

'She lives at 75 Hertford Way, Gloucester,' Bayliss replied as the inspector jotted the details down. 'I suppose I'll have to tell you – you'll find out anyway. Her husband's called Craig.'

He muttered to himself, 'There's going to be hell to pay now.' Shaking his head, Bayliss continued, 'Her parents live in Spain. Oh my God. They're going to be devastated. She's their only daughter and the love of their lives.'

He placed his head in his hands again and stared at the carpet.

'What was the shop called that she visited?' asked Vickers.

'Très Belle. It's in the High Street.'

'Oh, I know where it is,' said Vickers with a nod.

'How long has Mrs Goodhope been married?' asked Roscoe.

'Let me think,' said Bayliss. 'She's twenty-nine now and she told me she got together with Craig when she was twenty-four, so five years.'

'What's the state of the marriage?' asked Vickers. 'Is there a divorce going through?'

'Their relationship had gone from matrimony to acrimony,' he said. 'She hadn't got round to a divorce, but I'm pretty certain Craig knew about me. At least, I'm sure he had an inkling.'

'What sort of work does Craig do?' Roscoe asked.

'He's in sales and marketing.'

'So, you're a journalist, Mr Bayliss?' said Roscoe, leaning back on his chair. He watched him closely, like a doctor eyeing a patient with a serious rash.

'Yes. I used to work on one of the Gloucester papers, but I'm freelance at the moment.'

'So, how did you get mixed up with Mrs Goodhope?'

'Online dating,' said Bayliss.

'How long had you been going out with her?'

'Off and on, over two years.'

'Two years?' said Roscoe. 'I'd say, if that husband hadn't had at least an inkling after all that time, I'd be extremely surprised.'

Bayliss shook his head again. 'All the time we've been talking, a worrying thought's been running through my mind,' he said.

'What's that?' asked Vickers.

'That Craig might have found out we were going away to Warwickshire for the weekend and come over here to confront us,' said Bayliss.

Chapter 6

After assuring Cynthia Ecclestone that it would be safe for her to travel to the nearby village of Norton Prior to see her relatives, Sunita Roy left the witness in her room. She walked back to the landing where the stairway and lifts were. While peering through the glazed door leading to Candy Goodhope's corridor, she spotted two forensic staff examining the door.

Sunita made her way along and found the chief inspector was inside Room 224, talking to stern-faced Home Office pathologist Dr Silas Reynolds. She wondered briefly where her partner, Tom Vickers, had got to. They had been intending to spend time in the hotel ballroom, where the bride and groom had been due to host a dance before leaving for their honeymoon. She'd heard the event was being cancelled.

The stout, middle-aged pathologist, wearing a white gown and rubber gloves, had his back to the window and was bending over the woman's body while Roscoe was crouched down beside him.

'Come in, Sergeant,' said Reynolds, 'but take care where you put your feet. I was just telling Gavin here that it makes a change inspecting a body in such luxurious surroundings. He usually drags me out of my comfortable home to some grimy riverbank or some cold, uninviting woods to view a corpse.'

'Sadly, we don't have any control over where killers choose to strike,' Roscoe muttered as Sunita entered, slipping some plastic gloves from her pocket and putting them on. 'Ah, Sergeant. Come and take a look at this. It's a little gruesome, but it's important to know what we're dealing with here.'

Sunita, who no longer felt faint, stepped into the middle of the room and looked down at the victim's pale face. She could see red marks round the woman's neck.

'This poor young lady,' said Reynolds, 'is in her late twenties, she's one hundred and seventy-five centimetres tall with a northern blue butterfly tattoo on her right breast. She's suffered a severe blunt trauma injury to the head. I don't know if you can see but she's got a laceration on the side of her head measuring four centimetres – probably from being struck against one of those woodland prints on the wall. Then, while in a minimally conscious state, it appears this hand towel's been used as a ligature to throttle her. That action's caused decreased cerebral blood flow and deprived her of oxygen, resulting in cyanosis.'

'That means she turned blue,' Roscoe explained to his sergeant, who'd appeared puzzled by the term.

'Affirmative,' said the pathologist. 'This has led to asphyxia and rapid neuronal death. During the strangulation, which fractured bones in her neck, I suspect the victim was unable to put up a struggle because she was dazed from the earlier head injury. The ligature marks round the neck appear at the level of the larynx – it would have been higher if we were dealing with death by hanging – and the nature of the marks tell us the killer throttled her from a frontal position. Also the ligature mark on the skin is more prominent at the front.

'Further evidence of strangulation are the petechial haemorrhages – these spots on the eyes and face, which have occurred after blood escaped from the capillaries–'

Sunita interrupted him. 'Dr Reynolds, we have a witness who, believe it or not, observed the attack on this poor lady through the window. She says the woman was standing in full view when she was struck by a man.'

The pathologist glanced behind him at the window and nodded.

'Yes. It makes sense the attack took place behind me,' he replied. 'Afterwards, it looks as though the assailant seized her feet and hauled her across the carpet to the position where the body is now. I've been speaking to Dr Ling in forensics. She is checking whether microscopic fibres from her trousers became embedded in the carpet while the victim was being dragged.'

'So strangulation led to her death?' said Roscoe.

'Yes, old fruit,' Reynolds replied. 'The procedure is we've got to take the body to the mortuary at Queensbridge Hospital, and, once official identification's taken place, we'll need to carry out a physical examination. We'll start by studying the airways. What's happened is that external pressure to the veins and arteries has resulted in unconsciousness, depressed brainstem functions, and ultimately asphyxia and death. One can assume at this stage that she would have died rapidly from vagal reflex cardiac arrest.'

Sunita, who was standing by the bed, noticed a small black handbag on the cabinet and she turned towards the chief inspector.

'I take it that's Mrs Goodhope's bag,' she said. 'Anything much in it, sir?'

'It was found under the woman's legs,' the chief inspector replied. 'Forensics have seen it. Have a look inside.'

While the two men continued discussing the body, Sunita delved into the black leather Saint Laurent bag. It contained a pen, keys, a purse, hand sanitiser, lipstick, tissues, a hairbrush and comb, a mirror, a nail file, sunglasses and contraceptives.

'No mobile, sir?' she asked the chief inspector.

'Forensics have taken it away,' Roscoe replied as Sunita opened the pink purse. It contained credit cards and paper receipts but no cash. She carefully studied each of the five receipts in turn.

'This is interesting, sir,' she said, holding one out for Roscoe to see. 'It's a receipt for a transaction yesterday at a Queensbridge branch of Lloyds. It's for six hundred pounds.'

Roscoe stood up and flexed his legs for a moment. He stepped past Reynolds and examined the piece of paper.

'Yes, that *is* interesting,' he said. 'But I think we should leave Silas alone now. We're probably disturbing him.'

'I'm all right,' muttered the pathologist. 'I'll be on my way in a minute. Just got to arrange for the body to be taken to the mortuary.'

While Roscoe asked Reynolds about the body's removal, Sunita glanced inside an open wardrobe door. Shelves were stacked with cosmetic and styling products, hair extensions and, she thought, enough filming equipment to make a Hollywood movie.

The two detectives stepped outside a few minutes later and continued discussing the death in the corridor.

'I wonder what Mrs Goodhope wanted that money for,' said Roscoe. 'You don't normally take that amount with you in cash these days when we're all using bank cards to pay.'

'Maybe she'd been planning to make a big cash purchase in Queensbridge,' Sunita suggested.

'Maybe. Did Mrs Ecclestone have anything interesting to tell us?'

'Most of it was mundane, sir,' she replied. 'But there were a couple of details which might help us. She said the man had large hands and a gold ring on one of his right fingers.'

'Well, at least that's something, I suppose,' said Roscoe.

'Is DI Vickers still in the hotel?' she asked.

'Yes. I've asked him to speak to the manager about CCTV round the building,' said Roscoe as he answered his ringing phone. 'Here he is now. Yes, Tom.'

Sunita managed to overhear part of what Vickers was telling the chief inspector. It was something about some of the hotel cameras being out of action.

After ending the call, Roscoe turned towards her.

'Just our luck,' he said. 'The camera that covers the back door stopped working on Thursday. Dozens of people are accustomed to using the rear entrance door every day and it looks like, as far as today goes, we haven't got images of a single one of them.'

Chapter 7

By the time the chief inspector reached his detached house on the northern edge of the town, it was after nine o'clock and becoming dark.

After locking his navy-blue BMW in the garage, he walked wearily to his front door and turned the key in the lock.

'I hope your supper isn't ruined,' his blonde wife, Helen, called from the kitchen. 'Why didn't you tell me you were going to be late?'

'Sorry, darling,' he said as she entered the hallway, wiping her hands on an apron. 'Everything became a little chaotic. I got called out to a death at one of the hotels.'

'Was that the incident at the Queensbridge Arms Hotel?' she said. 'I heard all the sirens, and then some of my customers at the tearooms said a hotel guest had been attacked.'

'News travels very quickly round these parts,' said Roscoe, kissing her on the cheek. 'Yes, it was a woman. A bit gruesome. I don't think Tom Vickers was very happy. He was best man at his friend's wedding today and the reception was in the same building. He made his speech in the afternoon, but the dance in the evening had to be called off.'

'Was your sergeant with him?'

'Yes. Mind you, they were in the right place. They were standing right by the reception desk when another guest reported it.'

The couple continued discussing the incident for a few minutes while Helen heated up his beef lasagne meal and served it at the kitchen table. She then went upstairs so he could enjoy his food in peace.

Later, their twenty-five-year-old daughter, Melody, came down, listening to music on her earphones. She took off her headphones when she realised her father was back.

'How's it going, Dad?' asked Melody, her mousy, brown hair arranged in a pixie style.

'Another exhausting day, love,' he replied. 'Not going anywhere tonight? You're usually out on a Saturday.'

'Yeah. Alex is picking me up in a minute.'

'Listen, you're young and up to date with all the new trends,' he said. 'Does the name Candy Goodhope mean anything to you?'

'That must be Candy who does the beauty videos,' she replied. 'I was with her earlier today.'

'What? Are you serious?'

'Of course. Mum let me have a long lunch break from the tearooms, so I went shopping and ended up at that new beauty salon, Très Belle.'

Roscoe was astonished to hear that his daughter had been in the victim's presence just hours before the murder.

'What do you know about her?' he asked.

'Well, she's got millions of followers on social media. She owns a string of beauty parlours and had just announced she's opening her first shop dealing with ocular beauty, which she's calling Candy's Luscious Lashes. She's brought in an expert lash artist.'

'What on earth's that?' asked Roscoe, feeling as foolish as a clown at a funeral.

'Someone who enhances a woman's natural beauty with eyelash extensions,' said Melody. 'Candy trains women to become beauticians and is regarded as a mentor for those entering the beauty business. But this morning she was giving away free hair transformations, dying girls' hair in lime green, flaming orange and cherry red.'

'I expect that livened things up for the Saturday shoppers,' he remarked. 'I mean, if they saw a string of young women emerging into the high street with colourful hairstyles.'

She nodded before adding, 'The only thing is…'

She paused to watch for her father's reaction.

'What's that?' he asked.

'Not everyone was ecstatic about her visit to Queensbridge.'

'How come?'

'She's got some serious rivals who are intensely jealous of her. One's Kaylee Cavendish, who calls herself a beauty guru. They're at each other's throats all the time.'

'In what way?' he asked, finishing his meal and pushing the plate aside.

'They're forever mocking each other in public and encouraging their followers to make spiteful comments on websites. But I think Candy eased off on that front recently, fearing she was losing some of her supporters over it. It's not good for business, is it, Dad? Making unkind comments about your rival?'

'I suppose not,' said Roscoe, leaning back in his chair and relaxing.

'But things really kicked off last week when Candy revealed to her fans that she was going to be appearing in Queensbridge at the new salon. Kaylee went crazy because she regards the town as her personal and private domain where she should reign supreme.'

'So, what happened?' her father asked.

'Kaylee and her boyfriend, Luke, threatened to try and stop Candy from entering the shop. But, in the event, the demo they'd planned fizzled out. She couldn't get enough supporters. She's now threatening to boycott the shop because they invited Candy.'

'Isn't this just a silly row between two women who've become too big for their boots?' asked Roscoe.

'No, Dad. These two women have both built up a massive following which the beauty companies are very aware of. They both sell their own products as well as appearing online, on videos and on television. They're both creating multi-million-pound businesses and are becoming wealthy on the back of it all.'

'Did you actually speak to Candy?' asked Roscoe.

'Don't be silly, Dad. You couldn't get near her.'

'How did she seem?'

'Happy, bubbly.'

'How do you know so much about these two women?'

'For anyone interested in beauty products and hairstyling like me, you can hardly miss them on social media sites, Dad,' she replied. 'Come to think of it, I read somewhere this week that Candy was threatening to take Kaylee to court over something – that's how bitter the rivalry's grown between them.'

'Are you aware of the death at the hotel this evening?' he asked.

'I heard something. Mum was watching the television news earlier and they said a woman had been found dead in suspicious circumstances. Oh my God!'

She clamped her right hand round her mouth in shock.

'You don't mean…?'

Her father nodded.

'I'm afraid so. We're not officially releasing the name to the public for a few days. The body won't be formally identified until tomorrow. We need to give the family time to get over the initial shock. But we're fairly certain the woman who died was Candy Goodhope.'

Chapter 8

The countryside in Warwickshire and Worcestershire was at its most serene as Sunita Roy and Tom Vickers set off on their thirty-five-mile journey to Gloucester on Sunday morning.

Vickers' white Audi A3 passed through picturesque villages and lush green fields as the sun emerged from behind the clouds, bringing the promise of a warm summer's day. Here and there, Sunita caught sight of pinkish mayflowers and white cow parsley peering out among the hedgerows.

They skirted the towns of Evesham and Tewkesbury before approaching the M5 motorway.

'The way things are going, we should be at Craig Goodhope's house by half past eleven,' said Vickers.

'What did you make of Candy's boyfriend, Jack Bayliss?' asked Sunita.

The question took her partner by surprise. Vickers cast his mind back to the previous evening. He tried to remember the distressed man in his early thirties with blond hair and no tie, whose shirt had been unbuttoned at the neck.

'He seemed a pleasant enough guy, and I felt sorry for him. He looked genuinely shocked when we told him of

Mrs Goodhope's death,' he said. 'I don't think the DCI was so sure about him. He said if you invited him to a picnic, he might run off with the hamper.'

'You don't think he had a furious row with her over something, attacked her and then disappeared from the hotel for a while?' said Sunita.

'Well, he'd have to be a bloody good actor, if that was the case. Turning up at seven o'clock, looking fresh as a daisy, and going through a charade of pretending he didn't know his girlfriend was dead.'

'Has anyone checked with the tyre company that he actually bought a new tyre?' she asked.

'Not yet,' said Vickers, 'but the receipt for the tyre gave a time of half past five, and it looked genuine.'

She shrugged. 'That's the time the job was finished. The time to pay,' said Sunita. 'The tyre firm is less than a mile away. He had plenty of time to return to the hotel, throttle Candy and make off somewhere for a while.'

Vickers sighed. 'If you'd been there in reception yesterday like the DCI and me, I don't think you'd be suggesting that,' he said. 'He seemed like a broken man when we explained, as gently as we could, how Candy had been found dead. By the way, did you see his car? I took a look at it in the car park.'

'No, but I saw in the file that it's a Tesla Model 3.'

'Yeah. Great car. Anyway, did Mrs Ecclestone have anything else to say?'

Sunita shook her head.

'Not really. I told you about the gold ring, didn't I?'

'Yes. So there's not too much to go on.'

'No. We'll just have to hope Dr Ling in forensics comes up with something. How did you get on with the hotel manager over the CCTV?'

'We've got a whole set of front-door footage to plough through but nothing for the back,' he said.

'And from what we've learnt from our stay,' she said, 'huge numbers of guests park in the car park and then use the rear door to come in.'

'Exactly,' he said.

'If someone was really determined to get inside, all they had to do was wait by the rear door for someone with a pass and then follow them in,' she said.

He nodded as their car joined the motorway.

'Maybe whoever it was who killed her phoned round the hotels to see if they had a Mrs Goodhope staying with them,' Sunita said.

'That kind of information's meant to be confidential.'

'I know, but if they knew she was staying somewhere in the Queensbridge area and didn't know exactly which hotel it was, it wouldn't take long to phone round and bluff the information out of some unsuspecting receptionist.'

'That's true,' Vickers said.

'Mind you, once inside, an intruder still would've had to find what room she was in.'

'That would've been trickier,' said Vickers.

'I suppose they could have asked someone in reception directly,' said Sunita. 'You've already checked with the manager, haven't you, and all the staff claim no one asked for Candy's room number?'

'That's right.'

'So maybe, if it was an intruder that killed her, they looked up the room number on the hotel register while the staff were busy,' she suggested.

'Very hard to do that. The desk was manned constantly, according to the manager.'

'Well, the other option – if they didn't get the information from the woman herself – is they could have knocked on doors on each floor, claiming confusion about the door numbers and asking if they'd seen a striking-looking woman in a red trouser outfit with blonde hair.'

Vickers scowled. 'The intruder might get lucky with that, but that's a big risk,' he said. 'A guest disturbed by a stranger is likely to call reception and complain. Who've we got checking all the front-door footage?'

'Probably Brett Dawson will be making a start on that tomorrow.'

'In that case, let's hope that whoever it was, came in through the front door.' He paused. 'Do you know, this case bears all the hallmarks of a crime of passion? The man and woman in the window. The angry words. The man striking out and then choking her. Mark my words – unrequited love is at the heart of this.'

'Far too early to say,' she replied. 'I feel so sorry for Candy, you know. Young woman barely out of her twenties. She's beginning to make her mark in the world and then her light is snuffed out like a candle in a gust of wind.'

'Yes. It's a tragedy,' he agreed. 'I feel sorry for the parents as they've lost their only child.'

'Not forgetting the husband,' she said, 'unless he's behind the murder.'

'When are the parents going to ID the body? Any idea?' asked Vickers as the car left the M5 and headed along the A40 towards Gloucester's northern suburbs.

'Yes, they're flying back today and the DCI's taking them to the mortuary tomorrow morning,' Sunita replied.

'Rather him than me,' said Vickers.

* * *

After a further twenty minutes, the pair arrived on a new, private residential estate on the outskirts of the city. The Goodhopes lived in a top-floor, two-bedroom flat in an apartment block built twenty years earlier which overlooked fields.

Vickers parked outside the main door. Sunita was reaching for the door handle when he unexpectedly touched her arm.

'I don't think we should bring up Jack Bayliss's name to the husband,' he said. 'Not unless he mentions it himself. We don't want to get him riled up after we've broken the bad news to him.'

'I'm with you on that, Tom,' she said as they both climbed out.

After pressing the intercom button, they were buzzed in and made their way in the lift to the third floor.

Craig Goodhope looked despondent as he opened the oak door to his flat but quickly ushered them in.

He led the detectives past cardboard boxes in the hall, which Sunita suspected contained hair and beauty products. Seconds later, they found themselves in a light, airy living-room with a grey, three-piece suite. Beneath a television in the corner was a shelf filled with beauty awards and trophies.

'You're aware that your wife was found dead in the Queensbridge Arms Hotel?' said Vickers.

'Yes, a constable came round to tell me last night. He said there was a good chance it was her. She was found inside the room she booked and it was clearly her handbag, judging by the contents.'

'Yes,' said Vickers. 'Your wife's parents will be able to confirm it when they identify the body tomorrow.'

'I was too upset to see her.'

Goodhope, who was short in stature and with long, blond hair in a ponytail, stood in the centre of the room with his eyes fixed on the inspector. Then, without showing any emotion, he gazed down at the floor.

'It's unbelievable,' he said. 'Just unbelievable. Obviously, I'd been hoping that there'd been some kind of mistake. You know that it was someone who looked like my wife that had died. But no such luck.'

'We're so sorry for your loss,' said Sunita, tapping his arm.

'Well, it's come as a complete shock to me,' he said. He slumped down onto the settee with his head in his hands.

‘The last thing Candy said to me was “I should be back Sunday night about seven and I’ll cook supper”,’ he said. ‘And then she was gone.’

Chapter 9

'When exactly did you last see your wife?' asked Sunita, sitting down beside Craig Goodhope on the settee and slipping a small, black notebook from her jacket pocket.

'Friday morning,' he said, turning towards her. She noticed his eyes were red from crying. 'Must have been about a quarter past eight. She said she was going to one of her salons. Which is in Bristol.'

'Do you have the address?' asked the sergeant.

'Ashtree Grove,' he said, rubbing his right eye with the back of his hand.

Vickers stepped in front of them and settled down in an armchair.

'You obviously knew she was going away for the weekend?' he asked Goodhope.

'Yes, she had one of her beauty events in Queensbridge. Then she was going shopping in London and going out to the theatre.'

'And you weren't expecting to see her again until seven o'clock on Sunday night?' Sunita asked.

'That's right. There've been several of these weekend trips over the past year. I don't mind. It gives me a chance to meet up with my mates.'

Goodhope leaned forward and placed his head in his hands. Then he glanced up, and Sunita saw him crying.

'Are you all right?' she said. 'Do you want to do this some other time?'

'No. I'll be all right,' he insisted.

Sunita offered to make some tea, but Goodhope declined.

'That's kind of you, but I'll be all right.'

'I was just wondering,' said Sunita, 'whether I could take a quick look round your flat?'

'What for?' he asked.

'A detective needs the fullest picture possible of how a person lived their life,' she said. 'An insight into their world can sometimes steer the investigation into a totally different direction.'

'Sunita once solved a murder after finding an expensive necklace and a bus ticket in someone's bedroom,' remarked Vickers.

'Oh, Tom. It wasn't as simple as that,' said Sunita, glaring at her partner.

'Please go ahead and search, DS Roy,' said Goodhope. 'In view of what you've said, I'm happy for you to have a look around. We must do all we can to catch the scum who did this.'

Sunita stepped into the hall while the two men remained chatting. She peered inside three of the cardboard boxes in the gloomy hallway. They contained bottles of hair dye, cosmetic products, soaps, shampoos and perfumes.

More beauty products were stacked in the shower room and the small second bedroom.

When Sunita pushed open the door to the main bedroom, she was taken aback. The spacious room was boldly designed with turquoise walls and a lush cream carpet. The bed was draped in purple and white linen. A hairstylist's chair and sink stood in the corner while small portraits of beauty pioneers Elizabeth Arden, Helena

Rubinstein, Estée Lauder and Charlotte Tilbury featured on one of the walls.

So this was where the trailblazing beauty innovator rested her head at night, Sunita thought. What a tragedy that her life should have been cut short at the age of twenty-nine in a soulless hotel room.

Sunita pulled open the cream doors of the two double wardrobes to find nearly all the space consumed with colourful dresses, skirts, trouser suits, tops and leggings – enough clothes for Candy to have staged several fashion shows, if she had wanted to.

She wondered where the husband stored his clothes.

A search of wardrobe drawers revealed nothing of interest – mainly underwear, old phone handsets and day-to-day medicines. But Sunita was jubilant to find a black laptop tucked away at the back of one of the drawers beneath some unopened packets of women's knickers.

'A little more work for John Hepworth,' she told herself as she picked it up and carried it into the living-room. Hepworth was the force's digital forensic analyst.

'Did this laptop belong to Candy?' she asked Goodhope, who remained in the same seat on the settee.

He nodded.

'We'll have to take it for examination,' she told him.

'That's all right,' he said. 'You have to do what you have to do. Listen, now you're back, I need to ask you both something that's obviously been on my mind. Can you tell me how Candy died? The policeman that called round didn't have the details. All it said online was that a woman guest hadn't responded to first-aiders and that the death was unexplained.'

'I'm afraid your wife was found with a ligature round her neck,' said Sunita, resuming her place beside him.

'Oh my God!' he replied. 'She was strangled?'

'Yes.'

'I hope it was quick.' He raised his hands to his face.

'Must have been,' said Sunita, although she knew from her knowledge of similar cases that a victim could take several seconds to lose consciousness and that the transition to being brain dead could last for five or six minutes.

'Sorry,' he said, bursting into fresh tears. He left the room, returning two minutes later, wiping his eyes.

'Are you going to be OK?' she enquired.

He nodded.

'Yes, my brother and his wife are coming round in a minute. I'll be fine,' he said.

Sunita decided to move the conversation on quickly.

'So how was Candy planning to spend today?' Sunita asked.

Goodhope shrugged his shoulders.

'I don't know,' he said dismissively. 'Meet up with her friends, I suppose. She's been talking about wanting to see Leamington Spa.'

Vickers coughed.

'Did you never accompany your wife when she went off for the weekend?' the inspector asked.

'What? You're joking, aren't you? It would bore me rigid, watching her dolling up some bimbo. Nah, if that's how she wants to spend her time, good luck to her. She's been making good money out of it, and that helped both of us.'

Vickers continued, 'So was there never an occasion when you joined her on her weekend away?'

'I went with her once,' their host admitted. 'We took a trip up to Birmingham. I've never seen such a busy place. Never again.'

Sunita knew they would eventually need to ask Goodhope whether he was aware that the beautician had booked into the hotel with another man. She recognised she would have to be tactful.

'Tell us about Roxanne and Tiffany,' she said. 'Did they stay with your wife in the hotel?'

'I'm not sure. I think both of them would have just driven over to Queensbridge for the day. Roxanne is a stylist and Tiffany's a videographer. They both live in Gloucester.'

Sunita glanced briefly across the room at Vickers.

'There's something that probably hasn't been mentioned to you before,' she continued. 'The point is that…'

'Your wife wasn't booked in alone,' Vickers explained.

'How do you mean?' said Goodhope.

'There was someone else with her. The hotel register has the names Mr and Mrs Goodhope.'

The bereaved husband frowned and looked down at the plain, beige carpet.

'I see,' he said.

A heavy silence hung in the air.

'Well, it definitely wasn't me,' he said, glancing at them both in turn. 'Do you know who it was?'

'Yes, we do,' said Vickers. 'Were you aware your wife might be having an affair?'

'I won't lie. There were one or two little signs.'

'Such as what?' asked Vickers.

'Well, things haven't been right between us for a while. She sometimes hid her phone. I came back once and she'd left her laptop on. I sat down beside it. She rushed over and slammed the lid down.'

'I see,' said Vickers.

'So, who is the bastard?'

'We can't really give you his name at the moment. He's obviously a key witness.'

'Maybe he killed her,' Goodhope suggested.

'We're keeping an open mind at the moment,' Sunita interjected.

She turned round in her seat so that she was directly facing Goodhope. 'Maybe you already know who this man is?' she asked.

Goodhope said nothing. He simply gazed out of the window.

She repeated her question, but their host merely shook his head.

'What we don't want is for you, all keyed up over the death of your wife, having any rash, spur-of-the moment thoughts,' she told Goodhope. 'In other words, we don't want you deciding on your own to go looking for this person and take some kind of citizens' justice – you know, taking some kind of retribution. That wouldn't be right. It's for the police to investigate these kinds of crimes, find the real perpetrator and for the court to dispense justice.'

'All right, I've got the message,' said Goodhope. 'But I haven't a clue who this guy was that, according to you, was staying at the hotel with Candy.'

'So long as our advice to you is understood,' she added. 'Don't worry. We'll get to the bottom of who killed your wife. It may not be quick, but we'll get there and we obviously don't want anyone taking the law into their own hands.'

Vickers leaned forward in his seat.

'Mr Goodhope, can we ask where you were last night between five and seven?'

'Yes,' he replied. 'I went to Gloucester with a couple of mates. We went to the Blue Anchor then onto the Dog. I think its full name is the Dog and Partridge.'

'If you could give us your friends' names and addresses, that would be very helpful. Did you have a meal over there or just drinks?'

'Just drinks.'

'Mr Goodhope,' said Sunita, 'can you think of anyone with a reason to harm your wife?'

Goodhope shook his head and quickly replied, 'No.'

'Perhaps you'd like to think about the question,' she continued.

He paused as his eyes wandered around the room. He shook his head again.

'I know there's a lot of rivalry in the beauty business,' he said. 'There are a lot of people on social media who were envious of Candy's success. But I can't think any of them would have felt strongly enough to go over to Queensbridge and kill her. She told me she'd received a few funny messages but said that went with the turf.'

The detectives exchanged glances.

'All right. I think it's time to go,' Sunita said as the pair stood up.

'Are you sure you'll be OK?' Vickers asked their host. 'I mean, is there a neighbour or relative you can…'

'I'll be fine,' Craig Goodhope insisted, getting up. 'As I say, my brother will be here soon. He's always been a good support to me in difficult times.'

'We've got your phone number,' Sunita assured him. 'As soon as we get any positive news, we'll call you.'

'Yes,' said Vickers, shaking his hand. 'We'll try to keep you regularly informed of what's going on.'

Goodhope wrote his friends' details on a scrap of paper, which he handed to Vickers. Then he led his visitors back through the hallway and the inspector drew open the door.

'We'll be in touch,' he assured the husband.

Sunita paused. She was glancing down at a small table where a small notepad and pen lay beside a landline phone.

'Come on, Sunita,' Vickers said as Goodhope shut the door behind them. 'Let's go and get some lunch.'

'I'm coming,' she retorted, running behind him towards the open lift door. The pair quickly returned to the car.

'I know he was upset,' she said. 'But I was surprised how lucid he was.'

'Grief strikes different people in different ways,' muttered Vickers as he started the car.

'By the way, you didn't notice what I saw on the writing pad by the front door, did you?' she said.

'What's that?'

'The registration number of Jack Bayliss's car.'

Chapter 10

Shortly after arriving at her desk in CID on Monday morning, Sunita Roy braved the light rain and left the modern, four-storey building. As she hurried along the path at the side of the building, she was thinking back to their interview with Goodhope. The team would have to keep an eye on him. He'd denied knowing about his wife's partner. He was clearly lying.

She pushed open one of the two glass doors that led to the new forensics department and smiled at the receptionist sitting behind a screen.

'Is John Hepworth in?' she asked.

'Yes, he's been here for ten minutes,' said the man. 'I'll just let him know you're here.'

After Hepworth had been alerted by intercom, she climbed the stairs to the first floor and pushed open the door marked 'High Tech Crime Unit'.

Hepworth, who was six feet tall with dark-ginger hair and a perpetual solemn expression, rose from behind a large bank of computers as she stepped into the huge, brightly lit room.

'Good to see you, Sergeant,' he called out as he took a few steps towards her and gave her a brief wave. 'Not much fun, working over a Bank Holiday weekend, is it?'

'No, but think of the extra pay,' she said.

'Hardly worth bothering about,' he moaned.

'You said you'd got some information from Candy Goodhope's phone,' she continued.

'Yes,' said Hepworth, resuming his seat at his desk.

She drew up a chair beside him while he pointed to a monitor on the wall displaying a mobile phone screen.

'That's Candy's phone,' he explained. 'I may as well start by showing you some of the photos she took on Saturday morning.'

Hepworth scrolled through a series of images that seemed to have been taken inside a beauty salon. In the first sequence of pictures, a young woman with bright-green hair was sitting in a styling chair. A woman of similar age with ginger hair was attending to her while a slightly older woman was filming them with a video camera.

'Right,' said the sergeant, 'I believe that stylist is called Roxanne. She works with Candy at her salons, and the blonde woman with the video camera must be their friend Tiffany. Does Candy appear in any pictures, John?'

He nodded.

'She's in the next batch. Look.'

Sunita recognised Candy immediately as she emerged in the next set of photographs, clowning around with Roxanne. Candy waved and smiled at the camera, presumably at that point being operated by Tiffany.

The sergeant was at once drawn back to the moment, two days earlier, when she'd found the murder victim's body on the hotel room's dark-red carpet.

She was wearing the same white, sleeveless top. For the first and probably only time, Sunita was able to appraise her while in a light-hearted mood. Candy appeared to be a convivial, carefree spirit. She was a young woman revelling in the joys of life.

'Can you let me have pictures of Roxanne and Tiffany to take away with me?' she asked.

'Of course. No problem,' he said.

'By the way, have you seen any videos on Candy's website or on social media?'

'I had a quick look early this morning before coming into work,' he said. 'There's a video on Instagram, but it doesn't do much more than show Candy and Roxanne styling hair and doing make-up. All the talk between the two of them is related to the task in hand. There are similar pictures and videos on her website and other sites.'

Hepworth spent twenty minutes showing Sunita what the murder victim had posted on various sites. He then went on to display a set of pictures featuring members of the salon staff.

'I haven't started on her laptop yet,' he added.

'The guy at the left-hand side of these new pictures looks very out of place,' Sunita said, pointing out a man with a shock of black hair and a small beard.

'Yes. There were two men in the salon pictures. That guy and a blond-haired man, who's very casually dressed,' said Hepworth.

'That would be Jack the journalist,' said Sunita. 'Tom Vickers showed me a picture of him.'

'Well, Jack's not in all the pictures, but this guy *is*, and, as you say, he looks off-base,' said Hepworth, giving a weak smile. 'Feel a bit sorry for him, in a way. I'm wondering if he could be Mark Tanner.'

'Who's Mark Tanner, and why do you think it might be him?'

'I've gone through all Candy's most recent texts and WhatsApp messages,' he explained. 'He's Roxanne's boyfriend. He's mentioned in a couple of texts as someone due to visit the salon along with Roxanne. He was planning to stay for an hour or two and then he was going off to play football in Birmingham – one of the last matches of the season.'

Sunita shrugged.

'Oh well, that's the answer then. The guy in the images must be him,' she said. 'Quite a serious expression. So out of place among all the glitz and glamour of the girls.'

Hepworth nodded.

'Yeah. He looks as if he's got something on his mind, wouldn't you say?'

* * *

By the time she returned to the CID office on the first floor, she found her colleague, DC Brett Dawson, working hard, scrolling through CCTV footage on his desktop computer. He seemed as engrossed as a chess player within reach of a winning move.

'How are you getting on, Brett?' she asked the slim, twenty-seven-year-old detective constable, who had spiky, blond hair and an earring and was known for his juvenile sense of humour.

'Morning, Sarge,' he replied. 'Not got anywhere yet. The boss was trying to reach you. He says the parents have identified the body. It's definitely Candy Goodhope. They're devastated, as you can imagine.'

She nodded.

'Anyway, getting back to this, so far I've seen about thirty people arriving and twenty leaving the hotel through the main door,' he said.

'Well, have a look at these faces,' she said, putting a brown envelope down on his desk and pulling out the photographs of Roxanne and Tiffany she'd received from Hepworth.

'These are the two women who spent a large part of Saturday morning with Candy,' she explained. 'Have you seen either of them?'

'Yes, I have,' he said. 'Hold on.'

He spent a few minutes trawling through the footage, examining the hazy black-and-white images of the pavement outside the revolving doors.

'Here we go,' he said eventually. 'I think this is the pair. They're entering the hotel at around half past two.'

Sunita leaned over Dawson's shoulder and peered at the screen.

'Yes. That's Roxanne and Tiffany. But Candy should be with them.'

Dawson tapped a few keys on the keyboard.

'She arrives a couple of minutes after them, carrying her laptop,' he said.

Sunita was confused for a moment at the mention of a laptop.

'I suppose she must have had more than one,' she said out loud, without meaning to.

'Sorry, Sarge?' asked Dawson.

'It's all right, Brett,' she said. 'I was remembering that I found a laptop at her home. This means she must have had two. Anyway, I'm starting to wonder why all three women came to the hotel,' said Sunita. 'I suppose Candy might have wanted to show them her room.'

'More likely they wanted to have a drink in the courtyard,' said Dawson. 'It was sunny for most of the afternoon, and it's a popular place. They've got a great bar.'

'You're right. We'll have to take these pictures down to the hotel and talk to the bar staff.'

Dawson raised a finger, signalling he had remembered something.

'I nearly forgot,' he said. 'Candy went to the bank that day. One of the team's been to Lloyds Bank in Queensbridge and picked up footage from the bank's internal camera. Hang on.'

Within seconds of finding the footage on his computer and playing it, a grey figure could be seen entering the banking hall.

Sunita leaned over her colleague's shoulders. The figure joined a queue of customers. She was carrying an object that resembled a laptop.

'It's fairly obvious that's her, Brett,' she said. 'But you'd better wind it on. You know what waiting times are like in a bank.'

The pair discovered that Candy, recognisable because of her long hair and racy outfit, was kept waiting in the queue for nearly ten minutes before a dark-haired cashier in a green blouse beckoned her forward.

They watched as Candy spent several minutes apparently assuring the cashier of her identity before a large sum of money was counted out, placed inside a white envelope and handed across.

'Doesn't look like there are any likely suspects in the queue behind her,' Sunita muttered, standing upright again and taking a few paces back towards her own desk. 'No men in check shirts with large hands and a ring. It's mostly women in their fifties and sixties.'

He nodded.

'I'll go back over the time when Candy was waiting in the queue – just in case we've missed anything,' he said.

'Thanks, Brett.'

'By the way, I've heard a rumour that the DCI's son may be joining us,' he said. 'Is that right, Sarge?'

'Who told you that?' Sunita asked.

'Someone in the canteen mentioned it.'

'Yes, he's starting tomorrow,' she said.

'I hope he's going to pull his weight. We're already one down since Omar Khalid sprained his ankle in the gym.'

'He's been a constable for five years and he's been working for Stratford CID for the past few months. He should prove a valuable asset.'

'I can't help feeling he's only been taken on because he's the DCI's son,' said Dawson.

Sunita shook her head.

'People are bound to say things like that,' she admitted. 'But the guy should be given a chance to prove what he can do.'

Sunita spent the next few minutes trying to reach Roxanne and Tiffany. Candy's Gloucester and Bristol salons were closed for the week following the owner's death. A message on the firm's voicemail explained staff were devastated over the tragedy and were taking time off to cope with their grief. However, they'd had the good sense to include an emergency phone number, which Sunita immediately called.

She found herself speaking to Roxanne, who was currently visiting Tiffany's flat in Gloucester.

'I need to speak to you,' said Sunita. 'How long were you planning to stay over there?'

'A few hours. We're just chilling,' said Roxanne in a soft West Country accent.

'Stay right there, both of you,' Sunita said. 'If you just give me the address, I should be with you in about an hour.'

As she collected her fawn jacket from the coat stand, she glanced over Dawson's shoulders at the screen he was viewing.

'Any updates, Brett?' she began. Then she stopped herself. Looming into view, swinging a sports bag, was a man she vaguely recognised.

'Can you zoom in on that guy?' she asked her colleague.

Dawson pressed some keys to enhance the image.

'Is this footage still related to the middle of the day?' she asked.

'No, Sarge,' he replied without glancing up. 'This is around three o'clock.'

'Well, that guy's Mark Tanner, Roxanne's boyfriend,' she said. 'I can't understand why he'd be at the hotel at three when he was meant to be in Brum playing football.'

Chapter 11

Tiffany Edwards lived in a ground-floor flat in a rather dilapidated nineteenth-century, three-storey house in the centre of Gloucester. Rubbish spilled from a series of bins standing in the building's small front garden, which was fronted by black iron railings. White paint was peeling from the façade.

Sunita Roy rang the bell and had to wait several minutes before Tiffany appeared in the doorway and invited her into a dark, dingy hallway.

'You'll have to take us as you find us,' said blonde-haired Tiffany in a soft south-of-England accent. She was nursing a fair-haired baby that appeared to be asleep.

Tiffany wore a pink tracksuit in keeping with her relaxed mood, and showed her into a light, airy front room, which reminded the sergeant of an art room from her school days. There was an easel in the corner and the main wall was covered with paintings, prints and photographs, all competing for space.

Roxanne was sitting on a brown leather settee with her eyes focussed on her phone. She looked up and smiled as Sunita appeared.

'Sorry to call at such a sad time,' said Sunita, producing her warrant card. 'DS Roy. Can I sit down?'

'Of course,' said Tiffany, drawing up a chair from the corner of the room for their visitor.

'I know you were both in Queensbridge two days ago at the High Street salon,' said the detective. 'How did Candy seem that morning?'

'She was just her normal bubbly self,' said Tiffany, sitting down beside her friend. 'You should have a look at her websites and see what she posted on social media.'

'Yes, we've done that,' said Sunita. 'As you say, she seemed upbeat. But had there been anything troubling her, as far as you know?'

Roxanne shook her head.

'No,' she said. 'I'm not going to lie. There've been a couple of girls who didn't like the way we dyed their hair at the Gloucester salon a few months ago. But you never get a hundred per cent approval. Not in Gloucester, anyway.'

Removing her notebook from her pocket, Sunita asked when the three women brought their demonstration to a halt at the salon.

'We must have finished about midday,' said Roxanne. 'We then spent some time posting videos and pictures online. After one o'clock, we went to the Crown and Sceptre and, with a bit of wheeling and dealing, managed to get a table for lunch, although we hadn't booked.'

'All three of you?'

'Yes.'

'And what happened after that?'

'Then we spent some time looking round the shops,' said Tiffany, as her baby stirred in her arms.

'Were you with Candy when she withdrew some money from a bank?' Sunita asked.

Tiffany nodded.

'We waited for around ten minutes while she got the money. Then we all carried on up the High Street.'

'You didn't notice anyone hanging around, watching her, while she got the money?'

'We were too busy chatting,' Tiffany admitted as her baby stirred again.

Distracted as the infant began to cry, the detective remarked, 'He's been good.' She stood and peered into the child's face.

'It's a girl. Olive,' said Tiffany.

'You're so lucky,' said Sunita.

'Yes, I know.' Tiffany smiled. 'Candy caught up with us and suggested we go for a drink in her hotel. So we did.'

'We've got a receipt for the money she withdrew,' Sunita continued. 'It was for six hundred pounds. Do you know what she needed it for? It wasn't to pay you two?'

They both shook their heads.

'I get paid on a Friday directly into my bank,' said Roxanne.

'I'm freelance and get paid monthly,' Tiffany explained.

'So, what time did you reach the hotel?' asked Sunita, recalling her earlier conversation that day with Brett Dawson while viewing the CCTV footage. 'About two thirty?'

'Must have been something like that,' said Roxanne.

'And how long were you there?'

'Till about five o'clock,' said Tiffany.

'Did you have a lot of drinks over that time?

'You could say that,' Tiffany said. 'Candy was well-hammered.'

'Hammered?' said Sunita. Her phone beeped, signalling she had received a text, but she chose to ignore it.

'Yeah,' said Tiffany. 'Proper gazeboed, you could say. She'd had a string of rum and Cokes. I wasn't keeping up with her. I had to drive back for Olive.'

'So you helped her up to her room and then left?' asked Sunita.

'No,' said Roxanne. 'We just left her in the courtyard.'

'When you knew she was heavily drunk?' said Sunita.

'Not being funny, she was fine,' said Tiffany. 'She wasn't incapable. Otherwise, we wouldn't have left her.'

'She was all right,' Roxanne added. 'You know how it is, don't you? Autopilot kicks in.'

Sunita didn't know. She rarely drank alcohol and, on the rare occasions she sampled wine – such as at Gary's wedding, she'd never drunk it in such quantities that it would affect her mental or physical performance. She was shocked by the women's relaxed attitude towards heavy drinking but passed no comment.

'So it was around five that you left the hotel?' Sunita asked them.

'Yes,' said Roxanne. 'We both had to get back. Look, Candy was all right, honestly. There were loads of other people there.'

'Was she talking to anyone when you left?'

'There was a bit of banter with some fellas from a nearby table,' said Tiffany. 'But Candy was giving as good as she got. She just told us when we left that she was going up to her room and she'd see us on Tuesday morning, after the Bank Holiday.'

'What happened to your boyfriend, Mark?' asked Sunita, gazing directly at Roxanne.

'How do you mean?' said the ginger-haired make-up artist.

'He came to the hotel as well, didn't he?' said Sunita.

'Yes, for a while,' said Roxanne, 'but I don't see how that's relevant.'

'Everything that happened that day that had a connection with Candy – whether directly or indirectly – could be relevant to our investigation,' she said. 'So how come he was at the hotel at three o'clock? Did he come to join you?'

Roxanne shrugged her shoulders.

'You clearly know more about what happened to us that afternoon than you're letting on,' Roxanne said. 'Yes, Mark was with us.'

'What happened about the football?'

'The match was abandoned because of flooding.'

'So, Mark was with you at the hotel?'

'Yes. Most of the time.'

'How do you mean "most of the time"?'

'At one point, he went off to move his car, and then he went to meet up with his sister, who was shopping in town,' said Roxanne.

'Is he working at the moment?'

'No. He's trying to get work in the building game.'

'Did he leave at the same time as you?'

'Yeah. At around five.'

'What door of the hotel did you use when you left?'

'The rear exit. Why?'

'I just wondered. Listen, do either of you know of anyone with a reason to harm Candy?'

Sunita found herself staring at two blank faces. They both shook their heads.

'No,' they said in unison.

'Cast your minds back to the scene in the courtyard before you left,' said Sunita. 'Can you describe any of the men? For instance, the men at the next table?'

'They were beefy, rugby-playing types,' said Tiffany. 'They were drinking lager. One had long, greasy hair. Most had short hair. I might recognise one or two of them if you showed me a picture.'

'It's the same with me,' said Roxanne. 'I was with Mark, so I wasn't in the mood for chatting to blokes or anyone, for that matter. I might remember the guys if I was shown some pictures.'

'I think those guys left round the same time as us,' Tiffany added.

'One last thing,' said Sunita. 'Did Candy have any particular plans on how she was going to be spending the rest of the weekend?'

'She said something about wanting to catch up with one of the shopping channels,' said Roxanne. 'Otherwise, just chilling.'

'There's just one other thing. Were you both aware Candy was having an affair?'

The pair exchanged glances, both unsure how to react to the question.

'Yes. We both knew,' Tiffany admitted sheepishly. 'His name's Jack Bayliss, but we thought it was none of our business.'

'I think it was just a brief infatuation,' Roxanne added.

'All right,' said Sunita. 'We'd better leave it there.' She slipped her hand into her pocket and drew out two personal cards, which she handed to Roxanne and Tiffany.

'If anything important occurs to you, please call me. I'm sure you want to catch the maniac who killed your friend.'

'We do,' they chorused.

After returning to her car, Sunita remembered the message she'd received while at Tiffany's flat.

She checked her phone and discovered it was a text from John Hepworth.

> *Been trying to reach you. Someone sent Candy two threatening phone messages, and it looks like the same person added some toxic information to an online profile.*

Chapter 12

While waiting for the evening meal to cook on the Aga, Sunita Roy stepped into her sitting room and cast her eyes around at the two leather settees, the dining table and chairs and her grand piano.

'This place needs a spruce-up,' she told herself.

She fetched her vacuum cleaner and a duster and busied herself tidying the room for half an hour.

Just after seven o'clock, she heard the sound of a car engine and guessed that her partner had arrived.

She stepped into the hallway, and opened the front door with a smile.

Tom Vickers, radiating joyful energy like a happy child, locked his car before hurrying across the gravel forecourt towards her.

'How did it go with Craig Goodhope's friends?' she asked as he kissed her on the cheek.

'Fine. They both support his story,' said Vickers.

'That was a given,' she remarked as he followed her into the five-bedroom former schoolhouse.

'Tea's nearly ready,' she said. 'I've only got to wait for the rice.'

'Great,' he said.

Vickers walked into the sitting room, opened himself a can of lager and poured it into a glass.

'Are you having some wine, Sunita?' he called out.

'It's all right. I've got an orange juice,' she replied as she brought in some plates which she laid out on the dining table. She then fetched in their meal of grilled salmon.

After they had eaten, Vickers drew his chair away from the table and leaned back.

'That's what my family in Wolverhampton would call 'bostin' fittle',' he said.

'What's that – a good meal?' she asked.

'Not good, Sunita – brilliant.' He stepped round the table, bent down and kissed her on the cheek.

'Thanks, love,' he added.

Once the plates had been cleared away, the pair relaxed together on one of the settees.

'So, tell me about your trip to Cheltenham,' she said while topping up his glass of lager.

'Well,' said Vickers, 'I saw both the men that Craig said he was with on Saturday evening, Aaron Bradstock and Bruce Cummings. They confirmed they went to the two pubs Craig mentioned. They met in the first pub, the Blue Anchor, just before three o'clock and watched the football match between Bournemouth and Chelsea, which ended at around five. Then they moved onto the second pub, where they stayed until around eight.'

'So, who was doing the driving?' she asked.

'Craig, apparently, which, of course, meant he was only able to have a couple of drinks.'

'What happened at eight o'clock?'

'Craig took them home and then went back to his flat.'

'Looks like a sound alibi,' she remarked.

'Yes, but I'll be speaking to staff at both pubs – just to make sure they haven't simply concocted a story.'

'Definitely worth doing,' said Sunita, pouring herself a small glass of wine. 'Look, there's something I've got to tell you. As we both must realise by now, social media could well be at the heart of this case. Candy was an acclaimed influencer and clearly made some enemies while building up her career in the beauty business.'

'Yes, bound to happen,' he agreed.

'Right. Well, about two hours ago, I received a message from John Hepworth. Someone sent Candy a message threatening that they were coming after her and would put her in a box.'

'God.'

'Someone's also meddled with some of her profile pages, posting derisive comments.'

'What sort of comments?'

'Well, Candy had her own slogan which accompanied some of her videos. It was a line from a song. It's something about signing off with sweet candy kisses. Some joker changed the wording on certain web pages to read "sweet panty gussets".'

Vickers laughed and then immediately regretted it.

Readopting his serious manner, he said, 'Can John find out who it is that's been harassing her? Maybe it was that Kaylee Cavendish that the boss spoke about.'

Sunita nodded. 'Maybe,' she said.

Vickers placed his glass of lager down on a small table beside him.

'Perhaps it's going to be a matter of find the troll, and you'll find the killer,' he suggested. 'Does John have any idea how long it might take him to track the person down?'

'No. I asked him that, and he said it might take a few days or even a few weeks.'

'Well worth pursuing,' said Vickers.

'Anyway, before I spoke to John, I went over to Gloucester and met Candy's two assistants.'

'Roxanne and Tiffany?'

'Yes. Roxanne, who's a stylist, mentioned two women who hated the way Candy styled their nails a few months back.'

'Goes with the turf, I suppose,' said Vickers. 'You can't be at the top of your game in the fiercely competitive beauty business without getting flak from some customers.'

She explained how the three women went to the Courtyard Bar after lunch and Candy got drunk.

'Really?' said Vickers, shaking his head. 'A young businesswoman with the promise of a bright future and she behaves like that.'

'Then, at five, they left her highly intoxicated,' said Sunita. 'You'd have thought they would at least have helped her to her room.'

He nodded.

'Roxanne's boyfriend, Mark, wasn't with them all the time,' she continued. 'He went to move his car and meet his sister.'

'We'll have to speak to him,' said Vickers, sipping his lager. 'Goddammit. We're no closer to discovering the truth. We know nothing about the man in her room or how they knew each other.'

Sunita shrugged.

'Well, it certainly looks as though she met the guy sometime between five o'clock, when her friends left, and six o'clock,' said Sunita. 'Because our witness, Cynthia Ecclestone, watched Candy arguing with the man just before ten past six.'

'It's quite a narrow window in time,' Vickers remarked.

She nodded.

'Yes, and it's going to be crucial that we have a good chat with all the bar staff as soon as possible, because it's as clear as the fresh morning air that Candy Goodhope ran into her killer at that hotel bar.'

Chapter 13

After carefully steering his car into his parking space at police headquarters in St James Street on Tuesday morning, the chief inspector turned off the engine.

Turning to his passenger, he said, 'Well, here we are. The start of a new era.'

His son, George, aged twenty-seven, glanced across from the passenger seat.

'Yes, two Roscoes in one CID.'

'I've always been proud of you, George, and you've all the makings of a fine detective.'

'Thanks, Dad. I'll work as hard as I can to continue making you proud.'

Roscoe led his son up the flight of stairs to the CID office on the first floor. As they entered the open-plan department, they could see Sunita Roy and Brett Dawson pinning photographs onto the whiteboard at the far end, close to the chief inspector's private room.

'You remember George, don't you, Sergeant?' he asked Sunita.

'Of course,' she said, shaking the young constable's hand and smiling.

'And this is Brett Dawson, who's a detective constable like you,' said Roscoe.

'Pleased to meet you, mate,' said Dawson, who was the same age as George.

'Right, I'll find you a desk, and then I've got a meeting to organise,' said Roscoe, unlocking his door and hanging up his jacket.

* * *

Half an hour later, detectives and uniformed officers involved in the Candy Goodhope case began gathering in CID, taking up chairs and, in some cases, sitting on the tops of desks.

The chief inspector emerged from his room and clapped his hands.

'Thank you all for turning up so promptly,' he said. 'Before I get this briefing under way, I've got one important task to perform. To welcome a new recruit, my son George, whom many of you already know. For those of you who are unaware, he's been training with Stratford CID, and I've invited him to join us here for a few weeks while DC Khalid is off sick.'

George Roscoe, who was sitting on a desk near the front of the group, turned round, shyly smiling and waving at his new colleagues.

'Now, before we go any further, I ought to let you know the post-mortem on Candy Goodhope was held this morning,' said the chief inspector. 'The provisional cause of death has been given as ligature compression to the neck.'

A string of mumbled comments drifted round the room.

'Now, DS Roy,' Roscoe continued, 'would you be kind enough to tell us about the various characters you've got pinned to the whiteboard?'

Sunita nodded.

'Certainly, sir,' she said. 'The first picture, most people here will know, is of Candy Goodhope, the murder victim. We obtained this photograph from her husband Craig.

'The second picture shows the hotel room where Mrs Goodhope's body was found, and the third shows a view of customers in the hotel's Courtyard Bar sitting at six-seater dining sets. The table where Mrs Goodhope and her assistants were drinking during the hours before her death is the one nearest the camera.'

Vickers interrupted her.

'Could I ask something, guv?' he asked.

The chief inspector nodded.

'We know Candy is something of a celebrity. She's appeared on TV breakfast shows and one of the reality shows. There's a good chance she'll have been spotted in town by members of the public. They may even have stopped her for selfies.'

'That's a good point, Tom,' said Roscoe. 'I'll get the media team to put out a statement to the press, asking for shoppers and customers at the bar to come forward if they had any encounter with her during her time in Queensbridge. Sergeant, would you like to continue?'

Sunita nodded. 'Moving along, this guy with the blond ponytail is Craig Goodhope, the victim's husband,' said Sunita, pointing to the fourth image. 'He's been eliminated from inquiries for the moment because he's short in stature – only five feet five inches tall. Our key witness who watched the entire murder was clear that the pair in the window were about the same height.'

Her boss interrupted.

'Mr Goodhope has a solid alibi too, but that doesn't rule him out altogether,' he said. 'He might have arranged for someone else to visit Queensbridge and get rid of his wife.'

Brett Dawson was sitting beside George Roscoe. He turned towards the chief inspector.

'Sir, I'm getting bank details together for both the Goodhopes,' he said. 'I should have them tomorrow.'

'That should be extremely helpful,' said Roscoe. 'So, the next picture, if I'm not mistaken, is of Jack Bayliss.'

'Yes, sir,' said Sunita, pointing to the picture of the smiling journalist posing in a pub garden. 'Mr Bayliss was staying with the victim at the hotel. We know he paid for a replacement tyre for his sports car at half past five because we've got a receipt from the tyre company. But the tyre firm is only in Marina Gardens, and he could have walked to the hotel in less than ten minutes.'

'Didn't one of the team ask him about Mrs Goodhope's withdrawal of money from the bank?' said Roscoe.

'Yes,' she replied. 'He knew nothing about it.'

The chief inspector frowned. 'He can't be ruled out as a possible suspect.'

'Second to last on the board is Kaylee Cavendish, who's described as a bitter rival of Mrs Goodhope's,' Sunita continued. 'DC Dawson's been checking her out.'

'Yes. She's got a strong alibi,' said the blond-haired constable. 'She was at a restaurant with friends, and the proprietor's confirmed this.'

'Last of all, we have Mark Tanner, who's Roxanne Hayes' boyfriend,' said Sunita. 'He comes across as a rather shady character. On the few brief occasions he appears in Candy's videos or photographs, he's keeping his distance, and twice he seems to be scowling towards Candy.'

'I'm afraid, Sergeant, a lot of men would sympathise with his situation,' said Roscoe. 'For most of the time, he's the only man in the salon. No surprise if he looks and feels out of place.'

'Well, his behaviour certainly appeared strange after they all left the salon,' she said. 'He originally went to the Courtyard Bar along with his girlfriend Roxanne, but he kept leaving her and going off on his own. We're told he went to meet his sister, who was shopping, but we don't yet know if that's true.'

'We certainly need more information about him,' Roscoe agreed. 'But, before that, we need to speak to bar staff and build up a picture, if possible, of who the other customers were in the bar. Sergeant, I'd like you to go over there this morning. Take Dawson with you and see what you can find out. We need answers to several key questions: Did Mrs Goodhope meet someone after her arrival in Queensbridge who had a reason to kill her? Did she meet someone in the Courtyard Bar or some other part of the hotel after her friends left? Was there someone prowling round with evil intent inside the hotel?'

He paused before continuing. 'Then there's the money. For what reason did she withdraw six hundred pounds from the bank? Her friends said the money wasn't intended for them, so who was it for? Was the money taken by the killer in a robbery gone wrong? Was the money taken to make it *look* like a robbery? Finally, we need to ask: what were Candy's plans for the following day, the Sunday, and does that have anything to do with her death?'

'Whoever it was, sir, I'd lay money that it was someone she knew,' said Vickers.

'Why do you say that?' the chief inspector asked.

'Just the fact that the pair were together inside her hotel room and that they were arguing near the window. That suggests to me that, on the balance of probabilities, she knew the man and had invited him in.'

Chapter 14

The headmaster rose from behind his antique Victorian desk and stretched his legs. Then he stepped across to the large Gothic window and stared out as groups of pupils hurried across the gravel paths for their next classes.

He was wondering if he should ask one of his secretaries to make some tea when his phone rang.

Returning to his high-back chair, he lifted the receiver.

'Yes, Heather?' he said.

'Mr Wimbush,' said his polite, softly spoken secretary, 'I've got a lady on the line who's demanding to speak to you.'

'It's not another parent complaining about the new date for the Speech Day, is it?' he asked.

'The lady won't tell me what it's about.'

'Have you got her name?'

'She won't give me that either.'

'Very well. You'd better put her through.'

After a lengthy pause and two clicking sounds, he could hear breathing.

'This is Mr Wimbush,' said the grey-haired schoolmaster. 'How can I help?'

'Steven, it's me,' his caller announced.

'Miranda, I've told you never to call me when I'm in my study here,' he snapped.

'I think you've blocked my mobile number.'

'I haven't blocked you,' he said.

'Well, I've tried your mobile several times over the past few days, and I always get your voicemail,' she said.

'Then leave a message.'

'What's the point?' she said. 'I know you won't call me back. Oh, Steven, I've missed you so much.'

'Miranda, you know things are different now,' he said in a voice which was calm and cultured but imperious. 'You know what my thoughts are.'

'I can't stop thinking about you, Steven, and I've bought you a special present.'

'Miranda, you know what I've said. We can't meet up for the moment. We've got to try and move on.'

'Come and see me tonight. I'll cook you your favourite meal,' she said in silky, persuasive tones.

'It's very tempting, Miranda, but Samantha's unwell, and it would be unkind for me to leave her alone tonight.'

'Is that the same Samantha that you've promised to leave for good on countless occasions but never found the right opportunity?' asked Miranda.

'Shush,' he said. 'Heather's only in the next room. I don't want her overhearing us talking about personal matters.'

'Come over to Abbots Green to see me tonight, Steven,' she implored him. 'Tell Samantha you've got to visit the parents of one of the boys or something.'

'No, Miranda, I must be firm with you.' The tone of his delivery was as careful as a muted trumpet. 'I really can't come over this evening.'

She was silent for a moment.

'Are you still there?' he asked.

'Yes,' came a tearful voice. 'I can't stop thinking about you, Steven. But you've shut yourself off from me. You're indifferent. All the good times we've had together seem to be of no consequence to you. They're just a series of pretty memories.'

'Don't be ridiculous, Miranda. You know I enjoyed our time together, but sadly I can't see you for the moment.'

'It doesn't have to be like this,' she said. 'Come on, Steven. Come round at eight o'clock, and I'll cook for you again.'

'I'll see what I can do. I won't promise. I'll come if nothing crops up,' he said.

'Do the best you can,' she said. 'We need to talk.'

Then she ended the call.

The fifty-five-year-old head of Biddington Hall School replaced the handset on its cradle. He leaned forward and placed his head in his hands. *Omne initium difficile est*, he told himself, recalling a Latin proverb about difficult beginnings.

Heather, his auburn-haired secretary in her mid-forties, knocked and poked her head round the door.

'Was that all right, Mr Wimbush?' she asked. 'The lady seemed quite agitated.'

The headmaster gazed across at her.

'Perfectly all right, Heather,' he replied. 'Just a worried parent.'

'I've got Brendon waiting in the corridor outside the office, wanting to see you,' she continued. 'Shall I tell him you're busy?'

Wimbush glanced at his watch.

'No, it's all right. Tell him to come in,' he replied.

The school caretaker, a gaunt-looking man of medium height with dark, close-cropped hair, was in his thirties. The head had been talked into employing him as a favour when the previous incumbent had retired after several decades of loyal service.

'Mr Wimbush, these new hours you've given me aren't working,' Brendon Blake said after entering the room and shutting the door behind him.

‘Sit down and tell me what the problem is,’ said Wimbush.

‘I used to come in at a quarter past seven and the first thing I did was test the alarms, which meant teachers and pupils weren’t inconvenienced,’ he said while making himself comfortable on an upholstered chair. ‘Now you’ve got me starting at eight, I get nothing but complaints about the noise. Not only that. You’ve got me hanging around in the school until the cleaners have finished, and some nights I’m still here at six o’clock.’

‘Do you know why we had to change your hours?’ asked the head.

‘Something to do with the cleaners, wasn’t it?’ said Blake.

‘Correct. Prior to the change in hours, they’d wait until you’d left the main building at a quarter past five and then skip their work. They’d spend a few minutes chatting and then make tracks.’

‘So, on top of everything else I’ve got to do, I’ve become the cleaners’ overseer,’ he moaned.

‘I wouldn’t describe it like that,’ said Wimbush.

‘Oh? How would you describe it then? It seems to me I’m being put upon for all the jobs no one else in the school wants to do.’

Wimbush gazed across the desk at his slightly dishevelled employee who was looking pale with signs of stubble around his jaw.

He’s right, of course, the headmaster told himself. The previous caretaker had been an all-rounder, capable of juggling a variety of roles. They had been expecting similar proficiency from Blake, but he’d failed to live up to expectations.

‘I can’t do anything about it at the moment,’ said Wimbush. ‘The term will be over in a few weeks. I’ll speak to the bursar and see if something can’t be done. But I’m glad you’re here. There have been a couple of incidents reported to me.’

'Oh yeah? And what sort of incidents would they be?' the caretaker demanded.

The head leaned back in his chair and rested his hands on his desk.

'Well, the Friday before last and on Thursday of last week you were at least an hour late arriving for work, even though you live on the premises,' said Wimbush.

'That's because I wasn't very well,' said Blake.

'On Thursday, Mr Newbold went round to your flat to see what had happened, and he was astonished to find you were engrossed in playing some kind of game online.'

'That was the nosy bastard, was it, who knocked on my door and peered through my window?' said Blake.

'I'll thank you to mind your language. Mr Newbold was simply doing his job,' said Wimbush. 'So what have you got to say about this? You weren't ill at all.'

'Well, I had something important to do. That's all.'

'Look,' said Wimbush, 'if you've got something important to do, you should do it in your own time – not the school's. I'm sorry, Brendon, but I'm going to have to give you a verbal warning that you're at risk of losing your job if your behaviour doesn't improve.'

'I can't understand you taking that attitude,' said Blake. 'You know I've been under pressure because of the new hours.'

'Can I take it that you've heard and understood the school's side of the story, and that you're prepared to buck up your ideas?'

The disgruntled employee stood up and folded his arms.

'All right,' he said. 'I'll do my best.'

'Good. That's the right attitude,' said the head, leaning back on his chair in his black academic gown.

Without saying another word, the caretaker left the head's first-floor study, closing the door behind him.

The headmaster watched a few minutes later as Blake emerged from the building and began following the path that led to his small ground-floor flat.

He couldn't help noticing that, as the caretaker approached one of the flower borders, he drew his right foot back and kicked the low stone wall in frustration.

Chapter 15

The sun crept out from behind the clouds soon after midday on Tuesday, bathing the Warwickshire countryside in its rays, as Sunita Roy and Brett Dawson set off for the Queensbridge Arms Hotel.

The fields and meadows they passed were speckled with mauve foxgloves and yellow cowslips while some of the hedgerows were drenched in hawthorns' white blossom.

'Judging by the progress we're making, we should arrive at the hotel just before the lunchtime rush,' said Dawson.

'We don't have to worry,' she replied. 'The head barman knows we're coming. By the way, I'll be getting a call any moment from Tom Vickers. John Hepworth has been looking into Candy's phone and social media accounts. He found out it was Mark Tanner who sent the threatening messages.'

They were just leaving the M42 motorway and joining the A435 road when Sunita's phone began to ring. She glanced at the screen which confirmed it was her boyfriend.

'How's it going?' she asked, switching to hands-free. 'Has Mark Tanner made a full confession?'

'Sadly not,' said Vickers. 'We're on the Troutbeck estate but can't find him. Can I check with you? Is it definitely 67 Keswick Drive?'

'That's right, Tom,' she said. 'He's staying with his sister.'

'Well, there's no reply at the address.'

'That's a nuisance,' she said. 'I don't want to call his girlfriend, Roxanne, because she might tip him off that we're looking for him.'

'No, don't do that,' he said. 'Tell you what. We'll have a word with the neighbours. I've got George Roscoe with me, by the way. The DCI thought it would be good experience for him.'

'Well, let's hope you don't lead him astray,' said Sunita.

Fifteen minutes later, she drew into the hotel car park. She and Dawson got out and made their way round to the main entrance.

As they reached the glazed doors to the open-air Courtyard Bar, they spotted half a dozen customers sitting at tables beneath the parasols.

'Good afternoon, madam,' said a man in his thirties in a smart, navy-blue tunic. He was a short distance inside the bar, wiping a table. 'Can I get you both a drink?'

'Are you Mr Buckley?' Sunita asked.

'Yes, that's right,' he replied in a north-east accent.

'We're from Heart of England CID. I'm DS Roy. This is DC Dawson.'

'Oh, of course. You wanted to speak to us. Ellis Buckley, head barman. Shall I call Tasha? She was also on duty on Saturday afternoon.'

'If you could,' said Sunita as the two detectives stepped inside the beer garden.

Buckley, a slim man of medium height with fair hair and a beard, stepped behind the counter, which was on the left of the bar, and disappeared into the kitchen. A few minutes later, he reappeared, accompanied by a young woman in her twenties.

'This is Tasha,' Buckley explained. 'Tasha Garvey. She did an extended shift on Saturday, working from eleven till nine.'

'Is there somewhere we can sit down?' asked Dawson.

'Is this OK?' asked the barman, pointing to a table in the corner.

'That'll do fine,' said Sunita, removing a rolled-up photograph of Candy Goodhope from her pocket.

'Can we start by asking if you remember seeing this woman on Saturday afternoon?' Sunita asked, once they had all sat down.

Buckley took a few seconds to study the image, which showed the young long-haired woman in a convivial mood, laughing towards the camera.

'Yes,' he said. 'That's Candy Goodhope, isn't it? She was here and a little the worse for drink by the time she left.'

'What's your first recollection of seeing her?'

'She turned up with three other people at around half past two,' he said with a solemn expression. 'I remember her because she was in a lively mood and there was a lot of banter.'

'Who were the people with her?' asked Dawson.

'There was a woman with fairly lengthy, curly, ginger hair and one with medium-length blonde hair. There was a guy with them who had a mop of black hair and a beard. I remember Candy because she came up to the bar and ordered the first round of drinks from us.'

'Do you remember what the women had to drink?' asked Dawson.

'One of them had a honey bee. I remember that,' replied Buckley with a smile.

'A honey bee?' said Dawson.

'Yes. Honey with white rum.'

'It's delicious,' remarked Garvey. 'It's very popular in my home country.'

'Where's that?' asked Dawson.

'Jamaica,' she said with a broad grin. 'It also needs a drop of lemon juice.' She turned to the sergeant. 'You must try it.'

'Not for me,' said Sunita. 'I'm not into alcohol much.'

The two staff members glanced at each other but said nothing.

'I think the ginger-haired woman had the honey bee,' said Buckley. 'The younger blonde had white wine and Candy drank Bacardi and Coke.'

'And the man?'

'He was drinking QB Bitter,' said Buckley.

'How many rounds of drinks were there?' asked Sunita.

'Quite a few,' he said. 'I personally served them three times.'

'And I served them twice,' said Garvey. 'But we weren't the only people serving. Sian Boyle was also working behind the bar on Saturday afternoon. She's not here today.'

'Where did they sit?' Sunita asked.

'Table Five,' said the barman. He stood up and walked past four sets of tables with benches until he came to a fifth table where a solitary man was sitting, drinking beer.

'They were sitting here, by the wall, next to the TV screen,' he shouted before returning.

'What about the man who was with them?' asked Dawson.

'A bit of an oddball, I thought,' said the barman. 'Scruffy black hair and beard. A bit of a restless character. He was on his phone a lot and he kept disappearing for long periods.'

'Do you recall seeing a man with dark hair, a check shirt and a ring on his right hand?' asked Dawson.

'No.'

'How many customers would you say were here?'

'I'd say about a hundred,' said Garvey. 'A lot of customers were watching the football on our flatscreen TV.'

Sunita glanced across the table towards him.

'We've been told there was a group of men who looked like rugby players sitting at the next table to Candy and her friends,' she said.

'That's right. Tom, Chris, Mark and Tony were there with some friends from Queensbridge Rugby Club,' said the barman.

'And there was some joking going on between the men and the women?'

'We didn't have much time to listen to conversations,' Garvey said. 'We were rushed off our feet. I hardly had time to blow my nose.'

'We're trying to form a picture of what happened to Candy between five and six o'clock,' Sunita continued. 'The two women with Candy said they and the man left for good at around five o'clock. Did you see them go?'

'Yes. Would you believe there've been a few cases of customers running off without paying? So the hotel manager's asked us to keep a closer eye on things. I'm sure they left around five, along with the rugby guys.'

Garvey nodded. 'That's right,' she said.

'So, Candy was left at the table on her own?' said Sunita.

'Yes, but not for long,' said Garvey. 'It was a nice afternoon and the place was heaving. After a few minutes, I noticed two men and two women came to the table and were chatting to Candy. I took more of an interest in her then because it was obvious she'd had a lot to drink.'

'About six or seven Bacardis by then?' asked Dawson.

'I'd say so. Maybe more,' said Garvey.

'Did you notice what she had with her?'

'I know she was carrying a silver laptop because I had to move it to the edge of the table to make space for drinks.'

Sunita glanced at her colleague as the two bar staff left them briefly to attend to a customer who was complaining about the lack of service.

'Sarge, I wonder what happened to the silver laptop. It wasn't in her hotel bedroom when we searched, was it?' said Dawson.

'No,' she said. 'Maybe the killer took it.'

As soon as Buckley and Garvey returned, Sunita asked them whether Candy was carrying a handbag along with the laptop.

'I didn't see a handbag,' said Garvey.

'Maybe she'd gone up and locked it in her room,' Sunita remarked.

'I think the four newcomers all work at Mondales department store on the High Street,' said Garvey. 'They've been in a few times before.'

'Can you describe them at all?' Dawson asked.

'Early twenties. One of the women had long blonde hair and glasses. They were fairly smartly dressed. One of the men had a black T-shirt on which said "I never argue". Candy shuffled along the table so they could all squeeze on. She chatted to one of the guys for quite a while.'

'What time was that?' asked Sunita.

'About half past five.'

'Did they pay by card?'

'Yes,' said Garvey. 'They were laughing and joking. One of the women whispered to me, "Don't judge us. It's been a hard week."'

'If you've got the names of the folk from Mondales that paid, that would be very helpful.'

'I'll see what I can do.'

'What happened next?' asked Sunita.

'Candy then left the table,' said the barmaid, 'and queued up at the bar for another drink, but we said we couldn't serve her.'

'We both felt she'd had too much to drink,' said Buckley, and Garvey nodded.

'I shouldn't think she was too happy about that,' Dawson remarked.

'That's right,' said Buckley. 'She took the news badly. She was standing by two men who'd been stuffing money into the fruit machines. She struck up a conversation with them.'

'Do you know who these men were?'

Both bartenders shook their heads.

'Never seen them before,' said Buckley. 'One of them was drinking whisky and Coke. I don't think the other one even bothered to buy a drink. They were both chancing their luck on the machines.'

'Can you describe them?' asked Sunita.

'One was a slim guy in his thirties with very short hair. I think he had a brown jacket. The other guy was a bit overweight and in his forties. He was going bald and had a bright-red football shirt and jeans.'

Garvey nodded in agreement. 'One minute Candy was talking to the two men, and the next moment she was gone. Not a word of a lie. No sooner she'd gone, one of the shop workers rushed over with her laptop and said, "I think that woman left this behind." I'd seen her heading into the reception hall and decided to race after her.'

'Was she on her own when you reached her?' asked Sunita.

'Yes, but I had to run like the wind to catch her before she got in the lift.'

Chapter 16

Taking one step at a time, Samantha Wimbush carried the porcelain serving dish filled with steaming beef stroganoff into the spacious dining room.

'Here we are, Steven,' she said, moving the vase of blue delphiniums out of the way and proudly placing the piping hot container on a mat in the centre of the long table.

'That smells good, Samantha,' her husband replied, patting her on the waist with his right hand.

Her grey hair was drawn back behind her head, giving a rather severe look. She removed his hand from her midriff.

'What sort of day did you have, dear?' she asked, gazing out of their dining room window. A few lights were flickering from the ground floor of the red-brick school building a few hundred metres away.

'I had to give that lazy idiot Brendon Blake a verbal warning today,' he said as Samantha put some beef, potatoes and vegetables on his dinner plate. 'He's completely unreliable. I don't know why I ever employed him in the first place.'

'You told me he had a good CV and people spoke highly of him,' said Samantha, scooping stroganoff onto her own plate.

'I think his CV details were largely fiction,' he said. 'I was badly misled and should have checked it thoroughly, but we were in a hurry to replace Gordon. I told you he was late for work, didn't I? Gareth Newbold went to his rooms last week and caught him browsing a casino website. I had half a mind to dock him some pay.'

'You'd be within your rights.'

'I decided not to, in the end. I just hope he changes his attitude now he's received his warning. I can't stand laziness. *Ignavum fortuna repugnat.*'

'Fortune disdains the lazy?'

'Correct.'

Then their phone rang in the hallway.

'I'll get it,' said Samantha, getting up from the table and hurrying out of the room. She had just turned sixty, but regular country walks had kept her fit, and she nimbly reached the hallway before her younger husband had even risen from the table.

Wimbush listened as his wife picked up the handset and said, 'Hello' three times.

She returned with an annoyed expression.

'No one there,' she muttered. 'Maybe one of the boys.'

'It's possible,' he admitted as he tucked into the crème brûlée dessert which Samantha had placed on the table earlier beneath a teacloth. A few minutes later, the phone rang again.

'I'll go this time,' he insisted, stepping quickly into the hall.

'Hello?' he said. He could hear a faint voice burbling in the distance.

'Hello?' he repeated.

There was still no reply, so he replaced the receiver and resumed his place at the table.

'Probably someone playing a joke,' he said. 'Maybe one of the boys.'

A few minutes later, Wimbush finished his meal in the large dining room, beneath their crystal chandelier. He wiped his mouth with a serviette and stood up before stepping across to the patio doors that overlooked their substantial lawn and drew the beige curtains.

He yawned.

'Do you know? I think I'll take Bessie for a walk,' he said. 'I need to stretch my legs after that lovely meal.'

'I think it's still raining,' Samantha said.

'It's stopped,' he insisted, parting the curtains a fraction and peering outside.

He kissed Samantha on the cheek before stepping into the hall. He collected the dog lead from one of the hooks on the coat stand and opened the kitchen door.

Their boisterous five-year-old golden Labrador burst into life, jumping up at him and barking.

After putting on his Harris Tweed jacket and clipping the lead on Bessie's collar, Wimbush opened the front door and led the dog down their driveway and out into the dark lane. He was right – it *had* stopped raining. But the only light came from the waning moon and the occasional orange glow of a streetlight, so he tapped his pocket to make sure he had his torch with him, just in case.

With Bessie straining on the lead, they walked past the school, past the four black-and-white timber cottages and then up the steep hill. Eventually, they reached the crossroads at the top of Rose Lane where a white signpost directed travellers towards either the town of Queensbridge or the village of Norton Prior.

At the junction was a small green with a wooden bench, which some residents considered to be a central point in the hamlet of Biddington. Wimbush sat down and tied Bessie to the bench armrest. Then he drew his mobile phone from his pocket and dialled a number which was listed among his contacts as 'School Supplies'.

After a few seconds, his call was answered.

'Oh, there you are, Steven,' said the gentle female voice.

'Miranda, why have you started phoning my home again?' he demanded.

'It's the only way I can get through. You were meant to be coming round to see me tonight.'

'I only said I'd try. It wasn't possible tonight. Can't you get it into your head that we're taking a break?' he said.

'Don't say that, Steven.'

Bessie looked up at him and whimpered.

'Quiet, Bessie,' he said in a low voice.

'Steven, have you got the dog with you?' Miranda asked.

'Correct. We're on a walk.'

'Let me say hello to Bessie.'

'Don't be ridiculous.'

'Steven.'

'Oh, very well.'

He placed the handset in front of the dog.

'The dog can hear you now,' he told Miranda.

'Hi Bessie. Have you been a good girl?' she asked.

The dog's ears pricked up and she began wagging her tail.

'She recognised your voice,' Wimbush admitted.

'Will you come and see me tomorrow?' Miranda implored him.

'Firstly, you've got to promise me you won't call me at work again and you won't call me at home,' he said.

'Provided you come and see me tomorrow, it's a deal,' said Miranda. 'I can cook for you, and we can have a talk about what's been troubling you.'

'I can only say that I'll do my best,' he said.

'But that's what you told me this morning, and you didn't show up,' she said.

'Miranda, I've got to go now. The dog's getting restless.'

'There's always some lame excuse with you, isn't there, Steven? Why can't we get back to the lovely relationship we had until a few weeks ago?'

'Oh, when I speak to you, we end up going round in circles,' he said. 'You know how I feel. I need time to think. We've had some good times, but I just feel things have reached a turning point.'

Miranda did not seem to be listening.

'Steven, if you let me down tomorrow, I can promise you I'm going to be really angry. I may even call Samantha and tell her exactly what's been going on.'

'You can't do that, Miranda. Samantha would never forgive me if she found out.'

'You should have thought of that before you embarked on your little romantic adventure with me.'

'Promise me you won't talk to Samantha. She's already got her suspicions. If she finds out the truth about us, she'll take me to the cleaners. I could even lose my position at the school.'

'I won't call her if you come to see me tomorrow evening.'

'I'll certainly do my best,' he said. 'Look, I've got to go. Bye.'

'Bye for now,' she said, ending the call.

Wimbush untied the dog's lead and led Bessie along the Queensbridge Road, which was surrounded on both sides by open fields. When he was approaching the humpback bridge over the River Avon, he turned round and led Bessie back towards their house.

'Steven, old boy, you've got yourself into a real quandary,' he told himself. 'What on earth are you going to do about Miranda?'

Chapter 17

Tom Vickers' Audi swept by the dull, grey, pebble-dashed houses of Grasmere Road and turned right into Coniston Road just after one o'clock. After passing rows of red-brick maisonettes, he turned into tree-lined Keswick Drive, where blocks of flats, three storeys high, vied for space alongside more of the dull, grey, pebble-dashed houses. He drew up outside number sixty-seven, a two-bedroom semi-detached house with all its front curtains closed, and turned to his passenger.

'Let's hope we have more luck this time, George,' he said as the two men got out. 'You look a bit shattered?'

'Our baby's not a good sleeper,' replied George.

Vickers strode through the open gate and stooped to move a child's purple ride-on jeep off the path. Then, followed closely by George Roscoe, he approached the front door and knocked. Immediately, they were greeted by the sound of barking.

'Good,' muttered Vickers. 'Looks like they're home.'

An excited French bulldog appeared behind the beige curtains in the front window, yapping furiously.

'Is your master home?' asked Vickers as he stared at the brindle-coloured pet. This only spurred the dog into barking even more furiously.

‘Stop it, Milo!’ said a female voice before a woman in her late twenties with long black hair opened the door.

‘Heart of England CID,’ said Vickers. ‘We’re looking for Mark Tanner.’

‘What do you want him for?’ asked the householder as the dog continued barking. Two grubby toddlers could be seen playing in the dingy hallway behind her.

‘Just need to ask him a few questions,’ said the inspector, showing his warrant card. ‘We understand he knew Candy Goodhope.’

‘I’m Denise, his sister,’ she said. ‘Hold on a minute while I sort out the dog.’

She closed the door and the detectives could hear her saying, ‘Stop it, Milo. I’ll have to put you in the kitchen.’

A minute later, she was back.

‘Is Mr Tanner around?’ asked Vickers, who was growing impatient.

‘He were here a short while ago,’ she replied. ‘I’ll just call him.’

They watched as she walked to the foot of the stairs and shouted, ‘Mark. Someone here to see you.’

At first, the house was silent, apart from the sound of one of the toddlers striking the tiled hall floor with a plastic hammer.

Then a hesitant voice pierced the silence. ‘Who is it?’

‘It’s the police, Mark,’ said Denise.

Vickers and the young constable waited patiently by the doorstep for the twenty-six-year-old suspect to appear. But minutes passed and no one emerged.

‘I’ll go and see where he’s got to,’ Denise told them before climbing the stairs.

George happened to glance over his left shoulder. He caught sight of an agile young man with black hair and a beard in a white shirt and dark trousers, sprinting down the street in the direction of Coniston Road.

‘Is that him?’ he asked the inspector.

'Yes, it is!' yelled Vickers. 'Get after him. I'll take the car.'

Denise Tanner watched bemused as George raced down the pavement after the unemployed labourer, who was fleeing like a fox with his tail on fire.

After running a short way along the street, Tanner turned right into Borrowdale Lane and headed towards a grove of low trees and dense bushes. George, who regularly trained at a gym near his Warwick home, proved to be fitter than the suspect. The distance between the pair was shortening, but he remained at least a hundred metres behind. His eyes followed as Tanner darted into the bushes and was lost from sight.

Vickers arrived in the lane and drove slowly along beside the constable.

'Did he go into that wood?' asked Vickers, letting his window down.

'Yes,' said George, slacking off for a moment. 'But as far as I know, he can't escape over the back. There's a factory with a high fence. He'll have to come out eventually.'

'I'll go and park round the corner,' said Vickers. 'I've called the control room and they're sending one of the canines, but that may take some time.'

As Vickers drove away, George arrived at the edge of the grove. Taking a methodical approach, he walked along the pavement beside the bushes, searching for the slightest glimpse of a white shirt as he went.

For a while, there was no sign of the wanted man. But the moment he reached the far end of the trees, Tanner dashed out of his hiding place and careered back up Borrowdale Lane like a greyhound sprung from a trap.

George resumed the chase, following as Tanner turned right into Coniston Road. Then, as swiftly as Tanner had re-emerged, he vanished again.

The constable had become distracted. He had glanced away briefly as a car similar to Vickers' Audi had glided past. When he looked back, the man was no longer in sight. George was annoyed with himself. How had the suspect managed to get away? Had he crept into one of the gardens? Had he concealed himself behind one of the vehicles parked along the street?

Vickers drove up beside the narrow grass verge as George came to a standstill on the pavement.

'I've lost him,' moaned the constable. 'He just vanished into thin air.'

'That boy's got something to hide, wouldn't you say, George?' said Vickers while parking his car and stepping onto the pavement. 'He made off from the house as if he'd got the fear of God in him. Hold on a minute.'

The inspector was staring at a blue van parked a few metres ahead of them. The name 'Norton Air Conditioning and Refrigeration' was emblazoned on the back and sides.

'If I'm not mistaken,' Vickers muttered to himself, 'the driver's door hasn't been closed properly.

He stooped down and crept along by the side of the vehicle. Then he snatched the handle and the door burst open. Inside was an indignant driver, sitting quietly and drinking tea from a flask.

'Sorry, mate,' said the embarrassed inspector. 'We're police, looking for someone. You didn't see a guy run past, did you? White shirt and dark trousers.'

The middle-aged driver was so surprised he nearly spilled his flask.

'With really black hair?' he asked Vickers.

A smile flickered across the inspector's face.

'Yes. Have you seen him?'

'He went down that alley between the houses,' said the driver.

'Thanks, mate,' said Vickers as George joined him.

'He's down the alley,' said Vickers, who at once began hurrying down the narrow lane which had wire-netting fences on each side.

Eventually, the pair arrived at the end of the lane, where there were sixteen garages. Fly-tippers had turned the paved area in front of the first two garages into a dumping ground. An old double mattress was propped up against one of the garage doors.

'You have a look behind the garages,' Vickers told his colleague. 'I'll check if any of the doors are unlocked.'

George stepped across a patch of grass beside the first garage and found the lane ended with a high piece of wire netting near the building's back wall. It was clear Tanner had not ventured beyond this point.

As he retraced his steps, a figure suddenly darted out from beneath the mattress and headed back up the alley at a furious pace.

Realising at once it was Tanner, George raced after him like a whippet after a hare, all the while shouting for him to stop. This time, the fleeing man was not so fleet-footed – perhaps he was tired after his exertions – and George managed to grab his shoulder before he could reach the road.

The breathless runner spun round and attempted to strike his pursuer in the face. But the young detective saw his fist coming and dodged the blow. He then unhitched his pepper spray canister from his belt.

'Stop resisting, or I'll use the spray,' he yelled as Tanner prepared to strike a second blow.

Once it was clear the suspect had no intention of heeding the warning, George squirted the canister towards him.

Tanner fell to his knees, clasping his hands over his eyes and swearing. Thereupon, the constable forced him to the ground.

Vickers arrived on the scene as his colleague was handcuffing him.

'Good work, George,' said Vickers. 'We'll have to go back to the house now and impound any phones, laptops and tablets.'

Tanner kept screaming, 'Get off me. Leave me alone,' while the constable fastened a pair of cuffs round his wrists.

Chapter 18

'Did you have a good lunch, Tom?' asked the chief inspector as he opened his office door and peered out. Vickers, who was sitting at a nearby desk in CID, nodded and smiled.

'Events conspired to make it a late lunch,' he replied while standing in the doorway.

'I trust you're not going to give our Mr Tanner a rough time because of it?'

'No, sir, although the very thought of sitting in the same room as him this afternoon gives me indigestion.'

'Come on,' said Roscoe, picking up a bundle of documents. 'Let's go and see what he's got to say for himself.'

'By the way, sir, we wouldn't have caught him if it hadn't been for your son. He raced after Tanner as if his life depended on it.'

'I suppose all those hours spent in the gym have proved worthwhile in the end,' said Roscoe.

Mark Tanner looked a sad, lonely figure when they reached Interview Room One on the ground floor. His black hair was unkempt. He was still wearing the white shirt and black trousers he had worn at the time of his arrest two hours earlier under the Malicious Communications Act of 1988.

Beside him at the table was a slim, solemn-faced solicitor Saleema Siddiqui, who was whispering in her client's ear. The chief inspector took a seat opposite the suspect and placed his pile of documents down on the table. Then he watched as the solicitor, with dark hair tied neatly behind her head, ended the conversation.

'I hope we're ready to proceed,' said Roscoe.

'Yes, I think so,' said Siddiqui. 'I've had a chance to discuss matters with my client.'

'Right,' said Roscoe as Vickers took a chair next to him. 'Well, the first thing we want to ask is why you fled when DI Vickers here called round to speak to you earlier?'

Tanner stared across the table. 'I don't know,' he said. 'I suppose I weren't in the mood for receiving guests.'

'Very often,' said Vickers, 'people who don't want to speak to the police and run off have got something to hide.'

'You've probably got rather a lot to hide, haven't you?' said Roscoe.

Tanner shook his head. 'No,' he said.

Roscoe glanced down at a sheet of paper on the table. 'I can see you've kept a very busy life,' he said. 'We'll dispense with the juvenile offences. Since reaching eighteen, you've been convicted of five burglaries, two assaults, two cases of possession of cannabis, one attempt to supply class A drugs, one of possessing a knife, and two offences of driving while disqualified.'

'My client's served his punishment for these offences,' said Siddiqui, 'and he's changed his ways. He tells me those offences, though regrettable, occurred before he fully matured.'

'I wonder if he genuinely has changed his ways,' said Roscoe. 'If he has, he might like to come clean and explain why he eluded us.'

Siddiqui whispered in her client's ear. Tanner glanced towards her and nodded.

'All right,' he said. 'I'll be honest with you. My driving documents ain't in order. I've had a few run-ins with you people, as you're obviously aware, and I weren't up for a load of questions.'

'You're quite correct,' said Roscoe. 'Your driving documents aren't in order. You were caught on Thursday of last week driving a Ford Puma without insurance and without a valid driving licence.'

Tanner nodded. 'Yeah, maybe.'

'There's no "maybe" about it. You've been banned from driving, haven't you?' Roscoe continued.

'Yeah, all right,' he replied.

'And that's why you ran away from me and my colleague earlier, is it?' asked Vickers.

'Yeah, of course,' said Tanner. 'I thought you were coming to see me about that.'

Roscoe frowned and gazed across at their suspect.

'That wasn't all we wanted to talk to you about, Mr Tanner,' said the chief inspector. 'We wanted to ask you about some nasty comments you've made online which were directed at Candy Goodhope. They've been traced to your personal accounts. In addition, you sent two threatening messages to her phone.'

Tanner took on the appearance of a startled rabbit, unsure whether to reply or make a dash for the door.

'You've got to be joking,' he said defiantly. 'Why would I do that? My girlfriend depends on Candy for her income. You've got your information mixed up. I'd never have threatened her.'

'We've got a fair bit of evidence,' said Roscoe, removing three website images from his bundle and passing the pages across the table.

'Have a look at these. The first is an image of Candy Goodhope's YouTube profile on 28 April. Someone changed a slogan to read "sweet panty gussets" instead of "sweet candy kisses". You'll see that ten years has been added to her age on her TikTok profile. The third page, which relates to an online beauty tutorial, contains the potentially libelous comment that some of her techniques are directly copied from other make-up artists.'

'No, no, no,' said Tanner, leaning forward and placing his head in his hands.

'Are these changes still live as we speak, Chief Inspector?' Siddiqui asked.

Roscoe shook his head.

'No, I understand Mrs Goodhope's IT manager negated the changes as soon as they were spotted. Our digital expert is currently examining your client's laptop, obtained from his home, and there are signs he used it to tamper with Mrs Goodhope's web pages. It's also clear Mr Tanner's phone was used to send her at least two anonymous messages, threatening that the sender was "coming after her" and would "put her in a box".'

'None of that were done by me. I swear,' Tanner insisted.

'These allegations are all new to me,' said Siddiqui. 'I'd appreciate a quiet moment with my client, if that's possible, Chief Inspector.'

'I can give you ten minutes,' said Roscoe.

* * *

As soon as the chief inspector and Tom Vickers returned to the interview room after the adjournment, Saleema Siddiqui announced that Mark Tanner wished to make some admissions.

'That's good to know,' said Roscoe. 'Perhaps you'd like to explain the situation then, Mr Tanner.'

'Yeah, all right,' he said, sitting upright. 'I'll be straight with you. I didn't really like Candy and I did tamper with stuff online about her. I also sent the messages to say she'd end up in a box – just to scare her a little. You've got to understand. I went to the same school as her in

Gloucester, St Mildred's, and she were a grass. I once played a joke on one of her mates during a lunch hour.'

'What did you do exactly?' asked Vickers.

'I played a childish prank. It were very funny at the time.'

'Not for the poor girl, I imagine,' said Vickers.

'Candy grassed me up to the teachers and the deputy head, Mr Wimbush, got to hear about it. I got into a load of trouble.'

'It sounds to me as though she was standing up for a pupil you bullied,' said Roscoe.

'No, I never did no bullying,' Tanner insisted. 'It were just a lark. God, ain't no one allowed a bit of fun these days?'

'So, you and Candy had a bit of history?' said Vickers.

'You could say that,' Tanner admitted, 'but that ain't the whole story. I didn't like the way she treated Roxanne. Roxy worked extremely hard for Candy and were never properly appreciated. She just used her.'

'So, you decided to take out your grievances on Mrs Goodhope by meddling with online information about her and threatening her life?' said Roscoe, who was staring directly into his eyes.

'It were never a real threat to her life,' said Tanner, shaking his head. 'It were just done to give her a little bit of a scare. That's all. Hey, don't you jump to any conclusions about me. It weren't me in the hotel room. I swear on my mother's life. Roxy and me left the hotel more than an hour before Candy were done in.'

Chapter 19

A tall, grey-haired figure trudged along the narrow country lane with the approach of nightfall. Whenever he was caught in the headlights of a vehicle, he would step onto the grass verge and wait until it had passed before proceeding.

The troubled man felt himself occasionally buffeted by the wind that swept across the open fields until he reached the outskirts of Norton Prior, where his continuing journey was partly sheltered by the cottages and terraced houses of Oxford Lane.

Eventually, he reached his destination, the Grade II-listed St John's Rectory, and walked up the drive, past three cherry trees abounding with delicate pink blossom.

The visitor strolled up to the late-Georgian building's Palladian-style porch and pressed the bell beside the entrance.

His friend, Revd Peter Hughes, rector of St John the Martyr Church, a convivial, grey-haired man in glasses, drew back the door and greeted him with a warm smile.

'Steven, where have you left your car?' asked the clergyman.

'I walked.'

'All the way from Biddington?'

'I enjoy walking. Also I'm feeling a bit down at the moment. It boosts you up. Walking also gives you time to think. You probably know the Latin expression "*solvitur ambulando*", don't you?'

The churchman nodded.

'It's solved by walking?'

'Correct,' said the headmaster, following the minister into the house.

Revd Hughes, who had been appointed by the diocese to take charge of the Norton Prior parish and two nearby rural parishes twelve years earlier, led Wimbush into his oak-panelled drawing-room.

The headmaster cast his inquisitive eyes around at dusty shelves laden with books covering the whole of the far wall, the mahogany dining table and chairs and the marble fireplace.

The rector invited his visitor to sit down on a white sofa while he settled into a high-backed armchair. A half-empty coffee mug, a daily newspaper, a copy of the Bible and a notebook were on a side table beside him.

After admiring a white vase containing pink and white roses and peonies which stood in the centre of the dining table, the visitor took his seat.

'Would you like some tea or coffee?' asked the host.

'No, I'm fine,' said Wimbush.

'We haven't seen you in church recently,' said Revd Hughes.

'No. I've been busy. Things have got on top of me.'

Revd Hughes frowned. 'You've missed a lot. I was especially pleased with the Lent Talks.'

'I'll make more of an effort from now on,' Wimbush promised. 'And how have you been keeping, Peter?'

'Well, I'm forty-nine this year. There've been a few occasions in the past when I've hurried upstairs and forgotten what I've come for.'

Wimbush shrugged. 'We've all been there.'

'But now I hurry upstairs, forget why and then have to lie down to recover.'

The headmaster laughed as the rector continued, 'Anyway, you didn't come all this way to ask about my health, I'm sure. Is it something to do with that so-called young celebrity who was murdered in the hotel? I read in the *Gazette* that she went to that school where you taught years ago, St Mildred's.'

'Correct,' said Wimbush. 'I was deputy head when she joined the school fifteen years ago. Nice girl, actually. Very sad about her death. She was as good as gold. But she was close friends with another girl. What was her name? Yes, Jemima. Now she was a precocious young woman. Full of herself. Got me into a lot of trouble, making false claims about me. I befriended her, and then she wanted me to help her cheat in the exams by giving her the exam paper in advance. I refused, of course, and she got nasty with me. There was a boy as well. Mark Tanner – nasty bully. Only proficient with computers and playing sport. You try and help them, don't you? But, very often, once they reach school-leaving age, *alea iacta est* – the die is cast.'

'Steven, you mentioned on the phone you've been depressed?'

'Correct,' said Wimbush. 'Look, we've been friends a long time, Peter. I'll be totally frank. I feel my life is at a crossroads. As you know, I'm married to a very sweet lady, Samantha. I'm very lucky. She dotes on me. But I'm afraid my marriage is under threat because of a past transgression on my part.'

'Do you want to reveal the nature of this transgression?'

'Not at present, Peter,' said Wimbush, 'but, suffice to say, I'm going through a bad time. Someone is putting me under pressure and I need advice from a minister of the church such as yourself before I do something stupid.'

'It's very difficult for me, as your parish priest, to advise you when I'm not privy to the full facts,' said Revd Hughes. 'Are you being blackmailed?'

The headmaster shook his head.

'Not exactly,' he said. 'There's no money involved, but there's pressure from someone. They're threatening to cause trouble and bring my world crashing down. I've been thinking of various ways I can counter this.'

'You can't go to the police?' asked the churchman.

'No crime's been committed, has it?'

'I see.'

'Actually, I've been thinking of giving up my job and moving right away from the area with my wife to avoid this ugly situation.'

'Sounds rather drastic. You told me last year you were happy as head of Biddington Hall.'

'I am, but I'm not getting any younger, and I was thinking about taking early retirement.' A brief smile crept across his face. 'You know what they say – quit while you're a head!'

'How old are you, Steven?'

'I'll be fifty-six next term.'

'Still sounds rather drastic,' said Revd Hughes. 'You could try telling your wife.'

The visitor fiddled nervously with his wedding ring.

'It would break her heart and she'd probably divorce me, which would break mine,' he replied. 'Oh, Peter, I don't know what to do.'

'You haven't thought of anything even more extreme, I hope?'

'I sometimes wonder if I should retaliate in some way… No, it doesn't bear thinking about. That's why I thought I'd better come to you and see if you had any ideas.'

Revd Hughes shook his head.

'Steven, you're at the pinnacle of your career,' he said. 'You're head of a reputable private school, which is a position you've held for eight years? Nine years?'

'Nine years.'

'You also have a lovely wife and grown-up children. I don't know what's going through your mind. You seem reluctant to tell me. But think very hard before you do anything foolish and throw all that away. Steven, although I regard you as a friend, I can only give you the same advice I'd give any of my parishioners. You must seek your solution in prayer, and, if you sincerely ask the Lord for help, I'm sure that help will come. You must be strong to stand up to temptation. As it says in James, Chapter Four, Verse Seven, "Submit yourselves therefore to God. Resist the Devil, and he will flee from you." If you seek God's help, I'm sure he will provide it.'

Chapter 20

Television vans were lined up along Queensbridge High Street on Thursday morning as journalists from London and the Midlands arrived for the chief inspector's press conference.

As Tom Vickers made his way up the police station steps, he was nudged by a slim, dark-haired young man holding some lighting equipment.

'Sorry, sir,' said the visitor.

'That's all right,' replied Vickers. 'Let me hold the door open for you.'

The inspector followed the lighting assistant into the media briefing room, which the chief inspector had commandeered for an hour. He at once stood stock still.

Half a dozen posters of the murdered woman, depicted in two different poses, had been fixed to the walls. There was Candy the Businesswoman with long, straight hair looking as though she was set for an important meeting. Wearing a charcoal-grey business suit, she was solemn-faced with her arms folded.

And there was Candy the Society Woman with wavy hair, a seductive smile and a vivacious personality. Dressed in a light-green summer dress, she seemed ready to charm an eager audience of admirers.

The stark word 'Murder' above her head seemed incongruous – just as it seemed strangely absurd to see a description of the last clothing she wore and a plea for information at the foot of each one.

Vickers had never seen the images before and they unsettled him. His mind was fleetingly transported back to the hotel room in Queensbridge, where the young woman's life had been abruptly ended.

Then he composed himself, strode to the far end of the room and climbed onto the rostrum, where two trestle tables had been set up. He took the chair that was closest to the windows and sat down. Reporters, broadcasters and photographers were beginning to fill the dozens of chairs arranged in rows near the platform. Behind them, cameras were being installed on tripods and under the glare of television lights. At the very back were two constables in uniform, keeping a watchful eye on proceedings.

The inspector recognised in the audience a journalist from the *Queensbridge Gazette* and one from *Midlands TV News.* Sitting alongside them by the windows was a face he seemed to recognise – a man with blond hair in a crumpled mauve suit with a tie knotted six inches below the neck. For the moment, he couldn't place him.

Over the next few minutes, sound and lighting engineers continued making final adjustments to their equipment beneath the high ceilings of the three-storey building. Then the chief inspector, looking stern but dignified, made his way through the growing throng of journalists, followed by Craig Goodhope. Vickers greeted them both with a smile and extended his hand to the husband, who shook it firmly.

'Good journey?' he asked Goodhope.

'Your boss kindly sent a car to pick me up,' replied the salesman.

'Good, well, if you're ready, let's get things started,' said Roscoe, tapping the microphone on the table in front.

'Ladies and gentlemen, I'd like to get this briefing under way,' he said while remaining in his chair.

After the room fell silent, he continued, 'First of all, for those that don't know me, I'm DCI Roscoe. Sitting beside me is my colleague DI Vickers and the third person on the platform is the husband of the deceased, Craig Goodhope. You'll all be aware that Mrs Candy Goodhope, was murdered at the Queensbridge Arms Hotel last Saturday evening at 6.15 p.m. She's been described as a social media star and influencer. The post-mortem found the cause of death to be ligature compression to the neck.'

He paused to allow some murmured comments to pass among his audience before resuming.

'We know for certain the perpetrator is male, but his age is uncertain. We understand from a witness he was wearing a blue, checked, short-sleeved shirt, he had dark hair and a gold ring on one of his right fingers. Mrs Goodhope had long, blonde hair, a white crop top and a red flared pants suit.

'Now the reason I've called this briefing is that we need to appeal to shoppers who were in Queensbridge on Saturday afternoon. This lady had been in the town during the morning to film a demonstration at the Très Belle Beauty Salon. She was dressed in a striking outfit and was, certainly for part of the afternoon, in the company of two female assistants. It's likely that the killer stole £600 in cash and a silver laptop belonging to the victim. If anyone remembers seeing her, and they've not already come forward, they should contact the incident room.

'We're also appealing to customers who used the Crown and Sceptre pub between one o'clock and half past one, where she had lunch, and customers at the Courtyard Bar in the hotel, where she spent the rest of the afternoon. The sort of information we're looking for is: Was she being followed? Was she involved in some sort of altercation? Was anyone seen acting suspiciously? We invite anyone with information, however trivial, to come forward. This was a talented young woman with her whole future ahead of her who was killed in a most brutal fashion, and we are determined to catch the perpetrator.

'I'm now going to ask Mr Goodhope if he'd be kind enough to say a few words.'

As the husband withdrew a piece of paper from his pocket and opened it on the table, Vickers recalled who the man in the crumpled mauve suit was. He tapped Roscoe on the arm and whispered, 'Guv, did you know Jack Bayliss is sitting down there?'

'Oh God,' Roscoe murmured back while peering at Candy Goodhope's boyfriend. 'We'd better prepare for trouble.'

Goodhope leaned forward slowly, his ponytail bobbing from side to side. Vickers thought he looked unwell. He appeared unshaven and his skin was pale.

'I'm sorry,' he began, eyeing Jack Bayliss, who was scribbling in a notebook. 'I'm not used to public speaking. You'll have to forgive me. I just wanted to say that last Saturday, the world lost an angel – my dear wife, Candy. She meant everything to me, and I've made a promise to help the police catch her killer.'

He began coughing, at which point a uniformed officer emerged from behind the podium with a glass of water. After a few sips, he regained his composure.

'Sorry,' he said. 'On Friday, she set off to work in her salon in Gloucester, and I was expecting to see her on Sunday night so we could spend the Bank Holiday Monday together. I thought she was doing a presentation in Queensbridge and then going shopping in London. All I want to say is that I want the cruel bastard who did this taken off the streets and locked up so that no one else has to go through the nightmare ordeal I'm suffering.'

He sat down looking distressed. Vickers patted him on the arm and asked if he needed to go outside for some fresh air, but he declined.

'Right, ladies and gentlemen, I know you're all bursting to ask questions,' said Roscoe, 'so I'd like to throw this meeting open to the floor.'

A husky-voiced man with a Birmingham accent in the front row raised his hand.

'Chief Inspector, Adam Bunyon from the *Gazette*. We understand a man from Queensbridge was being questioned in connection with the murder yesterday. Is that right?'

Roscoe glanced down at the journalist.

'That's correct, Adam,' he said. 'The man in question's been released under investigation.'

'Can you give his name and age?' asked Bunyon.

'No, I'm sorry. No details are being given as he's not been charged, although he remains a person of interest.'

A tall, dark-haired man near the back raised his hand. 'John Singleton, *Midlands TV News*. Chief Inspector, there've been reports that Mrs Goodhope may have been upset by comments left on her social media accounts. Do you believe the attack on her could be related to this?'

Roscoe shook his head.

'We don't know at this stage,' he said.

'She was a lady with celebrity status,' said Singleton. 'Is it possible she was being stalked?'

Roscoe shook his head again.

'There's no evidence of that,' he said.

A woman in her early twenties who was sitting near the front of the room raised her hand.

'Chief Inspector,' she said, 'Ryleigh Todd, Press Association. I'd like to ask Mr Goodhope what state of mind his wife was in recently. Had she been upset over anything?'

Goodhope, who was clutching a paper tissue in his hand, turned his gaze towards her.

'She was a great woman,' he said. 'She had the whole of her life in front of her. She was doing so well in her career and had been on the point of signing a contract with a TV channel to present a daytime show. So she'd been in an upbeat mood all week. But then it all come to an end.'

Silence descended on the room amid a wave of pity for the widowed man.

Roscoe leaned forward. 'We'd better bring things to a close, now. Thank you all for coming. Safe journey.'

All the journalists and broadcasting crews began to file out of the room. Goodhope stood up and informed the pair he was leaving. They shook his hand and thanked him before he made his way down the steps.

After switching the microphones off, Roscoe turned towards Vickers. But he was only able to utter a few words before they both became aware that a brawl had broken out near the exit door. Vickers leaped from his seat and raced to see what was happening. He was joined by the two uniformed officers who found Goodhope and Bayliss trading punches. The inspector clasped his arms around Goodhope in a bear hug and pulled him away. But the aggrieved husband put up a struggle.

'Let me go,' yelled Goodhope. 'It's time I dealt with that weasel-faced piece of scum.'

The two constables grappled with the journalist, who managed to shout back, 'Stop spreading lies about me.'

When Roscoe reached them moments later, he could see Goodhope had a cut lip.

'Calm down, both of you,' he demanded in a rare show of temper. 'Please try and control yourselves. This helps nobody.'

Several reporters had witnessed the incident. Cameras were flashing and both parties were being pestered for a comment. But Roscoe quickly ushered the press out while the two constables marched Bayliss away.

'Are you all right?' Vickers asked the injured husband.

'I'll survive,' Goodhope said. 'You need to have words with that Jack Bayliss. Candy must have been with him at some point, and he must know what happened to her. I wouldn't be surprised if he had a row with her and killed her.'

Chapter 21

Miranda Higley finished her breakfast of muesli, toast and coffee in the kitchen of her Worcestershire home and placed her plates and cutlery in the sink. Then a cry from the hallway startled her.

'Where's Dan?' said the voice, which was followed by a loud cackling laugh.

The retired teacher shook her head crossly while walking from the kitchen to the hall.

'Oh Gabriel!' she snapped. 'I wish you wouldn't keep telling me the same things all the time.'

'Tell the kids! Tell the kids!' yelled the African grey parrot followed by more laughter. 'Come in, dear.'

Now in her late forties, Miranda was a gentle lady with greying hair who had made up for her shortness of stature by developing a friendly but forceful personality. She was known for her acts of kindness while, at the same time, being unable to suffer fools gladly.

She brushed her fingers along the bars of her pet's cage, then she stroked the bird's head.

'Hello. Nice to see you,' said the bird.

She sighed as she stepped into the front room of her seventeenth-century country home, Myrtle Cottage, with its exposed timber beams and inglenook fireplace.

This was the third morning that week that Miranda's estranged husband, Daniel, had been due to work on renovating her garden room at the rear of the cottage. But it had turned ten o'clock and there was no sign of him. He hadn't even sent her a text message to warn her he would be late, which annoyed her. She had her little jobs to do.

'You couldn't trust him back then,' she told herself, 'and you can't trust him now.'

She turned towards the Welsh dresser where she'd placed her mobile phone and where the speaker for her Alexa device was kept.

'Hey, Alexa, turn on the light,' she demanded, using the voice-activated digital assistant that her son had helped her set up.

'OK. Light on,' came the robotic-sounding reply as her chandelier lit up.

Miranda began cleaning the cottage.

She had just removed the vacuum cleaner from its kitchen cupboard when her phone rang. She shook her head as Daniel's name appeared on the screen.

'Morning, Miranda,' he said. 'Do you mind if I don't work on the new floor this morning? Gill from the church needs someone to take her to hospital. Her son's got a last-minute dental appointment, and there's no one else. It means I'll have to do a lot of hanging around up there.'

Miranda raised an eyebrow.

'Are you talking about Gill Montgomery?'

'That's right. I told her I'd pick her up at a quarter past ten.'

'Oh, Dan,' she said, 'you're always full of excuses.'

At the sound of her estranged husband's name, a raucous voice from the hallway enquired, 'Where's Dan?' She ignored the bird.

'Look, I'm sorry,' said her caller, losing his temper. 'Do you want me to do the bloody job or not? I'll be free after lunch and then I can crack on with the flooring.'

Miranda was in a difficult situation. She could not afford a professional builder.

'All right,' she said. 'But I won't be here after lunch. I'm due at the village hall at two. Still, that doesn't matter, does it? You've got a key, haven't you? You can let yourself in.'

'Yes. Don't worry about me. I'll be fine.'

'You haven't put any of your tools away,' she muttered. 'They're exactly as you left them in the garden room. You always were untidy.'

Dan Higley, who spoke in a mellow, educated voice, was close to losing his temper again. 'That doesn't matter, does it? You're not going to use the room are you?'

'Just as well, isn't it?' she snapped back. 'When's the wood being delivered?'

'First thing tomorrow,' he replied. 'By the way, did you have a visitor last night?'

'No. Why do you ask?'

'Oh, I was passing by, on my way to see Richard, and I noticed a man standing by your gate.'

She frowned. 'What time would this have been?'

'About seven o'clock.'

'I was out,' she said. 'What sort of man was he?'

'Hard to describe. About my height. Light-grey clothing.'

She shook her head. 'I don't know who that could have been.'

'Never mind. Just thought I'd mention it.'

'Probably someone a bit lost. As you know, some of the house numbers are hard to find.'

'Right, I must be off,' he said.

'Dan, thank you,' she said. 'You're doing me a big favour.'

'No problem,' he said. 'It won't take me long to get the job done.'

She glanced towards the dresser where she'd placed her handbag.

'Do you need any money today, Dan?' she asked. 'So far I've only taken out enough to cover the timber and all the materials.'

'Don't worry about that for now,' he said. 'We'll sort all that out when the job's done.'

After ending the call, Miranda stepped across to the three leaded-light windows. She opened one nearest the front door and glanced at her early-summer blooms of roses, delphiniums, aquilegias, peonies and honesty beside her neatly trimmed box hedge. She turned her gaze towards the sky. Scattered showers had been forecast, but the sun had slipped from behind the clouds and was caressing the rooftops with its golden beams.

Her estranged husband had seemed rather ill-humoured, but she had expected that. Her solicitor had just sent him a letter asking about his sources of income – a subject he was sensitive about. She was more concerned about this mystery man who'd been loitering outside her home. Who could that have been?

Miranda walked down to the garden gate, past the red and yellow rose bushes, and glanced down the lane towards their only shop. Then she turned her head towards St Andrew's Church, a quarter of a mile away, up the gentle hill to the right. The quaint street of detached cottages and bungalows was deserted, apart from a solitary magpie pecking about the grass verge opposite, no doubt searching for grubs.

She found herself absent-mindedly reciting the ancient saying, 'One for sorrow, two for joy,' as she stepped back into the cottage and shut the door.

'Old wives' tale,' she muttered. 'His mate won't be far.'

She noticed the tools stacked by the stairs and sighed.

'They're going to be banished to the back of the house tomorrow,' she declared.

Half an hour later, Miranda was standing in front of her Welsh dresser, preparing to send an email to her son, when she thought she heard a knock on the door.

I wonder if that's Dan, she thought. Maybe, on his way to pick up Gill, he's remembered something he needed to tell me. Or maybe it's someone from the village hall.

Miranda drew back the door.

'Come in. I'm in the middle of something,' she said.

Chapter 22

Set in the heart of Queensbridge, Mondales was the town's only major department store, offering ladies' and men's fashion, beauty products, furniture, homewares and gifts. It had, for decades, proved a popular draw for shoppers, but online competition and increased business costs had prompted rumours that its days in the town might be numbered.

Sunita Roy found a parking space in a nearby supermarket car park just before ten o'clock on Thursday morning and, accompanied by Brett Dawson, began walking towards the high street shop.

'The shop workers we're looking for are Euan Saltwood and Eve Gallagher, aren't they?' said Dawson.

'Yes. I called Mondales yesterday afternoon,' said Sunita as they approached the glass doors. 'He works in the furniture department while she sells perfume. I think we'll try to speak to Eve first. The perfume section's not far from the entrance.'

'By the way, Sarge,' he said, 'why all those questions to Ellis Buckley about the drinks served to Candy and her friends?'

'I was testing his memory,' she explained. 'If he can't recall the drinks he served them, can he properly remember other, more important facts?'

'I thought he did very well. They were rushing around catering for more than seventy people,' he reminded her.

'I know,' she said, 'but I needed to find out how reliable he is as a witness. I reckon he passed the test.'

The pair followed a trail of floral aromas wafting through the shop's ground floor and stopped at the Chanel counter, where they learned Eve Gallagher had called in sick. They had more luck when they took the escalator to the first floor and reached the furniture department. A colleague of Euan Saltwood confirmed he was at work, currently attending to a customer.

Sunita spent a moment examining an armchair offered at a reduced price. Then a fresh-faced man in his mid-twenties with short, dark hair approached.

'Did you want to speak to me?' he asked with an anxious expression. 'I'm Euan.'

'Yes,' said Sunita with a nod while producing her warrant card. 'We're from Heart of England CID. It's all right. You're not in any trouble.'

'We wanted to talk to you about your visit to the Courtyard Bar on Saturday afternoon,' Dawson explained.

'What's this about then?' he said. 'Is it about the girl that was murdered?'

Dawson nodded.

'I won't lie. I had a brief conversation with her,' said Euan. 'There were four of us who'd been on the early shift. We went for food, did some shopping and then turned up at the bar.'

'The bar staff have told us one of your group spoke to her for a good few minutes,' said Sunita.

'That was probably me. I just asked if she was all right because I was sitting next to her and she looked pretty whammed,' he said. 'Of course, I didn't know who she was at the time. We talked about her favourite drinks and how she argued with her boyfriend when he got a puncture. I didn't half get a shock when I saw her face on the telly the next day. Candy Goodhope was her name, wasn't it? God, what an awful thing to happen.'

'What time did you and your friends get to the bar?' asked Sunita, resting on the side of the armchair she'd admired.

'I think we arrived just after half past five.'

'Were you the one wearing a black T-shirt saying, "I never argue"?' asked Dawson.

'No, that was Doug and, for the record, he's always arguing.'

Dawson laughed.

'You didn't see a man with dark hair, a check shirt and a ring on his right hand, did you?' he asked the shop worker.

'No.'

'How did Candy seem to you?' Sunita asked.

'At first, she was none too happy that we took over her table, but the place was jam-packed, and there was nowhere else. She wasn't totally coherent. She'd obviously had a few. She received a phone call from her boyfriend at one point. He'd apparently had a problem getting a tyre for his car.'

'Did you talk about anything else?' asked Sunita.

'Oh, she was full of herself, talking about how many followers she's got on social media and how famous she'd become. I switched off, to be honest. That sort of thing bores me rigid. She also said she was going to be visiting an antiques fair in Rugby the next day in the hope of buying some art for her flat.'

'Really?' said Dawson before whispering in his sergeant's ear, 'Maybe that explains the money.'

Sunita nodded while maintaining eye contact with the shop assistant.

'Do you remember Candy telling you anything else, Mr Saltwood?' she asked.

'No, that's about it. She said she was going to the bar to order another drink, and I promised to keep her seat for her. But then she got chatting to the two men at the slot machines, and I didn't see her again.'

'What did the slot machine guys look like?' asked Dawson.

'Apart from them losing a lot of money, I didn't pay much attention. They just looked like a couple of dropouts.'

* * *

A familiar voice interrupted the chief inspector's private thoughts while he returned to CID after lunch.

'What's up, guv?' asked DI Tom Vickers. 'You've got a face as long as Livery Street, as my old mother used to say.'

'Under the cosh a bit, Tom,' said Roscoe, who was climbing the stairs to the first-floor landing. He waited for his colleague to catch him up. 'I've had Norris onto me over that fight at the press conference. She said when we found out Bayliss was there, we should have prepared for trouble.'

'It's easy to say that with hindsight, guv,' said Vickers.

'You did well anyway, Tom – breaking up the fight.'

Roscoe patted the inspector on the back as he joined him outside CID.

'I hope Goodhope got his injured lip seen to,' said Roscoe.

'He said he'd call in at Queensbridge General and see a nurse. Do you know if they let Bayliss go?'

'Yes,' said Roscoe, approaching the doors that led to the CID office. 'He got a caution.'

'Anyway, you got the publicity you were after, guv,' said Vickers, who was heading towards the opposite corridor.

'How do you mean?' asked Roscoe.

'Didn't you see the lunchtime news on the BBC about the punch-up? *The Sun* are saying, "Massive brawl at murder briefing".'

'If that's what it takes to get people to come forward with information that might crack the case, then I'm all for it,' said Roscoe as he pushed open the door to CID. 'Let's hope we get some useful calls coming in over the next few days.'

* * *

Sunita Roy was waiting outside his room.

'How was your trip to Mondales?' he asked.

'We only managed to speak to one person – Euan Saltwood. He and three other shop staff were drinking with Candy from around half past five,' she said. 'Candy then moved on to speak to a couple of guys playing on the fruit machines.'

'Any description?'

'Not at the moment,' she said as they both entered his room and sat down.

'But there's something else we've picked up from the bar and shop staff. We know that Candy had two laptops. The black one that I retrieved from her home is with forensics. So far they can't find anything of interest on it. But there's a second one. I've just checked with Craig Goodhope. He's confirmed she had two and that the second is a 13-inch silver Apple MacBook Air. She had it when she got in the hotel lift, but it hasn't turned up in her room.'

'Interesting,' said Roscoe. There was a knock outside. 'Come in,' he called.

The door opened and his son's head appeared.

'I thought you should know we're getting reports of a woman being brutally attacked at her home in Abbots Green, near Evesham,' said the young constable.

'Any name, George?' asked Roscoe.

‘Miranda Higley, who works as a home tutor. Her husband found her unconscious and covered in blood on the sitting-room carpet.’

‘We’d better get over there,’ said Roscoe.

Chapter 23

It was half past three by the time the chief inspector and his sergeant reached the picturesque village of Abbots Green and found Myrtle Cottage, nestled among a row of red-brick and flint houses in Furnace Hill.

Several police vehicles in Heart of England livery were lined up outside, and, as the pair got out of their BMW, they recognised a white Kia Sportage belonging to senior forensic officer Dr Alice Ling parked a short distance down the lane. Across the street lay a grassy bank, some high hedges and trees.

'Beautiful place,' Roscoe remarked to Sunita. 'Strange I've never passed through here before. Anyway, let's find out what's happened.'

They walked to the cottage gate where slim, dark-haired PC Nina Kaur was standing guard. A member of Dr Ling's team was examining woodwork around the open front door.

'Good afternoon, sir,' said the constable. 'Dr Ling and the crime scene manager are in the front room.'

'That's fine,' said Roscoe. 'I'll catch up with them in a moment. Can you tell us briefly what's happened?'

'Yes, sir. The lady's called Miranda Higley. She took early retirement from teaching in Gloucester and worked from home as an English tutor. Her husband found her unconscious on the living-room carpet and called the emergency services. She's been taken to Queensbridge General. Not looking good, apparently. They don't think she'll survive.'

'What sort of injuries?' asked Roscoe.

'Various head injuries – possibly caused by repeated firing of a pellet gun or BB gun. She's in quite a state, according to Dr Ling.'

'Any sign of the weapon?' asked Sunita.

'No,' said the constable. 'Not so far.'

'What about the husband?' asked Roscoe. 'Is he around?'

'Yes, sir,' she said with a nod. 'That's him over there.'

She pointed to a slim, grey-haired man with black-framed glasses who was pacing up and down on the opposite pavement, puffing on a cigarette and looking extremely agitated.

'His name's Daniel Higley,' she added.

'Is that his grey Volvo parked further down the lane?' asked Sunita.

Kaur nodded.

The chief inspector turned round. 'Sergeant, perhaps you should go and have a chat with Mr Higley,' he said. 'I'll have a word with Dr Ling.'

The chief inspector strode up the red-brick path, ducked his head beneath the doorway and disappeared inside.

Sunita waited for a van to drive past before crossing the lane.

Higley, had finished his cigarette and was stamping it out on the ground with his foot as she approached.

'Mr Higley?' she asked. 'DS Roy, Heart of England CID. We need to have a chat.'

Higley, who'd been staring at the ground dejectedly, raised his eyes.

'Yes, of course,' he said, giving a weak smile.

'We can't go into the cottage or the garden,' Sunita explained. 'Our scenes-of-crime people are hard at work.'

'Of course.'

'So sorry to hear about your wife's injuries,' she said.

He nodded.

'Yes. I was told the police would want to talk to me, but I'm desperate to get over to the hospital and see how she is.'

'Just a few questions,' said Sunita.

'I'll tell you anything you want. You have to catch whoever did this.' Daniel Higley stood on the pavement beneath the shadow of some ancient ash trees and broke down in tears. 'She really didn't deserve this,' he muttered, shaking his head.

'What exactly happened?' asked Sunita.

'I should explain that we're separated, but it's amicable, and I've been doing some work for her – some DIY in what we call the garden room,' he said. 'I phoned her briefly this morning and explained I couldn't come till the afternoon because I had to take a woman to hospital. At a quarter past two, I turned up and… Oh, my God!'

He stopped speaking and stared at the ground before taking a tissue from the top pocket of his check shirt and blowing his nose.

'Sorry,' he said.

'I know this is difficult,' said Sunita reassuringly. 'But if we're to fully investigate what happened, we need to know what you saw.'

He nodded. 'Of course,' he said. 'I just found her in a pool of blood.'

'Do you think Mrs Higley could have banged herself on some furniture?'

Higley shook his head. 'No. The constable I spoke to thinks someone's attacked her.'

Sunita, who was writing in a small notebook, continued, 'You were saying that you arrived here at a quarter past two. What happened then?'

'I knew something was wrong as soon as I arrived,' he said. 'One of the leaded-light windows was wide open.'

'It's been a warm, sunny afternoon,' Sunita pointed out.

'Yes, but Miranda had told me she was going out. She had to be at the village hall at two o'clock, and she's very security-minded. She'd never normally go out and leave a front window open – there was a burglary round here last year. So I guessed she must be at home. Anyway I searched my pockets for the front-door key and, while doing that, I peered through the open window and got the shock of my life.'

'You saw your wife?' said Sunita.

'Yes. She was lying there, covered in blood.'

'Where was she?'

'On the sitting-room floor between the settee and the fireplace.'

He raised both hands to his forehead and closed his eyes.

'You said you had a door key?' said Sunita.

'Yes. Only so I could come and go while doing the renovation work. I've got my own place. So, anyway, I opened the door in a panic, thinking she might have fallen over and I might be able to revive her. When I got to her, I saw the blood on her head.'

'Was she lying face down?' she asked.

'Yes. She was on her stomach with her head towards the fireplace. I could see straight away she was out cold, though luckily she was still breathing. I did my best to revive her. I shook her gently.'

Sunita nodded.

'But it was no good,' he said. 'I don't know how I managed to call 999. I was shaking. I was all over the place. To think that someone had somehow got inside and…'

'What happened after that?'

'Well, the ambulance people turned up about a quarter of an hour later, followed shortly afterwards by the police.'

'You didn't touch anything in the cottage, did you?'

'Apart from tending to Miranda, no.'

'How old is your wife?'

'Forty-eight. I'm a year older.'

'How long had you been married?' asked Sunita.

'I think it's twenty-two years,' he said.

'So there aren't any children?'

'She's got a son, Barry, my stepson. He must be around twenty-seven. Oh, my God. He's going to be so upset.'

'Have you any idea, sir, who might have done this?' she asked, stroking her chin.

'No, I don't. As far as I know, she didn't have an enemy in the world. Oh, there's one thing I ought to mention. There was a man hanging around outside the cottage last night.'

'What time would this have been?' she asked.

'Around seven. Miranda told me she was out at the time. She said it was probably someone confused about the addresses. It's hard to find some of the door numbers.'

Sunita's curiosity was aroused. 'How do you know this?'

'I was passing by and I saw the man.'

'Any description?'

'About average height. Light-grey clothes. I didn't pay a lot of attention. I was driving.'

'She hadn't been expecting anyone?'

'No.'

'Can I ask when you and your wife separated?' she asked.

'Five years ago,' he replied. 'I don't want to go into the reasons, but I moved into a flat in Evesham.'

'No divorce then?'

'We're going through a divorce right now,' he said.

Higley paused. He gazed at her puzzled face.

'You're probably wondering why it's taken so long. The fact is I wanted to get back with her. The separation was entirely her idea, and I was just forced to go with it.

Miranda recently became different. She became more distant and, for some reason, she decided to see a solicitor and get the split formalised.'

'When was that?' asked Sunita.

'Two weeks ago.'

'You were against the whole idea of a divorce?'

'Yes, I still loved my wife and had hoped to win her back.'

After asking Higley to remain close by in case their chief inspector wished to speak to him, Sunita retraced her steps across the lane and entered the small front garden of the cottage. She had found it hard to believe the man's story entirely. She knew they would have to examine the couple's assets.

Divorce usually brought with it huge financial upheaval, she reminded herself. Moreover, it was an astonishing coincidence, she thought, that, in April, his wife had announced she wanted a divorce and, two weeks later, she had been found the victim of a vicious attack.

Chapter 24

Dr Alice Ling was crouched down on the sitting-room floor in a white suit and gloves as Sunita entered the hallway. A rather short woman, she wore bifocal glasses, and her dark hair, tied neatly behind her head in a ponytail, swayed about as she examined the carpet. The chief inspector was watching her work from the doorway.

'Dr Ling believes the lady was attacked with a nail gun,' said Roscoe.

'Yes,' said Ling. 'One of the paramedics called from the hospital. He's mentioned seeing tiny, circular puncture wounds on the head and chest. On top of that, the woman's husband has told us he was doing some flooring. We escorted him into the garden room earlier on, and the nail gun he was using has gone missing. It was a pneumatic nail gun which used three-inch nails. He'd borrowed it from a friend specially for this job.'

'So, whoever it was grabbed it and turned it into a weapon?' said Sunita.

'None of this is confirmed,' said Ling. 'At this stage, it's only a theory. Hopefully, when the lady comes round, she'll be able to tell us exactly what happened.'

Sunita was shocked by the suggestion a nail gun had been used in the attack. An horrific image of the middle-aged woman being set upon with such a device flashed through her mind, but she managed to suppress a shiver of disgust. She moved forward into the room as the full import of the disclosure registered with her. Then she stopped still, shaking her head in disbelief.

'Well, at least that ties in with what the husband's been saying,' she said. 'He told me outside that, although the couple are separated, he agreed to sort out her floor.'

'He's obviously a person of interest,' Roscoe replied. 'We may have to bring him in for questioning before the day's out.'

'There's no sign of a nail gun anywhere in the house,' said Dr Ling, taking to her feet. 'There are also no signs of anyone breaking in, either. The DCI and I were just saying what a bizarre choice of weapon it was.'

'Did the paramedic you spoke to give any information about how Mrs Higley was lying when they arrived?' asked Sunita.

'She was lying on her front in a pool of blood with her feet pointing towards the windows,' said Ling, who was now standing by the window. 'Her head was turned towards the fireplace.'

Roscoe had become quiet for a moment as though deep in thought.

'We'll have to make a thorough search of the cottage, the garden and the whole area for any weapon,' said Roscoe.

'If you need to speak to him, sir, Mr Higley's by the garden gate right now, talking to PC Kaur,' Sunita said. 'I must say he seems very concerned about his wife and eager to get over to the hospital.'

'Don't be fooled by that, Sergeant. You'd be surprised by the number of concerned husbands I've collared in my time who've turned out to be domestic abusers.'

'So, how do we believe the attack happened?' Sunita asked. 'Did they go into the back room, grab the nail gun and assault Mrs Higley with it?'

'That seems to fit the facts,' said Ling.

'It's not possible that both she and the attacker were in the back room and that, after using the nail gun, they dragged her in here?' she asked.

Ling shook her head.

'No evidence of that, Sergeant,' she said.

'But she's definitely been attacked, hasn't she? I mean, suicide can be ruled out because there's no weapon at the scene.'

'Absolutely,' said Ling. She paused before asking, 'Do either of you have any knowledge of nail guns?'

They both shook their heads.

'In order for the nail gun to work in this case, the victim needed to be positioned against a solid surface,' said Ling. 'So the attacker would have needed to make sure her head was resting on the floor before they could use the device. Then they would have had to press the gun hard against her to make it fire.'

'Has anything been stolen from the cottage?' Sunita inquired.

'I've been asking about that,' Roscoe said. 'As far as we can tell, nothing's been taken–'

Dr Ling interrupted to say, 'The victim's handbag was over there on the dresser when we arrived. It's been bagged up now but, from memory, it only contained things like make-up, pills, keys along with a notepad and pen. They've all been safely removed by our team. But so far, we haven't come across her mobile.'

'Any money at all?'

'No, but there were two credit cards.'

'Poor lady,' Sunita remarked as Dr Ling launched into a conversation on her phone with one of her colleagues.

Sunita watched as her boss walked back towards the door and turned his attention fully towards her. He managed a faint smile.

'There was a bright moment earlier,' he said, lowering his voice. 'Apparently, Mrs Higley's parrot was squawking when the SOCO team first got here. Its cage was hanging near the stairs.'

'A parrot?'

'Yes, one of those African greys. It kept telling the crime scene manager, "Come in, dear. Nice to see you." It got on his nerves so he and one of his colleagues moved it into the garden room and put a tablecloth over the cage. That seemed to do the trick.'

'How funny,' whispered Sunita, breaking into a smile.

'Yes, the only light moment in what's been rather a cheerless afternoon, Sergeant. Anyway it's time I spoke to Mr Higley. Come on. You can introduce me.'

The husband was locked in conversation with PC Kaur when the two detectives emerged from the cottage. He was discussing his teaching career but broke off as soon as he saw the chief inspector approaching.

'You wanted a word?' he asked.

'Yes,' said Roscoe.

'I need to get over to the hospital,' said Higley.

'All in good time,' said the detective. 'Mr Higley, apparently you own a nail gun.'

'Yes. I've already told one of your officers it's disappeared.'

'We can't go into too much detail at this stage,' he said. 'We need to be absolutely certain it's been removed from the cottage.'

His eyes darted towards the rear of the cottage.

'I left it in the garden room, in the middle of the floor,' he said.

Roscoe shrugged. 'Listen, you're our main witness, and it's a bit awkward interviewing you in the street. We'll need you to accompany us to headquarters.'

'Oh, God. Is that really necessary? I need to visit the hospital and call Barry, our son – so I can break the news of what's happened to his mother.'

'Don't worry,' said Roscoe. 'Your wife is receiving the best medical care possible, and we've already taken steps to notify your son.'

'Do you have any idea who's done this terrible thing?' Higley asked.

'No, but I feel sure it won't take too long to identify the offender,' said Roscoe.

'Hey, I'm not under arrest, am I?' he said. 'You don't think I had anything to do with this appalling incident, do you?'

'We don't think anything at the moment,' said Roscoe. 'We're keeping an open mind, aren't we, Sergeant?'

Sunita nodded.

'We'd like you to accompany us voluntarily,' Roscoe added.

'I don't really have much choice, do I?' Higley complained as he followed them to the chief inspector's car.

Chapter 25

Sunita Roy's opinion of teacher Daniel Higley had softened over the previous two hours. After she first questioned him in Furnace Hill, she had harboured some doubts about the veracity of his account.

Now she wasn't so sure. The couple's long separation without divorce seemed to support his claim of wishing for a reconciliation. And if he had been the one to harm his wife, wouldn't he have fled the scene and begun constructing an alibi? What's more, if he'd intended for her to die, wouldn't he have delayed making his 999 call?

She watched for Higley's reactions as the chief inspector sat down beside her in the interview room at St James Street and stared across the table at him.

'Mr Higley, when was the last time you used your nail gun?' Roscoe asked.

'Yesterday afternoon, just before five o'clock,' the suspect replied in a quiet tone.

'And what were you using it for at that time?'

'I'd offered to help upgrade the conservatory and spent most of that day nailing plywood to the old floorboards.'

'What time did you stop work?' asked Sunita.

'I'd say it was about five o'clock.'

'And where did you leave the nail gun?' Roscoe asked.

Higley shrugged.

'I suppose I'm a bit of an untidy workman, to be honest,' he said, peering at the chief inspector over his glasses. 'I don't believe in packing tools away at the end of the day if I'm going to be using the same ones again the next morning. It seems a waste of time.'

'So, you left the nail gun on the floor, along with your tape measure, hammer, work bench and a couple of saws?' said Roscoe.

Higley nodded.

'Yes. My back began playing up yesterday afternoon and I decided to call it a day.'

'You used the nail gun for a short time?'

'Yes. The magazine holds fifty-five ring shank nails, and I only used about a dozen.'

'So, by your estimation, there should have been more than forty nails left in the magazine?'

'Yes. I charged the nailer up yesterday lunchtime, so it was ready to go.'

'That's a pity. If you'd allowed it to run down, it wouldn't have been available for use as a weapon.'

Higley nodded.

'I know. I feel really guilty about that now. I wish I'd packed all my tools away. Whoever got into the cottage and attacked Miranda might not have found it and used it against her.'

Roscoe raised an eyebrow.

'There are no signs of a break-in,' he pointed out.

'Someone might have got in through the open window, or she might have let them in through the door,' he retorted.

'Did you have a row with your wife over something?' Roscoe continued. 'She'd set her mind on a divorce, hadn't she? You were resisting the idea.'

'No, not at all,' Higley insisted.

'You opposed your wife's divorce petition, didn't you?' said Roscoe, glancing down at a sheet of paper in front of him. 'You told my sergeant here – and I quote, "The separation was entirely her idea, and I was just forced to go with it… I still loved my wife and had hoped to win her back."'

'That's all true,' said Higley, 'but we didn't argue. You seem to be implying I might have been the one to hurt her.'

'You're simply a person of interest at the moment. We just want to hear your side of events.'

'Listen,' said Higley, 'I was a maths teacher for twenty-four years. I've been a regular churchgoer and help out at the church. It was part of my role as a teacher to help young people find their moral compass. There's no way I'd have harmed her, and there's no way I'd have picked up the nail gun and used it as a weapon. The very thought of doing that absolutely disgusts me.'

'All right. All right,' said Roscoe. 'You've made your point. Nevertheless, you can't deny that you had reason to be annoyed with her. She wanted a divorce and you didn't.'

'Yes, that's true. But I wasn't annoyed.'

'How would you explain your response to the divorce issue then?'

'Well, I was disappointed. After all, if I'd fallen out with her over it heavily, I wouldn't have been doing the renovation work as a favour, would I?'

Roscoe grunted but said nothing. However, Sunita felt the man had made a valid point.

'Let's turn to your report of someone hanging around outside the cottage last night,' said Roscoe. 'Give us a description of this person.'

'It was a man of medium height. He'd got light-grey clothing. He was standing by the gate, staring towards the front door.'

'Why were you there at the time?' asked Roscoe.

'I've got a friend in Abbots Green called Richard. I was on my way to see him and take him out for a drink.'

'And the route from Evesham to your friend's address passed your former home?'

'Yes, it did.'

'We'll have to check with this Richard,' Roscoe said. 'If you pass on his details to my sergeant here, she can look into it.'

'I've no reason to lie about it.'

'I'm afraid your description of the strange man is about as helpful as a snow plough in the desert,' said Roscoe. 'Medium height, light clothing. Can't you remember anything else about him? His age, for instance? Hair colour?'

'No, except he may have been younger than me. I'm not sure. He had short hair.'

'Did he have a vehicle with him?'

'If he did, I didn't see one.'

'Are you sure you didn't make this up to divert attention away from yourself?' Roscoe asked.

'Not at all.'

'Sir, with your permission,' said Sunita. 'Mr Higley, we have to examine all the possibilities. You must admit that, at first glance, it obviously seems suspicious when a man opposing his wife's divorce petition should be the very person reporting a savage attack on her. Not only that. Early indications are that she was assaulted with a nail gun, and you were the person who brought a nail gun to the cottage.'

'All right,' he admitted. 'I can see that, maybe, I was in the wrong place at the wrong time. But surely, if I'd killed her, why would I have called the emergency number and hung around? I'd have fled the scene, wouldn't I?'

'Maybe your brain doesn't work that fast,' muttered Roscoe. 'Anyway, there's another thing. You told my sergeant you phoned your wife in the morning. What time was that?'

'Just after ten o'clock. I'd agreed to help a neighbour out by taking her to hospital, so I phoned to let Miranda know I'd be late calling round.'

'And you turned up in person at the cottage at a quarter past two?'

'Yes.'

'What did you do in the intervening four hours?'

'I took the lady to hospital.'

'Her name and address?'

'Gill Montgomery, Ivy Cottage, High Street, Abbots Green.'

'Which hospital was it?'

'Worcestershire Royal.'

'It took you four hours?'

'Yeah. I had to wait around for her and bring her home.'

'Didn't you stop anywhere for lunch?'

'I had a sandwich at the hospital.'

Sunita interrupted. 'Sir, with your permission,' she said, 'I'd like to ask Mr Higley a little more about his background.'

Roscoe nodded his approval.

'Mr Higley, you and your wife are both retired teachers,' she said, leaning back on her chair and folding her arms. 'Did you both work at the same school?'

Higley nodded. 'Yes, we met while working at the same grammar school in Gloucester. Miranda had been teaching there for two years when I joined the staff in 2000. It was love at first sight, I suppose. We started dating and got married a year later.'

Sunita exchanged glances with the chief inspector and dropped her hands onto the table.

'What was the name of the school?' she asked.

'St Mildred's High School,' he replied.

She strove to hide her surprise.

'But that's the school Candy Goodhope went to,' she said.

'I know. I did my best to teach her maths,' said Higley. 'Miranda had more success with her with geography.'

Sunita tutted. 'Why didn't you mention that before?' she asked, tapping her fingers on the desk.

'You didn't ask,' said Higley.

Roscoe interjected. 'So, you must have also taught a young lad named Tanner as well?'

Higley grimaced. 'There's a name from the past – Mark Tanner,' he said. 'I'd hoped to block him out of my mind forever.'

'Bit of a tearaway?' Roscoe suggested.

'Not much,' said Higley. 'Miranda had a hell of a time with him. She was his form teacher.'

Chapter 26

'Have you done much house-to-house before?' Tom Vickers asked George Roscoe. Both had been briefed by the chief inspector to join PC Nina Kaur and other uniformed officers calling on Miranda Higley's neighbours.

'A little,' replied George. 'There were a few break-ins in Stratford last year. Never done any after a murder before.'

'Nothing much to it,' Vickers continued as he parked in Furnace Hill just after 5 p.m. 'We'll try the neighbours each side. You start with the one on the left, Meadow View. You must know the sort of thing to ask – have they seen any visitors going into Myrtle Cottage? Any strangers or unusual vehicles? Have they heard any noise?'

While George walked up the concrete path to the detached house next door, Vickers took a few steps down the lane and entered the front garden of Trinity Cottage, a brick-and-flint property built in the same style as the murder victim's home.

He rang the doorbell. A stout, grey-haired, bespectacled man clutching a *Times* newspaper drew back the door.

'If you're selling something, we're really not interested,' he said.

'No, sir,' said the visitor, holding out his warrant card. 'DI Vickers, Heart of England CID. You probably saw all the police cars blocking the lane a short while ago.'

'Yes,' said the householder, lowering his voice and joining the inspector on the path. 'I've heard something terrible happened to poor Miranda.'

Vickers nodded. 'Yes, sir. The lady's been attacked.'

'Is she going to be all right?'

'We don't know yet. Last time anyone checked, she was in a critical condition.'

'Oh that's really awful. She's been such a good neighbour. Any idea–?'

'I'm sorry. I can't discuss the case, sir. But I wanted to ask, since you live next door, have you seen anyone visiting Myrtle Cottage at any time today?'

The householder stroked his chin and cast his eyes towards the garden path. Then he glanced back at Vickers.

'I usually sit by the front window, so I tend to see a lot of comings and goings,' he said, 'but I haven't been very well today so I've been resting upstairs. I saw Dan Higley this afternoon.'

'What sort of time would that have been?' asked the inspector.

'Some time after two because I'd come back from taking the dog for a walk.'

'Was Mr Higley entering Myrtle Cottage or leaving when you saw him?'

'He parked his grubby, grey Volvo and went inside. Why don't teachers ever wash their cars?' the man asked.

'I didn't know they didn't,' said Vickers. 'What sort of mood was he in? Was he angry at all?'

'I don't know, really. He just looked his normal self. He saw me looking out of the window and waved.'

'You knew both the Higleys quite well, sir?'

'Well, they've been neighbours for about fifteen years. Miranda does a lot for the village. Him, not so much. Of course, he moved out a few years ago and, at one stage, she took in lodgers to pay the bills. But Dan continued coming round from time to time.'

'Did you ever catch them arguing?' asked the inspector.

He shook his head.

'No. Do you know, I realise that, in the months before he moved out, they can't have been getting on. Hazel, my wife, says Miranda stopped doing his washing. But we never once heard them arguing. Peculiar, isn't it?'

'Have you seen anyone else in the street today – any strangers?'

'No.'

'What about last night at about seven?'

'No. No one. It's been quiet for a change.'

Vickers frowned. 'How do you mean, for a change?' he asked.

'Well, all this week there's been banging going on. Miranda told my wife out in the back garden they've been renovating the conservatory. Apparently, she roped Dan into doing it. Probably can't afford the prices builders charge these days.'

'He's quite a handy guy, is he?' Vickers asked, while noticing George hovering on the pavement, a short distance from the garden gate.

'I've heard he can turn his hand to most things. Inspector Vickers, isn't it?'

'Yes, that's right, sir.'

'He installed a new window in the kitchen a few years ago, Inspector.'

'Could I just take your name, sir?'

'Yes, it's Tyrrell, Martin Tyrrell. As I was saying, Inspector, there's been the sound of sawing and banging going on earlier this week. But today the place has been as quiet as the churchyard at the top of the lane.'

'No shouting?' asked Vickers.

'If there was, I missed it,' said Tyrrell.

'What about your dog?' asked the inspector. 'Wouldn't he respond to unusual sounds?'

'Him? He's as deaf as a post.'

Vickers thanked Tyrrell and walked back to the pavement where George was waiting.

'Any luck?' he asked his colleague.

'I've been chatting to an old lady on the other side,' said George. 'She didn't see anyone in Furnace Hill at all today until the ambulance pulled up just after half past two.'

'Did you ask about a stranger in the lane last night?'

'Yes. She said she was having her meal at the back of the house around that time,' George explained. 'But there was one thing of interest. She said she thought she heard someone shouting around half past ten in the morning.'

'Really?' said Vickers.

'Yes,' said George. 'It sounded to her like, "Don't you dare."'

'So, why didn't the lady do something about it?' said Vickers, shaking his head and frowning.

'She thought the noise was from the telly or it was the parrot yelling.'

'Might have been the television,' said Vickers. 'Anyway, that's definitely worth mentioning to your dad.'

The pair spent another hour knocking on doors in Furnace Hill but without acquiring any further useful information. They were about to drive away when George tapped Vickers on the arm.

'I've just had a thought,' he said. 'There's a village shop at the top of the lane, isn't there?'

'Yes,' Vickers said, 'but I think it must have closed at five o'clock.'

'It's just the sort of place where you can pick up gossip,' said George. 'You know, the place is probably a kind of information exchange for the village.'

'Yeah, but if it's closed?'

'The owners probably live nearby. They usually do,' said George. 'Also, they might have a camera.'

'Well, no one can knock your enthusiasm, George. Come on. We'll take the car up there.'

Vickers stopped his vehicle outside the single-storey premises, called Village Stores and Post Office. They guessed the shopkeepers lived in an adjoining house since its entrance gate was accessed from the shop's forecourt. George pointed out a CCTV camera above the shop door.

As soon as the constable had pressed the bell, a smartly dressed woman with curly, ginger hair swept back the door.

George explained they were from Heart of England Police and produced his warrant card. 'We're investigating a brutal attack on a woman down the lane and wondered if you'd seen any suspicious vehicles,' he said.

The woman nodded immediately.

'This is about Mrs Higley, isn't it?' said the woman, who revealed she was the sub-postmistress, Doreen Figg.

'Funny you should say that,' she said. 'I was just talking to my husband about it. There's a black car that's been picked up on our camera twice in the last few days. It comes past the shop and then passes slowly down the lane.'

'Does it stop at all?'

'Not as such. It slows down close to the Higleys' place as though the driver wants to peer through the windows, and then it pulls away.'

'That could be crucial for our investigation. What time of day would this have been?' asked Vickers.

'Once on Wednesday evening and once this morning.'

'Could you see anyone inside the vehicle?' asked George.

'No, but whoever it was seemed to be on their own,' said Figg.

'We'd like to take away the footage, if we may. We might be able to enhance it and identify the driver or pick up the registration number,' said the inspector.

Chapter 27

Tom Vickers drove through the wrought-iron gates of Ashiyana in Shawley Green and parked on the gravel forecourt. There was no sign of the house owner, although a white security light was shining from the porch and an orange glow glinted from wall lights in the living room.

He had hardly had time to open the front door with his key and let himself in when he caught the sound of Sunita's grey Mercedes approaching. She drew up behind his car and stepped out into the mild evening air.

'How was your trip to Evesham?' she asked, as he kissed her on the cheek.

'Made a bit of progress,' he said, following her into the house. 'One of the neighbours in Furnace Hill heard a woman shouting, "Don't you dare."'

'When was this?' asked Sunita.

'Around eleven o'clock this morning. It could just have been the TV. The village shopkeeper noticed a black car a couple of times, once this morning and once yesterday evening.'

'We're gradually making progress,' she said. 'Listen, I've got some salmon in the fridge. I'll put some rice and vegetables on. Are you hungry?'

'Starving.'

'You go and sit down. It won't be long.'

After their meal, Sunita joined the inspector in the living room.

'George was really helpful on the house-to-house,' said Vickers, who was sitting on the settee, sipping from a glass of lager. 'I'd forgotten about the village shop having CCTV, but it didn't escape George's attention. So we went up there and just as well we did. George has taken the disk from the CCTV and we'll have to trawl through it first thing tomorrow.'

'I think he's going to fit in really well,' Sunita said, 'although I've noticed Brett looking at him in a funny way. I'm wondering if he's jealous.'

'With George being the boss's son? Yes, that's a possibility. They're about the same age, aren't they?'

'Yes. They're both twenty-seven.'

Sunita fetched a glass of chilled orange juice from the kitchen before settling down on the settee beside him.

'The DCI's convinced the attack on Miranda Higley is an open and shut case. He's adamant the husband must have lost his temper with her. He also thinks Candy Goodhope's death is totally unrelated,' she said.

'Well, I'm inclined to agree with him on that,' said Vickers.

'Higley is a prime suspect in his wife's case. No doubt about that,' said Sunita. 'He may well have been motivated by the divorce petition. He's struggling financially, according to some background work by Brett and Wendy Hopkirk. Maybe he was battling to suppress his deep-seated anger and he flipped and grabbed the nail gun. But, all the same, I've got certain reservations. After all, it was he that made the 999 call and then he stayed at the cottage to meet the first responders. If he'd carried out the attack, wouldn't he have left the scene?'

'If you want my opinion, I tend to believe in Higley's innocence regarding his wife,' said Vickers. 'As you say, he made the 999 call. That strikes me as the behaviour of an innocent man. There were signs he'd loosened her clothing in an effort to help her breathe. At this stage, I think we have to give him the benefit of the doubt. It strikes me that someone else came to the house in the morning and carried out the attack, although there's no evidence for that.'

He added, 'We also have to remember that he's a churchgoer and retired teacher. Not an obvious suspect. And if he was so opposed to a divorce, would he have been putting in a new floor as a favour? To me, he's innocent but, like the guv'nor, I don't think the two cases are connected.'

'That's where I strongly differ from you,' said Sunita. 'The thing is Miranda Higley was a teacher at Candy's school in Gloucester – and she was Mark Tanner's form teacher.'

'Just coincidence, surely?'

Sunita shook her head. 'I don't think so. I've checked with the boss, and I'm going over to the school tomorrow to do some digging.'

'I'll come with you, if you like,' he said, taking another sip of lager.

'That would be cool,' said Sunita. 'I heard this afternoon that Brett's been checking with the friend Higley claimed to visit last night.'

'Richard Morris?'

'That's right. Richard's confirmed Higley visited him at his home in Abbots Green at around seven. So he might well have been passing Furnace Hill to see a stranger hanging about.'

'You see? Another sign he's been telling the truth,' said Vickers.

'The only thing is,' Sunita continued, 'that the stranger incident sounds so much like the kind of thing someone might make up as a distraction – to shift the focus of attention away from yourself. The implication is that this stranger had no good reason for being there and therefore might have had sinister intentions.'

'I know,' Vickers said. 'But isn't it possible this sighting might have been genuine?'

'Yes, it's possible. Oh, Tom, it's all so complicated. Anyway, if we suppose for a minute that it wasn't Higley that killed his wife, who carried out the attack? Tanner?'

'Tanner appears to be a bully and a thug,' he said, draining his glass, 'and probably capable of a vicious attack. Clearly, Mrs Higley had her work cut out if she was Tanner's form teacher. So what's your thesis, DS Roy? Years after leaving the school, Tanner suddenly remembers his hatred of Candy Goodhope and Miranda Higley and decides to end both their lives just a few days apart? And why wait so long? Why bottle up your resentment for years before taking your revenge?'

Sunita shrugged her shoulders.

'It sounds a bit far-fetched when you put it like that, but he's clearly a troubled figure, maybe capable of murder,' she said. 'Perhaps the two women fell off his radar and his anger was rekindled when he began dating Roxanne and moved to Queensbridge. Maybe, sometimes, lust for revenge can grow stronger with the passing of time.'

As their conversation continued, Sunita's phone began to ring.

'Maybe it's the guv'nor,' said Vickers.

She quickly confirmed, from a glance at the phone's screen, that it was the chief inspector calling.

'Yes, sir,' she responded. 'Everything all right?'

'Sorry to call so late. Just had some news from the hospital,' said Roscoe. 'Miranda Higley died just over an hour ago without regaining consciousness.'

Chapter 28

The following morning, as she prepared to set off for Gloucester with Tom Vickers, Sunita Roy received a call from her colleague Brett Dawson.

'Just wanted to update you on the car in Furnace Hill, Sarge,' he told her as she stepped from her front door and unlocked her car with the remote.

'I've only been able to identify the first part of the number plate from the CCTV,' he continued. 'The remainder is obscured with mud. All I've got is GL21. But it's a Volkswagen Passat.'

'So, it's a Passat that's two years old and that's all we've got?' she said. She slipped behind the steering wheel while Tom Vickers climbed into the passenger seat.

'Yes,' he said. 'The DCI wants me and George to find all two-year-old black Passats based within a twenty-mile radius of Abbots Green. Could take us a while.'

'Good luck with that,' she muttered under her breath. Then out loud, she said, 'You'd better start now, Brett. Listen, was the car only picked up twice on camera?'

'Yes. On Wednesday this week at 6.30 p.m. and on Thursday at 11.20 a.m.'

'Are there any other cameras in the village? Might be worth asking around. Maybe we could appeal for people with front-door cameras or dashcams to come forward,' she said. 'The more evidence, the better.'

'I'll do that, Sarge,' said Dawson.

'All right. So the car had a lot of mud on it?'

'Yes, Sarge. Looked like it had been driven through a farmyard.'

'Provided the driver hasn't put it through a car wash, that might prove key to you tracing it.'

'Let's hope so, Sarge,' he said before she ended the call.

* * *

Sunita Roy and her partner were in a sombre mood as they drove to Gloucester. The news of Miranda Higley's death at half past ten the previous evening had been fully expected, but it had nonetheless proved a shock to them both. They knew her passing, eight hours after Dan Higley's 999 call, would come as a monumental blow to relatives who had been praying for a miracle, and it served to give the investigation team a fresh urgency. They were now dealing with two murders.

St Mildred's High School stood on the northern outskirts of Gloucester, close to woodland. Built largely in the 1980s, the site consisted of two three-storey teaching wings behind a swathe of windows, a sports hall and a fourth building containing an assembly hall and performance space.

Sunita found a space in the visitors' car park at the end of their thirty-five-mile journey, and the pair followed a footpath to the main entrance. On the way, they glimpsed a central courtyard where a teacher was taking advantage of the warm weather to hold an open-air class.

Sunita marched briskly up to the reception desk in the main foyer.

'We're from Heart of England Police,' she explained to a slim, young blonde woman. 'I spoke to one of the school secretaries first thing this morning.'

'Oh yes,' the woman replied. 'We've been told to take you up to Miss Hardwick's office.'

'Is she the head teacher?' asked Vickers.

'No, she's one of our five assistant heads. The head teacher, Mr Murchison, is in Thailand, but we're sure Miss Hardwick will be able to help you. Just take the lift to the second floor and I'll get her to meet you on the landing.'

Sunita noticed Tom smiling to himself after hearing about the number of assistant heads. The blonde woman led them to the nearby lifts, where she pressed the lift button.

'Big place,' he said, leaning with his hand on the wall.

'Yes. More than a thousand pupils,' she replied.

The person who greeted them as they emerged from the lift was a slender woman in her early forties dressed conservatively in a skirt and jacket. She had rather unkempt light-brown hair and a cynical expression.

'You must be the lady that phoned this morning,' she told Sunita in a throaty voice.

'Yes, DS Roy,' said the sergeant, showing her warrant card. 'This is DI Vickers.'

'I'm Sarah Hardwick. Shall we go to my office?'

She led the detectives along a corridor and into a small, brightly lit room overlooking playing fields. Sunita imagined it was the kind of room into which anxious parents would be brought when their offspring had flouted school rules.

The visitors made themselves comfortable on the two chairs Hardwick provided before she settled down behind her desk.

'So what's this about?' said Hardwick. 'You mentioned a murder inquiry when you spoke earlier. Is this about Miranda Higley?'

'You've obviously read about it in the press this morning,' said Sunita.

'I saw it on the TV news,' said the teacher. 'The headmaster's been on the phone from Thailand. We're all devastated, as you can imagine.'

'We gather she taught geography,' said the inspector, 'and she was on the staff for twenty-three years until retiring two years ago.'

'That's absolutely correct,' said Hardwick. 'She was a wonderful teacher, a loyal friend to myself and others and achieved a lot for the school.'

'We're also investigating the death of one of your former pupils, Candy Goodhope.'

The teacher nodded.

'Of course, we knew her as Candice Cosgrove,' she said. 'I understand she changed her first name to Candy when she launched her beauty business, and then, of course, her surname changed when she married Mr Goodhope.'

'There are some other individuals who've also been drawn into our inquiries,' said Vickers.

'And they are?'

'Roxanne Hayes, Tiffany Edwards and Mark Tanner,' he replied.

'I remember all of them, along with Mark's sister Denise,' she said. 'I've been here eighteen years.'

'You should get stars on the wall, like the pupils,' Vickers remarked, trying to lighten the mood. Miss Hardwick ignored him.

'I don't remember Candy much,' she continued. 'She was in some of the higher sets. But I knew the others quite well. I knew Denise Tanner most. She went onto sixth form and then, sadly, dropped out after a year.'

Sunita leaned forward and rested her hands on the desk in front of her.

'Look, we're here because both the teacher and former pupil met untimely deaths,' she told Miss Hardwick. 'We're wondering if it's more than a coincidence.'

The teacher shrugged her shoulders and frowned.

'Well, I'm not sure there's any real connection, other than that they all spent a number of years here, in one capacity or another.'

Vickers leaned back in his chair and folded his arms.

'One way you can help us is by giving us some information about Mark Tanner,' he said. 'Do you have his files available?'

'I'm actually one step ahead of you,' Hardwick revealed. 'Since the horrific death of dear Miranda, I've discussed the matter with the head and we've both agreed to help you as much as possible. It's our duty, really. In view of that, I've already dipped into the files on Mark Tanner. They're here on my desk.'

She lifted up a brown cardboard folder lying on a plastic letter tray on the right of her desk and opened it.

'What do you need to know?' she asked.

'You could start off, if you wouldn't mind, by telling us what kind of trouble Mark got into while he was at the school,' said Sunita.

'Well, as you're no doubt aware, Mark Tanner had a troubled early life,' she said. 'I don't think I'd be giving too much away if I told you his father, whom he adored, left the family home in Gloucester when Mark was eight and Denise was ten. Their mother had a job in a supermarket and, on her income, they found it hard to manage. She remarried a year later and Mark's stepfather wasn't a good influence. He ran a trade in illegal drugs.'

'I'm not sure we were aware of that,' Sunita remarked.

'Mark was a disruptive influence at school. In Year Eight, he one day lit a cigarette in Mr Greaves' Tudor history class and refused to put it out. He claimed it was relevant because Sir Walter Raleigh brought tobacco to Britain.'

She glanced down at some paperwork. 'He got suspended over that,' she said. 'In Year Nine, he was caught smoking cannabis in the swimming-pool changing rooms, believing the smell of chlorine would have masked the smell of the drug. In view of his difficult background, it was decided to deal with this merely by suspending him.

'However, in Year Ten, he was involved in a couple of misdemeanours. He was found to have been bullying a fellow pupil, a girl. He also took a neighbour's car without permission and, while drunk, drove it into the side of the school minibus.'

'What happened on that occasion?'

'I'm afraid the then deputy head, Steven Wimbush, had no choice but to expel him.'

'Do you think Tanner retained any long-lasting grievance against either Candy Goodhope or Miranda Higley?' asked Vickers.

A heavy silence hung in the air. Hardwick gazed into the detectives' faces and, for a while, said nothing. She glanced down at her file of papers.

'Who knows what goes through the minds of these young people?' she said. 'I certainly don't know.' She paused again.

'I think, in view of the gravity of the situation, I ought to give you some additional guidance,' she continued. 'The bullying involved a friend of Candy's. On one occasion she opened her schoolbag and discovered someone had placed a live frog in it. A boy came forward and told the girl they'd seen Mark Tanner put it there. The girl was scared of Tanner and refused to make an issue of it but Candy disliked Tanner and reported him to his form teacher, Mrs Higley. Mrs Higley made a song and dance about it because he'd disrupted several of her geography lessons. Following the minibus incident, Mr Wimbush, acting on the authority of the headmaster, was obliged to expel the young man.'

After leaving the school premises, Sunita felt her decision to scrutinise the out-of-work labourer's school days had been extremely rewarding.

'I think that all puts Tanner right back at the top of the list of suspects,' she said as they returned to her car.

Chapter 29

Steven Wimbush stepped gingerly down the stairs of his house carrying a book and a briefcase at half past eight on Saturday morning. He pushed open the kitchen door and greeted his wife with a gentle smile.

'You've been up for a while, haven't you?' Samantha said. 'I thought I heard you banging about at around seven o'clock?'

'I was washing the car, and since then I've been working in the study.'

'You haven't seen the TV news, have you?' she said, drying her wet hands on a towel.

His smile faded.

'Why? What's happened?' he asked.

'You know that murder near Evesham two days ago?' she said.

'Heather was talking yesterday about a woman attacked in her home,' he said, gazing across the kitchen towards her. 'I didn't know it was a murder.'

'The woman died on Thursday evening, and police have just released her name. And guess what? It's that old floozy you used to work with.'

Wimbush shuddered and the colour drained from his cheeks. He turned back into the hall to collect his thoughts. Then he managed to recover his composure. He put his book down on the hall table and his briefcase on the floor nearby before stepping back to the kitchen doorway.

'Are you talking about the geography teacher, Mrs Higley?' he asked.

'That's the one. The one I caught you whispering to on the phone three years ago.'

'I've told you so many times – that woman was just a teaching friend who insisted on keeping in touch.'

'You were having some kind of affair with her, Steven,' she insisted.

'That's a misinterpretation of events,' he said. 'I had to visit her a few times to sort out some unfinished business relating to education matters.'

'Ha! A misinterpretation of events? Unfinished business? Are those the latest euphemisms for cheating on your wife?'

'I'd never cheat,' he insisted. 'So, tell me what it says on the news.'

'It says the woman killed was home tutor and former Gloucester teacher, Miranda Higley.'

His face turned pale. 'Are you sure?'

'Yes. She's died in Queensbridge General. Police named her after tracing next of kin.'

'Does it say how Mrs Higley died?'

'They're not commenting on how she died, but there's speculation in one of the national papers that the killer used a nail gun.'

'Oh, my God! Poor Mrs Higley. Did it say if the police have any clues as to who did it?'

'No,' she said.

Samantha placed her hands on her hips.

'Let's not mince words, Steven,' she shouted. 'I know precisely who she is. She's not simply an old teaching colleague. She's the old tart you had an affair with.'

'We were just friends,' he insisted.

'Steven, I know you probably slept with her. Don't try and pretend you didn't. I wouldn't mind betting that was her on the phone two days ago. I picked up the receiver, and there was no one there. When I tried to trace the call, it was number withheld.'

'You said yourself it was probably one of the boys,' he said.

'Steven, I'd love to be able to trust you again, but it's hard for me since I learned of your fling with that floozy.'

'Look, will you stop speaking in that vein?' he demanded. 'She was simply a woman I worked alongside in Gloucester. There really wasn't anything between us. Now you say she's dead.'

He paused. 'I wonder,' he said.

'What do you wonder?' she asked.

'If Daniel had anything to do with it,' he said, thinking out loud.

'Daniel?'

'Her husband, who taught maths. He could lose his temper on occasion, and I had to get him out of trouble a few times.'

Samantha sat down on a kitchen chair and glared across at him.

'It said on the news she'd been married three times.'

'Twice.'

'I suppose we shouldn't be surprised she's finally come unstuck. That's what happens to hussies. They play around with all manner of men, toying with their feelings, and, in the end, they get what's coming to them.'

'From the little I knew of her when we worked together, I really don't think she was that kind of woman,' he said.

'Shows how little you understand the world, Steven. It's clear to me she was exactly that kind of woman – the kind who drools at the whiff of a man's shirt.'

'You need to show a bit of compassion,' said Steven. 'Someone I worked alongside as a teaching colleague for eight years has lost their life and, by the sound of it, in a most horrific way. You seem to persist in a belief that we were far closer than colleagues. I've tried to convince you otherwise, but you won't have it. Fair enough, you're entitled to an opinion – even if it's a misguided one. But have a thought for people's feelings. This lady's just died and many folk, including myself, are going to be grieving for her. You know what they said in Rome? *Cum honore recordabor mortuos.*'

'And what's that supposed to mean?'

'Its meaning is precise – I will remember the dead with honour. If you can't say something pleasant about someone who's only just passed, I suggest we bring this conversation to a close.'

Samantha's mood suddenly softened as she watched her husband step backwards into the dark hallway and edge towards the front door.

'Steven, you can't go yet. You haven't had any breakfast, have you?' she implored him.

'I'm not hungry,' he snapped back.

While following him, she happened to glance out of the window.

'There's a police car outside with two men in it,' she said in a low voice. 'I wonder what they're up to?'

'Probably just checking for an address,' Wimbush suggested.

'I don't think so. They're staring at the house.'

* * *

George Roscoe smiled amiably towards his uniformed colleague as he and PC Derek Underhill got out of their Heart of England patrol car.

'This is where Wimbush lives,' he told Underhill, studying the scribbled jottings in his notebook. 'Steven Wimbush.'

Underhill, a genial and conscientious officer based at Queensbridge police station, shook his head in disbelief.

'My God! If it's the guy I think it is,' he said, 'he's headmaster of Biddington Hall School. They don't come much posher than him. That's the public school over there, behind the trees.'

'Doesn't sound a likely suspect for murder,' said George. 'I'm already sensing this will be a waste of time – like the other two calls we made this morning.'

The two men strode up the drive, past a garden mainly laid to lawn, and knocked on the solid oak door of the 1930s double-bay-fronted detached house. A garage stood on the left-hand side.

A tall, stern-faced, elderly man in a suit opened the door promptly.

'Mr Wimbush?' asked George.

He nodded to confirm his name as an exuberant Labrador came bounding into the hallway, barking incessantly.

'Bessie, be quiet!' Wimbush demanded before turning to his wife, who was behind him.

'Samantha, could you put Bessie in the dining room while I see what these gentlemen want?' he asked.

He switched his attention back to his visitors.

'Now, gentlemen,' he said, 'how can I help?'

'DC George Roscoe, Heart of England CID. This is my colleague, PC Underhill. I believe you own a black Volkswagen Passat,' said George.

'That's right. It's in the garage. I can assure you it's fully taxed and MOT'd.'

'We're not here about that,' George continued. 'We believe your car's been in the Evesham area twice this week.'

'Evesham? I don't think I've been over there.'

His wife came to the door.

'What is it, dear?' she asked, peering out at the visitors with a welcoming smile.

'I haven't been to Evesham, have I, dear?'

'No,' she said. 'Not to my knowledge.'

'To be precise, we're talking about the village of Abbots Green,' said Underhill. 'A black Passat with the same first four digits as on your number plate was seen over there on Thursday morning last week, at around 11.20 a.m. A similar car was seen near there the night before, just after 6.30 p.m.'

'Not me, officer,' said Wimbush. 'I wouldn't have any cause to go over there.'

'Fine,' said George. 'I suspected that might be the case. Do you mind if we just take a quick look at the car – as we're here?'

Wimbush shrugged.

'I don't see why not,' he said. 'I'll just fetch the garage key.'

Wimbush strode past his wife and collected the key from a hook on the wall.

He brushed past the policemen, walked round the front of the house and unlocked the garage door.

As the up-and-over door rose, the visitors' eyes rested upon a gleaming black Passat inside.

Underhill stepped into the garage and walked along the nearside of the vehicle, searching for any signs of it having passed through muddy terrain.

George, keen to impress his colleague, studied the offside of the car, pausing momentarily to open the driver's door and gaze inside. After a couple of minutes, George decided they'd probably seen enough.

'Come on, Derek,' he urged his colleague, who was lingering by the open car door. 'Time to move on.'

'Thank you for your time, sir,' Underhill told Wimbush, who was waiting by the front doorway. 'There's nothing for you to worry about. I don't think we'll be troubling you again.'

They returned to Underhill's car and began to drive away.

'I couldn't see any signs of mud, could you?' said Underhill as the vehicle travelled up Rose Lane towards the crossroads at the top.

'That car looked pristine – as though it had been recently washed,' said George. 'And you didn't see what I saw.'

'How do you mean?' asked the constable.

'If that guy Wimbush thought he could remove all traces of dirt, he's come a cropper,' said George. 'We've got to call in. I've taken a couple of photos on my phone as possible evidence. There was mud all over the pedals, in the footwell and on a rubber mat.'

Chapter 30

Sunita Roy was always reluctant to visit mortuaries. But she realised the importance of learning first-hand from the Home Office pathologist how Miranda Higley had met her end. So, with some reluctance, she set off for Queensbridge Hospital early on Monday.

The chief inspector met her outside the mortuary, at the rear of the nineteenth-century hospital in Market Street, and they pushed their way through the double doors.

After their nostrils had been assailed by the pungent smell of chemicals, they entered the cold, uninviting examination room. Oblivious to all around him, Dr Silas Reynolds was peering into the face of a corpse with a dome magnifier. As soon as he realised he had visitors, he stood back from the body. Sunita noticed the doctor's freshly cleaned chisels, knives, forceps and scissors were arranged neatly along a nearby bench.

'Ah, Gavin! Sunita!' Reynolds exclaimed. 'Very timely. I have the poor lady here for you to see, and I've nearly completed my report.'

He let them gaze at the pale, disfigured face of the retired teacher, lying outstretched on a stainless-steel table in the centre of the room beneath gleaming lights. The slim, silver-haired lady had a puncture wound in the centre of her forehead and a succession of further tiny wounds on the right side of her head. Her eyes were open and lifeless.

There she lies, thought Sunita. Less than four days earlier, she had been eating breakfast, perhaps chatting with her parrot and looking forward to helping out at the Abbots Green village hall. What a devastating twist of fate. She turned her face away while Roscoe maintained his gaze towards the corpse for a moment longer.

Reynolds peered at them both over his wire-framed glasses.

'It was definitely a nail gun, was it?' asked Roscoe.

'Yes, old fruit,' said Reynolds.

'I've only ever come across two deaths involving a nail gun. They involved chest injuries, and they were both suicides,' said the chief inspector.

'That's right,' said the pathologist. 'I believe I looked into one of those. Deaths involving penetrating craniocerebral injuries like this are extremely rare.'

'So, there's no doubt this was a case of murder?' asked Sunita.

'None at all. As pathologists looking into such incidents, we have to distinguish between self-inflicted injuries that occur through suicidal intent, accidental injuries and cases of homicide. In this case, the absence of the nail gun from the crime scene and of any evidence the lady was herself engaged in any DIY work clearly points to murder.'

Sunita was shaking her head.

'How do we know a nail gun was used and not some other, more commonplace weapon?' she asked.

'Altogether seven three-inch-long nails have been recovered from the victim's head,' Reynolds explained. 'Six left neat, circular puncture wounds to the right temporal region of the skull. Probably a pneumatic nail gun was used. The worst damage was done with a seventh shot which penetrated the skull just above the forehead in the midline.

'Doctors at the hospital carried out X-rays of the skull, which revealed a nail was lodged in the posterior cranial fossa with multiple bone fragments along its track.

'She was taken for a CT scan which showed the nail had passed through the septum, posterior hypothalamus and the midbrain – six centimetres above the glabella. This led to bifrontal contusion and intraventricular haemorrhage.'

'Serious brain injury?' Roscoe suggested.

'That's right, old fruit,' said Reynolds. 'Traumatic. Dead tissue was removed from the wounds and they were closed and the lady was attached to a Camino intracranial pressure sensor, but sadly the pressure in the brain rose steadily over the ensuing hours until she died at 10.35 p.m. on Thursday evening.'

'Dr Reynolds, weren't there also some chest wounds?' asked Sunita.

Reynolds nodded.

'Yes. Twelve other nails penetrated the chest wall and the left ventricular wall; three nails penetrated the middle and lower lobe of the left lung; and two nails were located inside the chest wall.

The doctor glanced at the two detectives, who had listened quietly to his every word and were now giving a passable impression of two bewildered tourists who, by accident, had gate-crashed a university lecture.

'On the positive side,' Reynolds added, 'this lady acted very bravely in her final moments. She tried to fight back. There are superficial lacerated wounds and abrasions on the back of both her wrists. These appear to have been caused by fingernails and clearly indicate a struggle at some stage.'

'At least, that's encouraging news, Silas,' said Roscoe.

'Yes,' said Reynolds. 'We're hopeful that skin cells recovered from beneath her nails may provide us with the killer's DNA.'

'Do we have any idea what time the attack took place?' asked Sunita.

'There's a wide margin of uncertainty because of biological variability in estimating a time,' said Reynolds. 'The best answer I can give you is that the attack would have occurred at some point on Thursday morning.'

'Dr Reynolds,' said Sunita, 'this means the attack took place well before the husband's emergency call just after quarter past two, doesn't it?'

'Judging by the rate of decomposition of the wounds, that's right. But to say any more might be misleading,' he said.

Roscoe pointed to a computer standing on a nearby worktop with a live screen.

'Is that your post-mortem report?' he asked.

'Yes, old fruit. It just says Miranda Higley died after traumatic penetration of the brain which caused a catastrophic haemorrhage. Put simply, the cause of death was penetrating brain injury.'

* * *

Once Sunita and Roscoe had returned to CID, DC Dawson revealed he had managed to trace Miranda Higley's solicitor.

'What have they got to say?' asked Roscoe as he prepared to enter his room.

'It looks as though the death of his wife has come at the right time for Daniel Higley,' said Dawson.

'How do you mean?' said Roscoe.

'Well, apparently Mrs Higley began divorce proceedings against her husband earlier this month, but because she's died, the divorce is immediately dispensed with. She'd intended leaving the cottage to her son from her first marriage, Barry Teague. Since she hadn't got round to making a will, Daniel Higley stands to inherit the cottage and most of her estate.'

'What does that mean in financial terms?' Roscoe asked.

'It means the murder's left him half a million pounds better off,' said Dawson.

Roscoe tapped his fingers on his desk while thinking about this new revelation.

'Where's Barry Teague, right now?' he asked the constable.

'I've been told that he's currently staying at Myrtle Cottage while he and Dan Higley plan the funeral,' he replied.

Roscoe turned towards Sunita, who was sitting by the door.

'Sergeant, you and Dawson had better get over to Abbots Green and see what the son's got to say about this.'

Chapter 31

The flint and red-brick cottages in Furnace Hill were bathed in a golden glow from the midday sun by the time Sunita Roy and Brett Dawson arrived in Abbots Green.

Sunita parked in the shade of the ash trees near the top of the lane and walked down the narrow pavement towards Myrtle Cottage. Dawson opened the wrought-iron gate and, for a moment, they paused to admire the clusters of yellow roses and blue delphiniums beside the brick path. Then Sunita knocked on the door.

Almost at once, an amiable man with dark hair appeared. Slightly overweight and short in stature – around five feet five inches tall, Sunita knew he was twenty-seven but thought he appeared a little older.

'Mr Teague?' she said. 'DS Roy and DC Dawson, Heart of England CID. Can we come in?'

He inspected her warrant card before inviting them into the hallway.

'Can we say how sorry we are at the loss of your mother?' she said.

'The whole family's devastated, as you can imagine,' he said. 'Shall we go through to the living room?'

'I have to say that my stepfather, Dan, has been a tower of strength,' he said as they sat down on the settee.

'Where's Dan?' called a voice from a corner of the front room.

Dawson laughed. 'I bet that parrot can be quite comical,' he observed.

'That parrot can talk for England,' said Sunita.

'And Scotland and Wales,' said Teague, walking across into the room and tapping his fingers along the bird's cage.

'I've moved him in here for company,' he explained.

'What's he called?' asked Dawson.

'Gabriel,' Teague replied. 'And in case you're wondering, he's no angel. Mum took him on when the previous owner moved abroad and he used to come up with some really choice language. And they're not cheap pets. What with food, vets' bills and insurance, they can cost a bit of money.'

'Where's the money? Where's the money?' squawked the bird.

'Shut up, Gabriel,' said Teague. 'He's just started saying that, and it's getting on my nerves.'

Like Dawson, Sunita found the parrot's noisy behaviour comical. 'How long are you planning to stay here?' she asked.

'My firm have given me leave of absence,' he replied. 'At least until after the funeral. I don't know when that will be. I suppose when the coroner releases the body.'

'It shouldn't be too long,' said Sunita.

'Oh, there was something Dan asked me to tell you,' said Teague. 'After the forensic people finished here on Saturday and said I could move in, Dan had a thorough look round. Some of his other tools have gone walkabout, as well as the nail gun. He's missing his circular saw, cordless drill and sander.'

Sunita removed a notebook and pen from the pocket of her light-grey jacket. 'We'll have to ask your stepfather about that,' she said, making a written note. 'Can I ask what you do for a living?'

'I'm an air-conditioning engineer. I work all over the Midlands,' Teague said.

'And you live in – is it Malvern?' asked Sunita.

'Yes. There's just me and my wife. She'll be joining me later in the week.'

'Do you have any idea who might have carried out this terrible attack on your mother?'

'No. I've been asking myself the question a lot over the past few days. She was the sweetest, kindest lady you could meet. I'm lost for words as to who could be responsible. Everything seems so unreal.'

'One suggestion that's been made to us is that someone with a grudge dating back to her time at St Mildred's High School could be behind what happened,' she said.

'How do you mean?'

'Well, for instance, there's a former pupil who was expelled, and it's been suggested he held a deep-seated grievance.'

'Who are you talking about? Perhaps I know them? I was at the school myself when we lived as a family over in Gloucester.'

'Mark Tanner.'

Teague grimaced. 'Oh, him. He was a troublemaker. I didn't have anything to do with him. He was in a class below me.' Teague sighed. 'So what's your theory? That he never got over being expelled and blamed my mother?'

'She was his form teacher.'

'Fair enough, but it doesn't seem like a strong enough reason to attack someone.'

'Unfortunately, some people brood over things like that for years,' said Dawson, leaning back on the settee and folding his arms. 'Then, one day, everything comes to the surface in an explosion of anger.'

'In any case, expelling someone isn't something my mother ever had any power over,' Teague continued. 'That's usually down to the head teacher.'

'Does the name Candy Goodhope or Candice Cosgrove mean anything to you?' asked Dawson.

'No.'

'She went to St Mildred's.'

'She must have been in a different year,' Teague replied.

'We need to know more of your mother's back story,' said Sunita. 'When did she actually retire from the school?'

'That would have been two years ago. She left a year earlier than she'd planned after an argument with the new head teacher.'

Sunita nodded. 'We've asked her bank for financial statements, but could you give us an idea how your mother was managing? I mean, we understand she and your stepfather separated five years ago.'

'That's right. That had been brewing for a while. Mum felt she couldn't trust him. She once said that the only thing you could rely on Dan for was to be unreliable.'

'Where's Dan?' said the parrot. Teague ignored the bird and continued, 'It was sad when Dan left, but to be honest, they seemed to get on better as soon as they started living apart. He'd continue to do odd jobs for her, and she sometimes invited him round here for a meal.'

Sunita paused to reflect on this answer.

'After splitting up with your stepfather, did your mother have any other relationships?' Sunita asked.

'Not that I'm aware of.'

'I imagine life might have become a bit of a struggle for your mother,' she said. 'She'd previously been used to running her home with two incomes.'

'Dan helped a little, but he had to pay rent on his flat,' Teague replied. 'In any case, Mum was a strongly independent woman who took pride in her financial independence.'

'So how did she manage?'

'She had her home tutoring work and she took in lodgers. There was a nurse, a gearbox engineer, a teaching assistant and a landscape gardener–'

Dawson interrupted. 'I've often wondered about having a lodger,' he said. 'It must be strange having to share your home with a stranger.'

Teague shrugged his shoulders. 'Well, they're only strangers when they first move in. After that, a lodger can become a good companion, and, of course, they help pay the bills.'

'What was the average length of time they stayed with your mother?'

'Some stayed a few months,' he replied. 'Two of them were long-stayers – the nurse and the gardener. They both stayed quite a while. She fell out a little with the gardener but solved the problem by recommending him for a job at Biddington School.'

'While we're on the subject of money, were you aware that your mother had started divorce proceedings?' she asked.

Teague nodded. 'Yes, she'd mentioned something about it.'

'You're aware that the death of your mother has financial implications and that far more of the family assets will now be passed to your stepfather than if a divorce had been finalised?'

'The solicitor pointed that out to me when I spoke to him on Friday afternoon, but, to be honest, my mind's been in turmoil since Mum passed. I'm more focused right now on matters like choosing hymns for the funeral.'

'I understand that,' Sunita said. 'Listen, while she was in her relationship with Daniel, did he ever lose his temper with her?' she asked.

Teague nodded. 'Like all couples, they had their ups and downs. There've been times when he's had a slanging match with Mum and other times when she's let rip at him.'

'Did he ever strike her?'

'There was one occasion when, she told me, he came home drunk and raised a hand to her. Of course, he was full of regrets the following morning and bought her flowers. But she warned him, if he did it again, she'd end the marriage.'

'So the same thing did happen a second time?' asked Dawson.

Teague nodded.

'Do you know I've never told anyone about this before – not even my missus, but I'm afraid it did happen again. And it was this that led to her ordering him to move out.'

'How did you feel about this show of violence by him?' Sunita asked.

'I could never have taken the lenient approach she took towards him,' he admitted. 'For me, it's unforgiveable to strike a woman – never mind twice. But Mum made me promise to put the first occasion out of my mind in the interests of family harmony.'

'You don't think your stepfather could be behind the attack on your mother on Thursday?' said Sunita.

Teague frowned. 'To be fair, that's never crossed my mind until now.'

Chapter 32

Breathing heavily and perspiring a little, the frenzied figure scurried from the car park in front of St James Street police headquarters on Tuesday morning and rushed inside. She sprinted up the stairs and burst through the doors that led to the CID office. After greeting DC Dawson with a wave of her hand, Sunita Roy knocked on the chief inspector's door and, still puffing and panting, opened it a fraction.

'Sorry I'm late, sir,' she said. 'Traffic on the motorway.'

'Don't worry about that,' said Roscoe, who was sitting in his office chair with his back to the window, talking to Tom Vickers.

The inspector, who was sitting by the door, glanced up with a smile. 'I was wondering where you'd got to,' he whispered.

'Now you're both here,' said Roscoe, as she drew up a chair, 'I wanted to let you both know we've had an extremely interesting call as a result of the press conference. Do you remember Justin Hemming, the assistant manager at the hotel?'

They both nodded.

'Justin has called Wendy Hopkirk in the incident room and told her about an ex-convict we might be interested in.

The hotel staff gradually get to know all the potential troublemakers who hang around Queensbridge town centre. One of the chefs recalled seeing a guy called Kevin Leggett in the Courtyard Bar on the day of Mrs Goodhope's murder and originally thought it wasn't important enough to mention to anyone.'

'Good name for a villain, guv – Leggett,' said Vickers.

'Well spotted, Tom,' said Roscoe with a grin. 'The guy's come forward after all the publicity about the brawl.'

'What was this Kevin doing on the day of Mrs Goodhope's murder?' asked Vickers. 'Trying to get customers to buy him a drink in the bar?'

'No. Apparently, he was just inside the door of the bar, playing on the fruit machines.'

'How can we find him, guv?'

'Apparently he's staying at a bail hostel in Queensbridge after serving a sentence for dishonesty offences and aggravated assault.'

'There's only one bail hostel I know of, guv, and that's McKinley House in Mill Road.'

Roscoe nodded.

'I think that must be the place,' he said. 'I'm minded to send the sergeant round with Dawson to knock him up. We've heard that Candy spoke to two men at the fruit machines. Perhaps he was one of them. We need to check it out.'

He turned his head towards Sunita, who had been listening intently.

'Anyway, Sergeant, you were telling me on the phone you picked up some useful intelligence from Mrs Higley's son, Barry, yesterday?'

Sunita nodded.

'Yes, sir. It appears a number of power tools were stolen from Myrtle Cottage. I've managed to contact Dan Higley and he's confirmed that.'

'But whoever it was,' said Roscoe, 'they left behind Mrs Higley's two credit cards, didn't they? That suggests robbery may not have been the motive.'

'Unless they simply failed to see them,' she said.

'We've finally heard back from Mrs Higley's bank,' Roscoe continued. 'She withdrew eight hundred pounds two days before she was attacked. So the question is: what happened to the money? It wasn't in her handbag and it's certainly not in the house. Our team has searched the place thoroughly. All I can surmise is that either she spent it or the killer stole it.'

'Perhaps she left the money out for her husband, Dan,' Sunita suggested. 'I'll check with him. I was going to mention that, apart from the missing power tools, I also learned from Barry that Dan has a violent streak.'

'Yes. There are obviously certain facts in the case, like that one, that point to the husband being a suspect in his wife's murder,' said Roscoe.

'Guv, could I mention the guy over in Biddington with mud in his car's footwell?' said Vickers.

'Yes. The headteacher. What's his name? Wimbush?'

'That's right, guv. So altogether, it means there are three guys with mud on or in their car with the number plate GL21.'

Sunita looked as shocked as if a party balloon had burst in her face.

'Wimbush – that's the name of the headmaster who expelled Mark Tanner,' she said.

'Really?' said Roscoe. 'That's a coincidence, isn't it? Anyway, I think we can put the matter of this head teacher on the back burner for the moment. I've got George wading through the list of other Passat owners, and I think we should wait for him to finish that before we decide on our next step. Right now, I want to turn our attention back to Mark Tanner. I'd like you to track him down, Tom, and find out if he's got an alibi for last Thursday. We should also have another word with his girlfriend, Roxanne Hayes.

Sergeant, can you go over to Gloucester and see if she can give us any steer on Tanner's activities over the past week?'

* * *

Wearing the same clothes as the week before, Mark Tanner opened the door to his sister's house just before midday to find Tom Vickers standing there. I hope he's put them through the wash since we last spoke to him, the inspector thought to himself.

Tanner stood in the hallway motionless while the French bulldog, Milo, barked furiously from behind the closed living-room door.

'Oh it's you again,' he said. 'What do *you* want?'

'Just a little chat, Mr Tanner. It won't take long and there won't be any need to take you up to headquarters.'

'All right. You'd better come in.'

'Who is it, Mark?' called a female voice from upstairs that Vickers recognised as being that of Tanner's sister.

'DI Vickers,' said Tanner.

'Do you mind if I don't come down?' Denise replied. Her brother gave no response. Instead he led his visitor into the small kitchen at the back of the house.

'What's it all about this time?' asked the unemployed labourer, taking a cigarette from a pack on the table and lighting it.

'Just need to know where you were last Thursday,' said Vickers, settling himself on a high stool beside a small breakfast bar.

'Thursday? Why? What's happened?'

'Just answer the question.'

'I'm pretty sure I was here. No, hang on a minute. I was over at Roxy's place in Gloucester. I was there from two o'clock onwards.'

'How did you get over there, Mark? You're banned from driving, aren't you?'

'I went on the bus.'

'It's a tough life, Mark,' said Vickers, suppressing a grin.

'The buses round here ain't too bad.'

'Your journey to Gloucester takes you through Evesham, doesn't it?'

Tanner nodded.

'That's right? Why do you mention that?' he asked the inspector.

Vickers was about to reply, but his phone rang and Sunita's picture appeared on the screen.

'How's it going, Sunita?' he asked, pressing the answer key on his handset. 'You've been speaking to whom? Hold on.'

He turned to Tanner, who was blowing smoke towards him.

'Can't hear. I'll just be a minute,' he said, glaring at Tanner before stepping outside with his phone.

'That's better,' he told the sergeant while standing by the open front door.

'I'm with Roxanne right now,' Sunita explained.

'Can you ask her whether Tanner was with her last Thursday morning?' he said.

After some muffled words were exchanged in the background, Vickers heard Sunita's voice again.

'Yes. Roxanne took the day off and they went to a nearby park,' she told him. 'But there's something else you ought to know, Tom.'

Chapter 33

Judging by the tone of her voice, Sunita Roy was about to make a surprising disclosure. Tom Vickers moved away from the door and stood in the middle of the lawn. He did not want Mark Tanner to hear.

'Roxanne's admitted that Tanner was once obsessed with Candy Goodhope,' said Sunita. 'He asked her out several times before he got the message that she wasn't interested, and he then switched his attention to Roxanne.'

'So, is that the reason he mounted that hate campaign against Candy?' Vickers asked.

'It looks that way,' said Sunita. 'I've just been speaking to both Roxanne and Tiffany. Apparently, the reason Candy didn't show any interest in dating Mark was because she knew Roxanne fancied him and didn't want to queer the pitch for her.'

Vickers smiled.

'I can't really imagine an enterprising woman like Candy would have been interested in a loser like Tanner,' he said in a low voice.

'Well, that's true as well,' said Sunita. 'But what this shows is that we really can't trust a word Tanner says to us.'

'Oh, I'd sussed that out already,' Vickers told her. 'Did you ask her about Miranda Higley?'

'Yes,' Sunita. 'Roxanne was reluctant at first to say much about Mrs Higley, but eventually, with Tiffany butting into the discussion, she admitted Tanner hated her because she got him expelled.'

Vickers ended the call and was about to return to the house when he happened to glance down a side alley. A few metres away, leaning against the side of the semi-detached house, stood a black electric scooter.

He returned to the kitchen, where Tanner's sister Denise had joined her brother.

'Is that your scooter next to the house?' he asked Tanner, who was stubbing his cigarette out in an ashtray.

'It's mine,' said Denise hurriedly.

'I was going to say,' said Vickers. 'You've got to have a valid driving licence to ride one of those – something you don't have, Mark.'

'I know.'

'You haven't been totally straight with us, have you?' said Vickers, resuming his place on the breakfast-bar stool. 'Your girlfriend's told us the real reason you turned against Candy. She refused to go out with you.'

'Well, since she's let the cat out of the bag, I suppose there's no sense in me denying it.'

'We're still trying to decide what action to take against you over the threatening messages.'

He shrugged his shoulders.

'What threatening messages?' asked Denise.

Tanner glanced fleetingly at his sister. 'I'll tell you later. It ain't what it seems,' he said.

'Luckily for you,' the inspector continued, 'your girlfriend confirms your story that you were with her in Gloucester at eleven o'clock last Thursday morning.'

Denise seemed puzzled but said nothing.

'I knew she would,' said Tanner.

'It's very convenient for you,' said Vickers, 'because that was the morning someone you used to know very well died unexpectedly.'

'Who's that?'

'Don't you read the papers or watch the TV news?' asked the inspector with a solemn expression. 'That was the day Miranda Higley died.'

Tanner stared down at the floor. Then he looked up.

'I knew someone had been attacked in Abbots Green,' he admitted. 'I didn't realise it was her.'

'Who is it, Mark?' asked Denise. 'Miranda Higley?'

'Yes, that old trollop who got me kicked out of St Mildred's,' he told her. 'She got done over at her house.' Turning towards Vickers, he said, 'Is that why you were asking me earlier about whether the bus went through Evesham?'

The inspector nodded.

'Now look, Mr Inspector,' said Tanner, 'I don't want no one getting hold of two and two here and making them four. The old biddy *did* get me slung out of school eleven years ago and I got stuck in a referral unit as a result. Yeah, I won't lie – she screwed up my life and made it hard for me to make a go of things. But if you think I took a bus over there, called in and knocked her about in revenge, you'd better think again. I didn't even know she lived in Abbots Green. I got the whole business about being thrown out of school out of my system years ago. In any case, if I was going to track her down and put her in her place, believe me – I wouldn't have waited eleven years.'

* * *

It was clear to Sunita that Roxanne Hayes was an unsophisticated, down-to-earth woman with a lively, sociable nature, even if she had missed out on a more extensive education. She nonetheless came away full of admiration for the ginger-haired beautician who spoke with a soft West Country burr.

She found Roxanne honest and trustworthy, although she still found it hard to comprehend why she had embarked upon a relationship with a known offender like Mark Tanner. Perhaps Roxanne felt sympathy for him and believed she could help him mend his ways. Or perhaps she was one of those women attracted to male villains by their confidence, dominance or masculinity.

As she drove away from Tiffany Edwards' house in Gloucester, Sunita's mind returned to the pitiful murder scenes in the Queensbridge Arms Hotel and Myrtle Cottage. Somehow, she could not imagine the brooding, black-haired Mark Tanner, despite his convictions for assault, engaged in an act of murder. Where was his motive? Redress for his expulsion from school years earlier? This was barely plausible to her.

While approaching Evesham, her mind focussed on Miranda Higley's estranged husband, Daniel. She had phoned him earlier, but he had been unable to shed any light on the mystery of the missing eight hundred pounds. He knew nothing about the money.

Here was a man facing financial hardship if a divorce went through. That formed a possible motive for murder. But he had spent his life in teaching, and inquiries seemed to confirm his moral probity. She found it hard to visualise him standing over his wife of twenty-two years with a nail gun. And, while he had had past contact with Candy Goodhope as her maths teacher, he hardly had a reason to end her life.

She also dismissed the likelihood of either Craig Goodhope or Jack Bayliss being involved in the deaths. Perhaps, as the chief inspector was tending to believe, the two incidents were unrelated.

However, her instincts were telling her the two cases had to be related… in some way. Both events involved defenceless women alone at the time of their deaths. The murders occurred within five days of each other and the locations were only nine miles apart. No outside weapon was used in either case. The killer used a towel to kill Candy Goodhope and a power tool found at the cottage in the case of Miranda Higley.

St Mildred's School linked the two victims. That had to be the key to the entire investigation. But most of the key figures with links to the school had severed their ties eight or nine years ago. Even the Higleys had ended their association with St Mildred's a good few years before.

Of course, a few hours after their arrival at Myrtle Cottage last week, the chief inspector had played down Sunita's suggestion of a connection. He had spun round in mid-conversation like an agitated student caught shouting in the college library.

'Why do you mention that?' he'd demanded as though it were a taboo subject. 'You think we might have a serial killer on our hands? I hope to God we haven't.'

'Not a serial killer yet,' she'd pointed out, 'but a double killer.'

He had walked away in a huff, but he was not alone. Tom Vickers also believed the cases were unrelated.

Regardless of that, there were a huge number of suspects, and she was more confused than she'd been with any previous cases. She was reminded of a comment Tom had made to her the previous evening. 'The deeper we probe, the murkier the waters appear to become.'

Chapter 34

While his sergeant was making her journey back from Gloucester, the chief inspector was planning an early lunch. He had just risen from his executive chair and stepped towards the door when his desk phone rang.

Always reluctant to speak to his superior, Chief Superintendent Norris – especially on an empty stomach – he glanced somewhat anxiously at the phone's screen. He was delighted to find it was a call from an unknown number. He picked up the handset and slid back into the seat behind his desk.

'Roscoe,' he announced.

'Is that the chief inspector?' asked a woman in a quiet voice.

'Yes. DCI Roscoe. Can I help?'

'I've been transferred to you from the incident room,' said the caller. 'I'm phoning you about someone I work for who's been behaving very strangely of late.'

Roscoe's stomach rumbled. His lunch was overdue.

'Is this urgent? Can I get someone to call you back later?' he asked.

'This is very difficult for me,' she said. 'It's about a murder.'

She had his full attention.

'In what way has this person been behaving strangely?' he asked.

'For the past week, he's been coming into work looking as though he hasn't slept,' she said. 'He's also been taking a lot of time off. He's just not his normal self.'

'I'm assuming you're quite close to this person. Is it your husband?'

'No. He's a work colleague. I'd rather not explain my connection,' she replied. 'Let's just say I have his interests at heart.'

'You mentioned murder,' said Roscoe.

'Yes,' she said. 'It's the murder of that woman in Abbots Green.'

Roscoe sat up in his chair. 'Miranda Higley?' he asked.

'Yes.'

'You think this man might have been responsible?'

'I honestly don't know. I'm worried he might have been involved in some way. Mrs Higley phoned him a week ago. He was annoyed that she rang, and, after the call, I noticed he was extremely upset.'

'Was he?'

'Yes. Then one of my friends was passing the rectory in Norton Prior a few evenings ago and saw him going into see the minister, who's a friend of his.'

'Could be a simple explanation for that,' Roscoe suggested.

Roscoe did not divulge that Revd Peter Hughes, the rector of St John the Martyr Church, was also a personal friend of his. Roscoe had first got to know him during the search for missing property tycoon Harry Bowers some years before.

'Was this person you're talking about at work last Thursday?' he asked.

'No,' she replied. 'He took the day off.'

'Any idea why?'

'I'm afraid not and I didn't ask.' She added, 'I can tell you that, since the news of her death came out, he's remained just as edgy. Sometimes he's been morose.'

'Could you tell me the name of the person you're talking about?' asked Roscoe.

'I'm not sure I should.'

'Your call is a bit of a waste of time, otherwise,' he said.

'All right. It's Steven Wimbush,' she said.

'Isn't he the headmaster of Biddington Hall School?'

'I don't think I should say any more,' said the caller. 'He's probably got nothing to do with it. It's just that I'm so worried about him. He's been a good boss – very kind to me. Do you know? I think I'll end the call now. I've probably gone too far already.'

'Could you tell me your name?' he asked.

'No. I've said too much,' she said. Then she hung up.

For a while, the chief inspector sat staring at the handset as it rested in its cradle. His head was crowded with questions. Should he phone the school and try to identify the anonymous caller with the gentle voice – and make sure this hadn't been some kind of hoax call? Why had the head teacher of the prestigious private school been having sleepless nights? What exactly was the relationship between him and the murdered woman? Was he in some way responsible for the woman's death?

Forgetting about his much-anticipated lunch, he took out his list of contacts and found the phone number for Revd Hughes. He dialled the number.

'Gavin, this is an unexpected pleasure,' said the clergyman as he answered.

'I need to speak to you about something,' said the detective. 'It's rather delicate and best discussed face to face. I wondered if you were going to be around over the next day or two? I'd appreciate it if I could call round to the rectory.'

'Of course, Gavin,' said Hughes. 'I'm available after lunch today. Can you give me an idea as to the nature of this delicate matter?'

'I'd rather not, if you don't mind,' said Roscoe. He had already calculated that this might turn out to be one of those pastoral cases that the clergy could be sensitive about. He wanted to be able to look into his friend's eyes and gauge his natural reactions to his questions.

* * *

Nearly an hour later, the chief inspector's car drew into the driveway of St John's Rectory. He switched off the engine and got out. After spending a moment admiring the cherry blossoms, he walked up to the porch and pressed the doorbell.

Revd Hughes opened the door with a broad smile.

'Good to see you, Gavin,' he said. 'Come on up to my study.'

He led Roscoe up to a cluttered room on the first floor of the four-bedroom house where he invited the detective to sit on a brown-leather settee. Roscoe found himself surrounded by portraits of both Christ and King Charles. Revd Hughes seated himself behind his antique desk.

'Peter, you'll understand in a moment why I felt we had to have this conversation in person,' said Roscoe. 'As you may know, we're investigating two murders. The one I've come to speak to you about is the more recent of the two, a victim called Miranda Higley.'

Hughes sat upright and folded his arms.

'I've seen in the *Gazette* and on TV the reports about her dreadful murder in Abbots Green, and I guessed you might be in charge of the investigation,' he said.

'That's right,' said the detective. 'Look, I received a call earlier from a woman who gave me the impression she might be on the staff at Biddington Hall. She was concerned about her boss, Mr Wimbush.'

Hughes raised an eyebrow.

'The headmaster,' he said while folding his arms. He looked like a man anticipating an awkward conversation.

'I understand this man, Mr Wimbush, might have been a friend of Mrs Higley's,' Roscoe continued, 'and he recently came to see you.'

'I can't deny that I did receive a visit from someone recently,' said the clergyman with a solemn face. 'But you must realise I can't discuss it. There's a matter of confidentiality here. My parishioners need to be able to trust the church when they approach us with pastoral matters.'

Roscoe had suspected that his friend would use such an excuse to withhold his cooperation. But was there any way he could use some guile to shed some light on the reason for Wimbush's visit?

The churchman was maintaining his stoical exterior.

'I can't tell you anything,' the rector continued. 'The relationship between a parishioner and his pastoral advisor is sacrosanct. Surely you can see that, Gavin? If the clergy were to report to police every time a churchgoer made an admission about their personal fears or feelings of guilt, they'd soon stop coming, and the whole principle of pastoral care would break down.'

Roscoe nodded. 'I understand what you're saying,' he admitted.

'All I can say to you as a friend, without betraying any confidence, is that the person who visited me – I can't confirm his name – was clearly a troubled individual.'

'Did you give him any advice?'

'I can't divulge that. I can only say that I provide anyone who comes to the church's door seeking help with the spiritual guidance that I believe is appropriate for them.'

Roscoe could appreciate the moral dilemma he had placed the rector in, but he felt frustrated that his friend would not help him more with his investigation. He leaned back on the settee, folded his arms and nodded.

'Look,' Hughes continued, 'I don't want to be unhelpful in what's obviously a murder inquiry. I can say that this person made no admission about anything, but I became concerned he might do something rash and I gave him some guidance.'

'We've got a number of suspects in the case already,' said Roscoe as he stood up, 'but I feel I ought to let you know that I intend to have a word with Mr Wimbush as a matter of routine.'

'You must act as your duty requires,' said Hughes. 'All I can say is that I trust, Gavin, that the man who visited me gained solace through the Lord at his moment of need and is entirely innocent of this heinous crime.'

Chapter 35

The chief inspector glanced at his sergeant as they drove through villages in West Warwickshire on Wednesday morning.

'You said his morning meeting was at ten o'clock?' he said while they turned onto the drive leading to Biddington Hall School.

'Yes. The woman I spoke to believed it wouldn't last long, sir,' Sunita replied.

'You didn't let slip who we were, did you?'

'No, sir.'

'Don't want him doing a vanishing act, do we?' he said as they passed school playing fields and drew up in front of the main school, a red-brick, early English Gothic building.

'Since John Hepworth enhanced the image of the number plate and confirmed it was Wimbush's car on the CCTV, I've been relishing the opportunity of tackling this man about it,' said Roscoe.

Fleetingly, he cast his mind back to his own education at a Birmingham grammar school during the 1980s. He had some fond memories but also some painful ones. In the end, the day he left to join the police had not come a moment too soon.

'School dinners, playing rugby, messing around with Bunsen burners – it's all coming back to me now, Sergeant,' he muttered after they parked and walked together towards the heavy oak entrance door.

'I imagine you were something of a swot, sir,' she suggested with a grin.

'A dedicated middle-streamer,' he replied. 'I just kept my head down and kept out of trouble as best I could. Unlike you, with your fancy grades and your law degree.'

'Like you, sir,' she said, 'I just worked hard on my course and strove to get on.'

'What possessed us to join the force then, eh?' he said, as they reached the door.

'Can I be of assistance?' asked a dark-haired man in his early thirties. Gaunt-looking and wearing a blue boiler suit, he had appeared from nowhere.

'We're looking for the headmaster's office,' Roscoe explained.

'You're in luck,' said the man. 'I had a meeting with him which has just finished.'

'Oh, he had a meeting with you?' asked Sunita.

'Yes, I'm Brendon Blake, the school caretaker,' said the man with a smile that exposed his crooked teeth. 'So, it's straight up the stairs to the first floor, and his secretary's office is right there. You can't miss it.'

'Thank you,' she said. 'You've been very helpful.'

'Don't mention it,' said the man before walking away.

The detectives passed through the door and climbed the stone steps to the first floor.

A smartly dressed, auburn-haired woman glanced up from behind a reception desk. Roscoe explained they needed to speak to the headmaster. She hesitated.

'I'm not sure if he's available,' she said. 'I'm his secretary. Who are you exactly?'

'DCI Roscoe, Heart of England Police,' he said. 'This is my colleague, DS Roy.'

'Just one moment.'

The woman brushed past the desk of a female colleague and disappeared into a door that led into a corridor.

'I think that might be the caller who tipped us off,' Roscoe told his sergeant in a low voice. 'I think I recognise her dulcet tones.'

The secretary returned two minutes later.

'You can go through,' she said. 'He's got another meeting but he's free for five minutes.'

She raised a hatch and passed through the counter. Then she led them into the adjacent passageway and through a door marked 'Private'.

Steven Wimbush rose smiling from behind his desk while his secretary returned to her own office, closing the door behind her. He stepped towards his visitors with an outstretched hand. When he realised the pair bore solemn expressions, his hand was swiftly withdrawn.

'Good morning,' he said.

'I'm sorry to trouble you,' said Roscoe, 'but we need to ask you a few questions. DCI Roscoe.'

He produced his warrant card and showed it to the headmaster.

'My colleague, DS Roy,' he added.

'What's this about, Chief Inspector?' he asked.

'It's about your friendship with Miranda Higley,' said Roscoe.

'As you probably realise,' said Sunita, 'we're investigating her death.'

'Yes, I *did* realise,' said Wimbush. 'Poor lady.'

'You knew her well, didn't you?' said Roscoe.

'I used to,' Wimbush said. 'I worked with her for eight years at a school in Gloucester, but that ended nine years ago when I was appointed the head here. It's a very sad business but I'm afraid I've got no information that could help you in your investigation.'

'We understand you drive a black Volkswagen Passat,' said Sunita. 'Can you confirm the registration number?'

After he had recited the number, she told him his vehicle had twice been seen in Furnace Hill, where Mrs Higley lived.

'Furnace Hill. Where's that?' he asked, returning to his seat behind his desk.

'Abbots Green, as you well know,' said Roscoe, who was gradually losing his patience. 'Where were you, Mr Wimbush, last Thursday?'

'I think I was here at the school,' Wimbush replied. 'I'm always here.'

'We've been informed you had the day off,' said Roscoe. 'Shall I check with one of your secretaries? Perhaps they could jog your memory.'

'Er, no,' he responded nervously. 'That won't be necessary. Maybe you're right. Maybe I had the day off. Let me look in my diary.'

He pulled back one of his desk drawers and drew out a blue diary. He flicked through its pages before stopping at a particular date in May.

'Yes. You're right,' he said. 'That's a little embarrassing. I lead such a busy life these days, I sometimes look back and can't remember my days off. One of the penalties of getting older. Have you read any Horace, Chief Inspector?'

'No. I'm afraid I haven't,' said Roscoe, shaking his head.

'He wrote some famous lines about the passing of time,' said Wimbush. '*Eheu fugaces labuntur anni.* Alas, the fleeting years slip by.'

'I can certainly sympathise with Horace,' Roscoe muttered. 'I can feel our morning slipping away as I stand here. Mr Wimbush, how did you actually spend your time last Thursday. Do you remember?'

'Well, I believe that was a day I spent with my dear wife, Samantha. Yes, that's right. We went shopping in Queensbridge. We had a coffee in the High Street. I bought her a new dress.'

'Why can't you tell us the truth, sir?' asked Roscoe, who was becoming increasingly impatient. 'Your Volkswagen Passat was caught on CCTV in the village of Abbots Green on Wednesday evening and Thursday morning last week.'

'There must be some mistake. It can't have been my car.'

'No mistake, sir,' said Sunita. 'We'd like you to accompany us to our headquarters for an interview under caution, and then we can show you the images.'

'Do I have a choice?'

'I'm afraid not, sir,' said Roscoe.

'Very well,' said Wimbush. 'Do I need a solicitor?'

'Your choice,' said Roscoe, who proceeded to read the police caution and advise him of his rights.

'I think I'd better ring my solicitor, Mr Huckabee, and then I'll need to have a word with my secretary,' said Wimbush.

'We've got a few minutes,' said Roscoe. He was reluctant to leave the room in case their suspect used the opportunity to conceal any evidence.

Once his arrangements were in place, the two detectives led Wimbush down the stairs and out into the car park.

'We'll also need to speak to you about Candy Goodhope,' said Sunita.

'I was devastated when I heard her life had ended so tragically,' Wimbush replied as they walked towards Roscoe's car, 'especially in view of what happened before.'

Sunita stopped abruptly in her tracks.

'How do you mean?' she said.

'Didn't you know? She nearly died a few years ago.'

Chapter 36

Less than an hour later, the chief inspector and his sergeant were peering through the one-way glass into the interview room at headquarters

'There sits a cunning old devil, Sergeant,' Roscoe remarked while they watched the headmaster speaking animatedly with his solicitor, Magnus Huckabee. 'We'll need to keep our wits about us.'

'It was interesting what he said about Candy Goodhope,' said Sunita. 'You know, about the school trip to Germany.'

'Yes,' said Roscoe. 'It sounds as though she was very lucky. She got out of her depth in a lake and started panicking. Luckily, someone dived in, dragged her out and gave her first aid. If she'd been in the water any longer, she probably wouldn't have made it.'

'Didn't Wimbush say it was Daniel Higley who dealt with the family afterwards?' she asked.

'Yes. Sounds like the school mounted a huge public relations exercise to steer the family away from making a complaint,' said Roscoe. 'Anyway, let's go and see what Wimbush has got to say.'

Steven Wimbush looked up as the detectives entered the room.

‘I hope this won’t take long, Chief Inspector,’ said the headmaster. ‘I’ve got a governors’ meeting later on.’

‘I’m sure we can get this wrapped up quickly,’ he said while switching on the recording equipment. ‘Now, Sergeant Roy, could you show Mr Wimbush and Mr Huckabee those two images from the CCTV.’

‘Yes, sir,’ Sunita said, taking two photographs from an envelope and taking a seat opposite the solicitor. ‘Here is your car, Mr Wimbush, on Wednesday evening last week. The time on the frame is 6.32 p.m. This second image was taken at 11.20 a.m. the following day, Thursday, which is around the time when, we believe, Mrs Higley was murdered.’

Wimbush stared at the two grimy photographs of a vehicle captured by the camera travelling down Furnace Hill.

‘I’ve got to admit that it does look like my car,’ he said.

‘Come on,’ said Roscoe. ‘You’re wasting everyone’s time. Admit that this is your car. Then we can move onto your explanation as to why you were there on those two occasions.’

Wimbush’s eyes remained focussed on the photographs. Then he turned his long, stern face towards the chief inspector.

‘All right. I was there,’ he said. ‘But I didn’t call on Mrs Higley. I drove past.’

‘You drove past slowly,’ said Roscoe.

‘OK. I drove past slowly.’

‘You knew she lived at Myrtle Cottage?’ said Sunita.

‘Yes. I knew she lived there. But I hadn’t travelled to Abbots Green to visit her. I was visiting my old friend Richard, who lives further on down the lane.’

‘Is this a man named Morris?’ asked Roscoe.

‘Yes. How did you know that? He used to teach at one of the Gloucestershire schools years ago,’ said Wimbush.

‘What time were you there on Wednesday evening?’

'Let me think,' said Wimbush, glancing at his solicitor. 'It must have been sometime between half past six and half past seven.'

Roscoe nodded. 'I believe this Mr Morris lives at an address called The Paddocks. Is that right?'

'Correct,' said Wimbush.

'Apart from you and Mr Morris, who else was at Mr Morris's house?'

'No one else. His wife died a year ago.'

Roscoe frowned.

'I'm afraid you're not being honest with me, Mr Wimbush.'

'How do you mean?'

'We've spoken to Mr Morris about another matter. He had a visitor around this time, but it wasn't you and they went out for a drink. So, I'm afraid you're going to have to do better than that.'

Magnus Huckabee, a stout, balding man, whispered a few words in Wimbush's ear. The headmaster gazed down at the table and then glanced back at the chief inspector.

'All right. I'll tell you the truth. Some time ago I had a brief affair with Miranda Higley, a matter of some personal shame. In the end, I decided to end it and focus on rebuilding my relationship with my wife, Samantha. But Miranda found it hard to accept that our relationship was over and threatened to confess all to Samantha. Of course, Samantha had her suspicions, but she never knew the full story, and I was determined to keep full details of the affair from her. Miranda began pestering me both at work and at home, and I became worried that she'd speak to Samantha and reveal the whole story.'

'You were concerned that your marriage might break down if the facts became known?' Roscoe asked.

Wimbush nodded. 'That's right, Chief Inspector. I'm afraid I spent a lot of time worrying about all this, and I thought I might be heading for a nervous breakdown. Things came to a head this month, and I'm ashamed to say it crossed my mind that the only way to protect my marriage would be to thrash things out with Miranda. To get her to stop.'

'Be very careful what you say, Mr Wimbush,' said Huckabee. 'Although this is a voluntary interview, anything you say now could potentially be used against you in any criminal proceedings.'

'I'm aware of that,' Wimbush replied, giving a nervous smile. 'All I was going to say was that, on the Wednesday evening, I passed the cottage and looked in through the front window. There was a light on in the corner, but I got the impression she was out. On the Thursday morning – my day off – I came back. But do you know? I looked through the cottage window and realised it would be useless trying to reason with her. I knew in my heart of hearts she was too blinkered to act with any common sense. But I also recognised at the same time that there was no way I could threaten her in any way and certainly no way I could ever harm a hair on her head. So I drove on down the lane.'

'You expect us to believe that, do you?' said Roscoe. 'The camera cannot lie, Mr Wimbush. There you were, outside the cottage in your Passat. This was around the time our Home Office pathologist believes the attack was committed. You had murder in your heart, and yet you sit there, expecting us to believe that you didn't venture inside. You sailed on by. So, by an amazing coincidence, someone else committed the murder, did they? Someone else had murder on their mind?'

'Correct,' said Wimbush. He glanced out of the window at the rows of cars parked outside. Then he looked back at Roscoe.

'I know my story may sound a little ludicrous – admitting I drove over there, thinking of threatening her but not proceeding with it. But I'm being completely honest with you, Chief Inspector.'

Roscoe shook his head.

'So someone else beat you to it?' he asked the head.

'No. Not at all,' said Wimbush.

'The life of the very woman who was blighting your world was terminated, and someone else took on the task. You didn't have to lift a finger. Do you really expect us to believe that?'

'It may be hard to credit, but it's the truth, Chief Inspector. You can't think I murdered that poor woman with a DIY tool, can you, for God's sake? You must accept my explanation because it comes from the bottom of my heart. *Veritas solet esse mara.*'

'I'm sure you're going to tell us what that means, Mr Wimbush,' said Roscoe.

'It means the truth is often bitter. Chief Inspector, after I'd returned to Biddington, I took my wife shopping in Queensbridge, an outing which had been planned for some while. I can show you the receipt for her new dress. I don't know if you'll believe me but I'd like to say I'm ashamed of going behind my wife's back in seeing another woman. I also feel extremely sorry for Miranda. She was a wonderful person, honest, hard-working and devoted to her pupils. She was also a marvellous companion, and the world is a poorer place without her.'

'It's also arguably a poorer place without Candy Goodhope,' Sunita remarked.

'You surely don't think I had anything to do with that woman's death, do you?' asked Wimbush.

'Where were you on the Saturday before last, out of interest?' asked Roscoe.

'I was watching our First Eleven playing cricket at the school against a team from Shropshire,' said Wimbush.

Roscoe nodded back but said nothing, while Sunita folded her arms and leaned back on her chair.

'Mr Wimbush,' she said, 'I've been meaning to ask you. There was a lot of mud on your car when it appeared on CCTV. Can you explain how it got there?'

Wimbush smiled.

'We were talking about Richard Morris earlier. I genuinely did visit him recently – although not on the day of the murder. He's got a smallholding at the bottom of a muddy track, and that's how the car got grubby. No big issue there.'

'Well, if you don't have any other questions, Sergeant, we'll wrap it up there. We'll consider your answers to our questions, and, in case we need you, I'd advise you to remain in Biddington.'

Wimbush shrugged his shoulders.

'I'm not planning to go anywhere,' he said.

'Good,' said Roscoe, 'and I'm going to leave you with a word of warning, Mr Wimbush. *Scitote quoniam peccatum vestrum adprehendet vos*.'

'You remember your classroom Latin, Chief Inspector,' said Wimbush as he stood up.

Sunita glanced at her boss with a puzzled look.

'Be sure your sins will find you out,' Roscoe explained.

Chapter 37

Sunita Roy and Brett Dawson had no difficulty finding McKinley House bail and probation hostel in Queensbridge late on Wednesday afternoon. It was the last building in Mill Road before the busy thoroughfare passed into open countryside.

As they walked along the pavement towards the large, detached Victorian premises, Sunita concluded the 'halfway house' was set in an ideal location for newly released offenders. They could be gradually reintegrated into the community without their presence being too intrusive for residents of the market town.

The pair had travelled there in the sergeant's car, which she had parked in nearby Fishpond Lane. After passing a nail bar and the shuttered premises of a derelict pub, The Woodman, they reached the double-fronted, two-storey hostel.

A slightly built man in his mid-fifties answered the door with a cold expression. When Dawson asked if Kevin Leggett was there, he gave no reply. He simply knocked on the first door along the hallway and called out, 'Kevin, it's for you,' before disappearing into the back of the house.

A balding, stocky man in his mid-forties emerged sheepishly from the room, rubbing his left arm and giving the impression of having been woken up.

'Sorry to bother you,' said Sunita, producing her warrant card. 'DS Roy, Heart of England CID. My colleague, DC Dawson. We wanted to have a chat with you because we've been told you were at the Queensbridge Arms Hotel eleven days ago?'

Leggett was nonplussed and scratched his head.

'Eleven days ago? That would have been a Saturday. Oh, you're talking about the day that woman got murdered,' he said. 'Yes. That's right. I called in at the Courtyard Bar.'

'Nothing to worry about,' said Dawson. 'We're talking to lots of people who were there – trying to build up a picture of what exactly happened that afternoon.'

'I'd invite you in,' said Leggett, 'but my room's in a bit of a state.'

'Don't worry,' Sunita assured him. 'So, what time did you get there?'

'Must have been just after five o'clock. Tell you what – there were this gorgeous blonde that I chatted to for a few minutes in the bar. Absolute stunner. That weren't her, was it? That Candy?'

'It probably was,' Dawson replied, guardedly.

'I thought it might have been. What a bloody tragedy.'

'Anyway, tell us what happened,' Sunita continued while slipping a small notebook and pen from her pocket.

'Well,' said Leggett, 'I'd been in Coral for a couple of hours with a mate, and I'd had a bit of luck with the gee-gees, so I were flying high.'

'How much did you win?' she asked.

'Fifty quid. My mate had to get home, but I wanted another drink, so I went to the Courtyard and played on the machines, trying to win more money.'

'Did your run continue?' asked Sunita, who was writing details down in her book.

'No. Lady Luck give me the cold shoulder, and I ended up putting most of me winnings into the bloody machines.'

'What sort of time are we talking about?' Sunita asked.

'About five thirty.'

'Do you remember who else was there?' she said.

Leggett shrugged his shoulders. 'It's hard to recall,' said Leggett. 'I'd had a skinful by then.'

'Were you by any chance wearing a red football shirt?' she asked.

'Yes. How did you know that?'

Dawson interrupted to say, 'We've been talking to lots of people, mate.'

'We've been told there was a second man playing the machines before Candy Goodhope came over,' Sunita went on.

Leggett looked down at the grey hall carpet for a moment, rapt in thought. Then he glanced back at her.

'Yeah, there were a bloke there. He kept waiting for me to stop and move away before having a go. Trying to win some of the cash I'd put in, I suppose.'

'Did he manage to win any money?'

'He had one or two little wins – same as me,' said Leggett.

'Can you describe this man?' she asked.

'Not sure I can. He were younger than me. Probably mid-thirties. I'd say he were slightly taller than me, but then most people are. He were slim with short, dark hair.'

'Any special characteristics – you know, tattoos, nose ring, earring. Anything unusual?'

'Not that I can recall.'

'Was he wearing a ring on his right hand?'

'I didn't notice.'

'What clothes was he wearing?'

'No idea.'

'What about the woman that joined you?' said Sunita. 'We've assumed up to now it was Candy. Can you describe her – you know, so we can be sure?'

'Yeah. She were blonde with longish, wavy hair. She'd a white top and red trousers and she'd a drink with her.'

'That was her,' the detective muttered. 'Any idea what she was drinking?'

He nodded.

'She told me it was Bacardi and Coke. God. She were three sheets to the wind. Well hammered. She were wobbling about all over the place. She kept putting her glass down on top of the machine I was on, next to her can of Coke. I know she tried to get another drink but she got turned away at the bar. They reckoned she'd had enough.'

'Sounds like the bar staff were just acting in her interests,' said Dawson.

'Yeah, but she weren't too happy about it. She were swearing about them when she came back to pick up what remained of her drinks.'

'So, you spent a while talking to her?'

'Yes,' said Leggett. 'I tried to have a bit of a chat with her, like, and I got out of her that she was staying at the hotel but not much else. She could hardly string together more than a few words at a time. In the end, she said she felt tired. She took her can of Coke off the top and wandered off.'

'What time did she leave?'

'I couldn't tell you precisely, but, at a guess, it could have been around twenty to six.'

'I see,' said Dawson. 'Was the man with the short, dark hair still playing on the slot machines when she left?'

'No, I think he left around the same time.'

'What was he drinking?'

'I think he was on shorts as well, but I can't be certain.'

'How much longer did you remain there after Candy had gone?'

'Not long. It must have been just before six when I went off for some food.'

Sunita paused for a moment to think.

'My boss is probably going to want the name and address of the guy you were with earlier,' she said.

'No problem. If you give me your book, I'll write it down for you,' he replied.

'By the way, what did you do after leaving the bar?'

'I stopped for a beef stew at the Apollo Tearooms in the High Street and then went home.'

Sunita smiled. She knew that, if she gave Leggett's description to Helen Roscoe, she would be able to confirm whether he ate at her restaurant or not.

'Hang on a minute,' said Leggett. 'I remember from the TV that the Candy woman were meant to have been killed in her bedroom sometime after six.'

Sunita nodded.

'So, if that's the case, I was one of the last people to talk to her before she died.'

'That's right,' said Dawson.

Chapter 38

The sound of a phone echoed round the CID office as Sunita Roy arrived for work early the following morning.

Surprised to find she was the first to arrive, she hurried past the desks and found it was her own phone ringing.

'Oh, you're there, Sergeant,' said a woman's voice after she lifted the receiver. 'I was about to give up.'

'Sorry. I've only just arrived,' Sunita explained to the caller, Dr Alice Ling.

'Could you tell the DCI I've just received some interesting DNA results? If you could ask him to call me when he comes in.'

'No problem,' said Sunita. 'Nothing you can share at the moment?'

'I think he ought to be first to know,' said Dr Ling before she ended the call.

Half an hour later, while sitting at her desk, Sunita noticed the chief inspector striding into the office, followed closely by Tom Vickers.

'Sergeant, we need to have an urgent chat,' he said while unlocking his room.

'Certainly, sir,' she replied.

Roscoe sat down behind his desk. Sunita followed Vickers inside and closed the door.

'I've been thinking about it overnight, and I'm convinced Steven Wimbush murdered Miranda Higley,' said Roscoe as the other pair drew up chairs. 'I want you to take charge of this work, alongside Dawson and my son, George. We need to find out if any motorists in Abbots Green have got dashcams and see if residents have got doorbell cameras. We also need to get a search warrant for Wimbush's home. I'll ask George to check out his alibi that he was watching a game of cricket, and we'll have to speak to this Richard Morris character again.'

He paused before continuing, 'I haven't mentioned this before, but you both may remember my old friend Peter Hughes.'

'The rector of St John's, guv?' asked Vickers.

'That's the guy. Wimbush is a friend of the rector, and I found out he visited him the day before the murder. Hughes didn't give much away, but it's clear Wimbush was suffering from some kind of crisis of conscience, and Hughes was concerned he might do something rash.'

Sunita frowned.

'Although Wimbush was at least twice in the vicinity of Myrtle Cottage, we've no evidence he went inside, sir,' she said. 'We've got no witnesses and no forensics. I watched him during the interview yesterday. I'm not convinced he'd have had the wherewithal to commit a murder. When he confessed he couldn't harm a hair on her head, it had the ring of truth about it.'

Roscoe shook his head. 'I can't agree, Sergeant,' he said. 'He's got an air of cunning about him. Although we let him go yesterday, I don't think it'll be long before we have to bring him back in.'

'Sorry, sir,' said Sunita, 'I forgot to mention that a few minutes before you arrived, Dr Ling was trying to speak to you.'

'Did she say it was urgent?'

'Not exactly,' said Sunita, 'but it sounded important. Apparently, there are some interesting DNA results.'

'All right. I'd better call her,' he said, reaching for his desk phone. 'You two sit tight for the moment.'

A few seconds passed while he dialled the number for the forensics department and waited.

'You've been trying to reach me,' said Roscoe as Dr Ling answered.

'Yes, sir. Do you remember the soft drink can and the glass tumbler found in Candy Goodhope's room at the hotel?'

'Yes, of course. It was a Coca-Cola can, and, presumably, the glass was the one she'd been drinking Bacardi from.'

'That's right, sir. The results are in. Mrs Goodhope's DNA is on the tumbler and also on the rim of the can. However, there's also someone else's DNA on the can.'

'Really. That's tremendous news,' he said, beaming with delight. He explained he was switching the call to loudspeaker so the others could hear. 'So, who is it?' he asked. 'I assume it's a man.'

'Yes, it's a man. His name's Kirk Blackhurst.'

'So, what can you tell us about Kirk Blackhurst?' said Roscoe.

'Well,' said Ling, 'he's male, Caucasian and he was born in 1989 in the town of Kendal in Cumbria, where he lived. He first went onto the database after a robbery in 2006. I'm sorry this has taken us a while.'

Sunita and Vickers gazed at each other in amazement.

'So, what the hell was he doing nearly two hundred miles away in Warwickshire at the beginning of May?' asked Roscoe.

'We can only hypothesise, sir,' said Dr Ling. 'People do move round the country, as you know – normally for work reasons.'

After the call ended, Roscoe shrugged his shoulders while gazing at his colleagues' surprised expressions.

'This investigation gets more mysterious by the minute,' he remarked. 'Have either of you come across this name before?'

They both shook their heads.

'No, sir,' said Sunita.

'We need to check the national computer,' said Roscoe. 'But this is a very valuable nugget of information. Could this be our mystery slot-machine player? It certainly suggests strongly that this Blackhurst fellow was sipping Coke with Candy Goodhope minutes before she died. Did they suddenly have a fall-out which led to him strangling her? We need to find this guy as a matter of urgency.'

Both Sunita and Vickers left the room. Less than an hour later, Sunita returned.

'Sir, I've found a little bit on Kirk Blackhurst,' she said. 'He's got form.'

'Has he?' said Roscoe. 'What for?'

'Low-level crime,' she replied. 'Burglary, assault, car theft.'

'Any picture of him? Any addresses?'

'Yes. I've found two pictures. And I've got an address for where he was last living in Kendal.'

'These are the custody images,' she said, handing over two printouts.

Roscoe studied the image of Blackhurst's full face and his side view.

'Nothing much to look at,' said Roscoe. 'Long, dark hair. Bit of a scowl. Deep-set eyes. Looks like a kid in his early twenties.'

'Yes, sir. His last conviction was at Carlisle Crown Court twelve years ago after he and two other men broke into a house in Kendal armed with a machete and stole jewellery and cash. He was jailed for four years.'

'Doesn't sound like that's long enough at all. I take it he's served his time now?'

'I'd imagine he has,' she replied. 'Let me see. He'd be thirty-four now.'

At that moment, Tom Vickers burst into the room without knocking, short of breath but with the exuberance of an astronomer who's just discovered a new planet.

'You're not going to believe this, guv,' he announced. 'Kirk Blackhurst went missing at sea eight years ago, and he's been officially declared dead.'

Chapter 39

The chief inspector slumped forward onto his desk with his head in his hands while he digested this bombshell announcement. Sunita shook her head in bewilderment as Vickers stood in the doorway.

Finally, Roscoe looked up. 'This is a jaw-dropping revelation, Tom,' he said. 'Before we do anything else, we need to get back to Dr Ling and ask her to run the DNA sample through the database again. We should make sure she does it personally – not let one of her staff do it – so there can be no doubt about it.'

'There's at least one other possibility, sir,' said Sunita. 'Kirk Blackhurst could have an identical twin. If the twin was in Queensbridge on the Saturday of Candy Goodhope's murder, that might account for the DNA result.'

Roscoe nodded.

'That's a good point,' he said, 'and something we've got to consider. Sergeant, as a matter of priority, we need to get our genealogist, Philip Gardener, to do some work on this guy's family tree.'

'I've got some more information on this guy,' said Vickers, who was clutching a piece of paper. He came into the room and sat down beside Sunita.

'Well, let's hear it,' said Roscoe.

'I've been in touch with an inspector in Merseyside. They've gone through their archives. He was last seen alive on a night ferry between Liverpool and Belfast on 23 April 2015. He's on a list of passengers who boarded on the Thursday night. He was spoken to by a crewman as they were about to embark, and nothing's been seen of him since.'

'So, he may have fallen into the Irish Sea?' said Sunita.

'That's what the inspector thinks. His frantic sister, who was staying in Belfast and waiting for him to arrive, reported him missing, and the coastguards and police launched a search. But the family never heard anything of him again.'

'That must have been devastating for them,' Sunita said.

'It was just a social visit to Northern Ireland?' said Roscoe.

'That's right. He was going to meet relatives,' said Vickers.

'You said just now that this Kirk had been officially declared dead,' said Roscoe.

'That's right, guv,' said Vickers. 'Last summer, a coroner made a declaration of presumed death after an application from the family and they've now got a death certificate. Guv, I've got a little more on his antecedents. Kirk had appeared in court as both a juvenile and adult offender on various counts – mainly burglary, shoplifting, criminal damage and possession of drugs.'

'At some point,' Roscoe interrupted to say, 'his DNA profile was obviously stored on the database.'

'That's right, guv,' said Vickers. 'Shall I carry on?'

'Yes, of course,' said Roscoe.

'A note dated October 2014 from Kendal Probation Office reports his probation officer's been encouraged by recent behaviour,' said Vickers. 'He suggested Kirk had set up his own building company and seemed sincere in his wish to start afresh.'

'I've heard that one a few hundred times,' said Roscoe, cynically. 'What do we know about this sister of his?'

'She's Hannah Griffin, who lives at 12 Pine Tree Grove, Kendal.'

Roscoe turned his chair and glanced briefly out of the window towards the children's playground across the street.

'So what do the lads up in Merseyside make of it all? Do they think it's a genuine case of a man falling off a ferry?'

'There's a suggestion he might have committed suicide, guv.'

'Where did you pick that up? From that inspector you spoke to?'

Vickers peered at the sheet of paper he was holding. 'There's a memo here from a Merseyside DCI, a guy called Geoff Harrison, guv. It's written a year after Kirk went missing,' he said, before proceeding to read the document.

> *Officers have been in constant touch with Mr Blackhurst's sister, Hannah Griffin. She is the main relative since his mother died in 2012. Mr Blackhurst's car was found in a public car park in Birkenhead a week after his disappearance, on 30 April 2015.*
>
> *A year has passed since Mr Blackhurst was originally reported as having fallen overboard from the Sea Goddess ferry.*
>
> *Following our previous appeals and continued investigative enquiries by detectives, we have seen a number of people come forward which has given us vital new information to help piece together what may have happened to him. Two of his personal friends have claimed that, at times, he suffered from*

> *depression, but there's not enough evidence at this stage to prove suicidal intent.*
>
> *We still need to speak to anyone who knew or might have spoken to Mr Blackhurst in the days, weeks, or months leading up to 23 April. Any information, no matter how irrelevant it may seem, could be the missing piece of the puzzle that helps us figure out what happened to him.*

'It's signed by DCI Geoff Harrison,' Vickers added.

'So what have we got here?' said the chief inspector. 'If it was suicide, and this Kirk Blackhurst chose a watery grave, his body is no doubt somewhere in the Irish Sea. Or perhaps there was some kind of accident. Whichever it was, there's a strong likelihood that the body will never be found. How does his DNA end up on the rim of a drink can at the Queensbridge Arms Hotel? I think we should also consider the possibility of a mistake at the lab where the drink can was analysed. I reckon they might have muddled up the results with someone's else's results – perhaps someone with a similar name.'

Vickers pulled a face.

'That somehow seems unlikely, guv,' he said.

'Yes, maybe, but we can't discount it. Cross-contamination and errors must happen from time to time in the best-run laboratories. I'm sure they're normally quickly spotted and rectified. It's unusual for incorrect results to go so far as to be passed on to officers in the case, but I'm sure this wouldn't be the first time. What are the other possibilities? We also need to consider the sergeant's point that a twin brother or sister was sipping from Candy's can. That's why the genealogist could prove so helpful here. Does this Kirk have a twin? We need to know.'

Sunita nodded.

'Either of those is a possibility – an error or an identical twin,' she agreed. 'But I'm not entirely convinced by the suggestion of suicide.'

'Whyever not?' said Roscoe. 'Surely it's a strong possibility?'

'There's no note, and DCI Harrison doesn't seem completely convinced, judging by that report,' she said. 'He's still appealing for information to fill in the missing piece of the puzzle, as he calls it. After all, he's the SIO in the case.'

'Maybe he's just being thorough. Wants to cover his back,' said Roscoe.

'Maybe,' said Sunita.

'Anyway, this lets Steven Wimbush off the hook for the moment,' said Roscoe. 'I want us to focus all our time and resources over the next few days on trying to get to the bottom of this. I want both of you to travel to Kendal and see the sister. Treat her with kid gloves, obviously. She'll no doubt be very upset when we explain the reason behind our visit.

'See if there are any other relatives we can speak to, and try to have a word with DCI Harrison. Meanwhile, I'll get George and Dawson to hit the phones and find out as much as they can from down here.'

All three of them stood up.

'There is, of course, one final option, sir, that I'm sure is in all our minds,' said Sunita. 'That he faked his death.'

'Yes,' said Roscoe with a nod. 'There's obviously a chance Kirk Blackhurst, whoever he is, didn't give up the ghost. Maybe it's like Mark Twain – reports of his death are greatly exaggerated.'

Chapter 40

Hannah Griffin's white, semi-detached house in Pine Tree Grove was on the western side of the market town of Kendal, on a hillside estate which lay just outside the Lake District National Park.

Sunita Roy and Tom Vickers caught a glimpse of distant Lakeland fells as her car drew up outside on a chilly, overcast Friday morning and they got out.

'I'm glad I made that phone call after all,' Sunita remarked, glancing across the pavement at the small front garden.

'Yes, after that journey yesterday of a hundred and seventy miles, it would have been a real hammer blow to find she wasn't going to be around,' Vickers admitted.

The sergeant led the way up the path to the front door, which was opened promptly by a tall, ginger-haired woman in her mid-thirties wearing a yellow T-shirt and ripped jeans.

'DS Roy and DI Vickers,' said Sunita, showing the woman her warrant card.

'Thank you. I'm Hannah. Please come in,' said the woman solemnly. 'I thought all the police interest would have faded away, now we've got a death certificate.'

They followed her through a small, dark hall into a bright, airy living room with patio doors overlooking a neat rear garden. An oil painting of Lake Windermere hung above the brick fireplace, while three photographs of Kirk Blackhurst, a short-haired, willowy man, smiled down from above a nearby bookcase.

Sunita stared across at the framed pictures. For a moment, she thought she noticed a resemblance to a face she'd seen in the recent past. She couldn't recall who it was, and her thoughts returned to the present. She heard the inspector ask behind her back, 'Have you had to take time off work to see us?'

'Yes. Just a couple of hours this morning,' said Hannah as the two visitors sat on a white, leather settee.

'What line of work are you in?'

'I work at a nursery down the road. I've got two kids of my own, and the work usually fits in well with our routine.'

'Are you married?' asked Sunita.

'Divorced,' said the woman, who spoke with a rather husky North of England accent.

'Oh, I'm sorry.'

'I'm not. I was well rid of Mr Dale Griffin.' There was an awkward pause. 'So what's this all about?' asked Hannah, slumping down into an armchair.

'It's a rather delicate matter,' said Vickers. 'We know you were obviously close to your brother…'

'Yes. I was. I think about him every day.'

'There's no easy way to say this,' said Vickers. 'Your brother's cropped up in one of our current cases in Warwickshire.'

'How do you mean?'

Sunita tried to smile sympathetically. 'To be precise, some genetic information from your brother has been discovered on a soft drink can,' she said. 'We're trying to find out how it got there.'

'That's weird,' she said. 'I'm confused.'

Sunita wanted to move the conversation on quickly before Hannah had time to consider the implications fully.

'Sorry to interrupt your train of thought,' said the sergeant. 'There's something important I must ask. Kirk didn't have a twin brother or sister, did he?'

Hannah looked as bewildered as a vegan offered a crown roast.

'No. There were just the two of us. I was born two years before him,' she replied, shaking her head.

'So, he was your little brother?' said Sunita.

Hannah nodded.

'I'm so sorry,' said the sergeant.

'You know what happened to him, don't you?' Hannah continued.

'Not really,' said Sunita, removing a small notebook from her pocket. 'It would be extremely helpful if you could go through the story.'

'All right. I've explained this so many times over the years, and it was such a long time ago now. It's strange. I don't find it so upsetting now to talk about it. We've got relatives in Northern Ireland, and, after Easter in 2015, we were invited over there, me and Kirk. I took the ferry on around 15 April, but Kirk couldn't make it because of work. So it was arranged he'd take the ferry from Birkenhead a week later and join us.'

'It's a long trip from Birkenhead, isn't it? An eight-hour crossing?'

'He worked late on the Thursday and wanted to use the night ferry so he could sleep in one of the cabins.'

'What sort of job did he have?' asked Vickers.

'He was running a small building company, KB Building Contractors, him and a mate. Well, I was waiting at the port for him early on the Friday, and he never came off the boat– Sorry. One minute.'

The pair could see tears beginning to trickle down Hannah's right cheek. She hurried into her kitchen and returned with a box of tissues, using one to dry her eyes.

'Are you all right?' asked Sunita.

'Yes. I'm fine. Sorry. I was talking about me waiting for my brother at Victoria Terminal in Belfast. Well, I made a big fuss and, although they had him listed as a foot passenger, there was no sign of him. A huge search was launched but he was never found, and last year I got him declared dead officially.'

'We've heard that his car was found in a car park,' Vickers said. 'His car keys were inside.'

'Yes.'

'We understand two friends told police your brother had been depressed. Had he spoken of ending his life?' asked Vickers. 'Officers from Merseyside I've spoken to say they made inquiries about whether he might have done that.'

'Well, everyone gets down from time to time, don't they?' she said. 'He did have a few money problems, but he assured me his new business was going well and he was going to be able to sort everything out. This Liverpool cop called Harrison gave me a bit of a hard time at one point. He came round here three times, asking questions. In the end, he seemed happy and left me alone.'

'So, what do you think actually happened to your brother?' Vickers asked.

Hannah paused briefly and stared at him.

'All I've been able to think over these past few years is that he might have met with some kind of accident while he was on that ferry. I think it's likely he went up on deck for some fresh air and fell overboard.'

'We understand a lifeboat was launched and coastguards notified,' said Sunita.

'Yes,' said Hannah. 'The coastguards said Kirk would only have been able to survive in the water for a short time. Weather conditions were getting worse with north-easterly winds gusting to force eight. The search was called off after a few hours.'

'We're very sorry you lost your brother,' said Sunita.

'Thank you. I appreciate that,' Hannah replied. 'Losing him like that caused all sorts of problems. It was a relief, in a way, when we were able to get a death certificate last year. It meant we could finalise everything. But Kirk will never be forgotten. Do you know that every February, to mark his birthday, I go down to the docks in Birkenhead and scatter petals?'

'That's a touching way to remember your brother,' Sunita murmured.

'But listen, I'm still confused,' said Hannah. 'What's this genetic material you were talking about? How does it relate to Kirk?'

'You've heard about DNA which gets left behind at crime scenes, haven't you?' said Vickers. 'A drink can was found in a hotel bedroom where a young woman died. Tests have confirmed it bore traces of Kirk's DNA.'

'But I don't understand. How could that happen? Unless something belonging to Kirk got transferred from Kendal to Warwickshire. Is that even possible?'

'Listen, Hannah,' said Vickers gently, 'it's crossed our minds that, just maybe, your brother might not be dead.'

'That's absolutely ridiculous,' she replied.

'But is it?' the inspector went on. 'Your brother's body was never found, was it? We're drawn to the conclusion that somehow he might still be alive.'

Hannah had been listening to his words with mounting horror and suspicion. Her reddening face was becoming contorted in anger. Finally, she snapped.

'Get out of my house!' she demanded. 'You come in here claiming to have new information about the loss of my poor brother. Then you come up with the ridiculous allegation that he might still be alive – just a year after we've gone through all the anguish of having him declared dead. You've really upset me now.'

As tears welled up in her eyes again, she snatched another tissue and blew her nose.

'We're terribly sorry to have caused you distress,' said Sunita while stepping towards the hallway. Vickers followed her without saying a word.

'How dare you come here with your preposterous suggestions,' Hannah shouted as Sunita opened the front door and the pair headed out into the warm summer's day. 'You're just a couple of ghouls.'

Chapter 41

'Well, that worked like a charm,' Tom Vickers remarked as he and Sunita Roy returned to her car and climbed in. She reached across from the driving seat and patted him on the arm.

'Don't worry, Tom,' she assured him. 'At some point, we had to raise the issue that her brother might still be alive.'

'I've been called a few things over the years,' he moaned. 'Ghouls is a new one on me.'

'We just had to tackle her about it,' said Sunita. 'It's something that can't be ruled out. I doubt whether there's been any mix-up at the lab or by Dr Ling.'

'We have to bear in mind there could also have been a mix-up with genetic sampling seventeen years ago when Kirk's profile first went on the database,' Vickers pointed out.

'True,' she said. 'But if so, there's probably nothing much we can do about that now. That's so long ago. Anyway, we now know there's no twin. Hannah reacted in shock at the suggestion and our family researcher emailed me this morning to confirm no other siblings. So, we seriously have to consider the possibility that Kirk faked his own death.'

Vickers nodded.

'You're right, of course. But we need to get away from here. She's obviously in a foul mood with us. How about going to get some tea somewhere in town? We can discuss the case, and I can put in a call to that DCI in Liverpool.'

'Why don't we just go back to the hotel?' she suggested. 'Their tea's awesome.'

Twenty minutes later, the pair were relaxing in armchairs in the sumptuous lounge bar of the Highgrove Hotel in the centre of Kendal.

'So what did you make of Hannah Griffin, then?' asked Sunita.

'Quite articulate, wasn't she?' Vickers said. 'But I suppose she's had to say the same words over and over again down the years.'

'I feel very sorry for her,' said Sunita. 'She obviously feels the loss greatly. Otherwise why travel eighty miles every year to sprinkle petals?'

He nodded.

'I know,' he said. 'But the problem is it's increasingly looking as though his death was a scam. So we must move onto the second logical question: did he fake it on his own, or is the sister in on it?'

Sunita leaned back in her armchair, which lay beside a sash window overlooking the bustling street outside.

'If it was a plot involving the sister, she's an excellent actress,' she said. 'But we certainly can't overlook that. And, after your second logical question, I can think of two more: was Kirk's life insured and, if so, has she made a claim?'

'You're right,' he said. 'That DCI in Liverpool would know. We'll have to get hold of him.'

Sunita took a sip of her lemon tea.

'I'll tell you something else we need to do,' she said. 'We need to track down Dale Griffin. He and Hannah clearly parted on bad terms, so there's a good chance he'll be ready to speak frankly – especially if it means getting his ex-wife into trouble.'

Vickers nodded.

'I'll call the office. Maybe they can find an address for him.'

Vickers stepped outside for a clearer phone signal and spent several minutes speaking to a CID colleague before returning.

'I've got George doing a bit of work for us,' he said as he sat down and reached for his coffee. 'I don't know, Sunita. If Kirk fabricated his own death, it's hard to see how he did it. The inspector I spoke to yesterday morning was adamant that the name Kirk Blackhurst was listed as having boarded the ferry.'

Sunita shrugged her shoulders.

'All I can think is that, within minutes of going on board, maybe he sneaked off down the exit gangway with staff who were leaving.'

'So, he never sailed?'

'Exactly.'

'How would he have passed through security?'

'I don't know. I wasn't there,' she said with a grin.

Vickers took a mouthful of coffee and glanced down at the oak floor. He shook his head slowly.

'I don't know,' he said.

'It was very convenient for them that Hannah was already over in Belfast,' Sunita continued. 'She was there to report him missing and kick up a fuss. And don't forget Hannah mentioned Kirk had had money problems, which is another sign he might have been thinking of doing something desperate.'

Her phone began to vibrate inside her pocket. She could tell from the handset's screen that George Roscoe was calling.

'Yes, George,' she said as she answered it.

'Hi, Sarge. How's it going?' he asked.

'Fine, thanks,' said Sunita as she cast her eyes around the bar. 'Making a bit of progress. How are things your end?'

'Dad's been badgering Dr Ling about the test results. He managed to get her to go over to the lab and kick up a fuss. She redid the tests herself, using the sample from the rim. She achieved the same results. Anyway I've got an address for you.'

Sunita drew out her notebook and pen.

'Who've you got for us?' she asked.

'Dale Martin Griffin. Date of birth: 12 January 1983. He's living at Flat 15A, Bakers Row, Kendal.'

'Any idea what he does for a living?'

'Taxi driver.'

'All right. Thanks, George,' she said as she ended the call.

Sunita turned to Vickers.

'Well, that's a bit of luck, Tom,' she said.

'What's that?'

'The ex-husband, Dale, only lives a few streets from here. I think we should go and see him next.'

'Good idea,' he said, finishing his drink. 'Come on.'

Leaving their car in the hotel car park, the pair walked up Highgrove Street, turned left into Bakers Row and found Dale Griffin's flat was on the first floor of a two-storey house, above a charity shop.

Vickers led the way down an alley to the door. He pressed a bell and waited.

At first, it seemed they might have wasted their time. They could not hear a sound coming from within. Then there was a faint rustling noise, the door was drawn back and an indignant, dark-haired man in glasses appeared.

'Yeah?' he demanded.

'Are you Dale Griffin?' asked Sunita.

'Depends who's asking,' he replied.

'We're sorry to trouble you. Heart of England CID,' she said, showing her warrant card. 'Could we come in? It'll only take a moment of your time.'

'I don't know,' said Griffin, stroking his stubbly chin. 'What's this about?'

'We've been to see your ex-wife. It's about her brother,' she continued.

'All right.'

He led them up a narrow, carpeted staircase to a drab sitting room and kitchenette.

'This is Kirk you're talking about, isn't it?'

They both nodded.

'I can't tell you much,' he said. 'I didn't really know the geezer too well.'

'How long were you married to Hannah?' asked Sunita.

'Four years. We ended it a couple years back after I lost me job. I was at home living on benefits, and she couldn't cope with it.'

'So, you drifted apart?'

'You could say that.'

'The main reason we're here,' said Vickers, 'is that we're looking into Kirk's disappearance.'

'Him going overboard, you mean,' said Griffin.

'Do you think it really happened like that?' asked the inspector.

'Well, no one really knows, do they?' said Griffin, taking a seat on a dining chair. 'There's two trains of thought. One is that he topped himself after feeling down. The other is that his disappearance was staged and that he's living happily in Northern Ireland, where his mum's from. Where did you say you're from again?'

'We're from Heart of England Police in the Midlands,' Sunita explained.

'So, how come you're involved?' asked Griffin.

'It's connected with a crime we're looking into,' she said.

Griffin frowned, clearly unable to comprehend how his dead ex-brother-in-law might be linked to a crime in Warwickshire or fully grasp why detectives from a hundred and seventy miles away had descended on him.

'Kirk was always trouble,' he continued. 'He had a few brushes with the law up here and dabbled in drugs. And he was always tapping Hannah for money. That's one of the things we argued about. One day he wanted five hundred quid out of money left by her father. I told her not to be so stupid and that he'd only waste it, so she said no. Do you know what? He turned around and said how could he go straight if he couldn't clear his debts. So she gave him the money, and he gambled it away. I know I shouldn't say this, but it was a godsend when he vanished.'

Vickers folded his arms and leaned against the doorway.

'You were saying there were two trains of thought – that he either ended his life or he's set himself up in Northern Ireland,' said the inspector.

Griffin nodded. 'Yeah.'

'Which of those theories do you lean towards?' asked Vickers.

'I don't think he'd have the brains to set himself up with a new life – especially since he was so dependent on Hannah. I reckon he was under a lot of pressure and took the easy way out.'

'Hannah mentioned that Kirk had a few money problems,' Sunita admitted.

'More than a few,' said Griffin. He gazed into their blank faces. 'You don't know, do you?' he said. 'Yeah, the idiot was more than two hundred thousand pounds in debt when he went over the side.'

Chapter 42

Shortly after midday, the two detectives set off on the forty-mile journey through the national park to the home of retired detective Geoff Harrison. The former Merseyside officer had agreed on the phone to see them at half past two. During the journey, they stopped at a country inn to have lunch and call their chief inspector back at the office.

'Kirk Blackhurst is believed to have been heavily in debt at the time he disappeared, sir,' Sunita told Roscoe as she sat in the pub garden, 'and it's looking more and more likely that he falsified his death.'

'You're suggesting it's a case of fake suicide, are you?' said Roscoe. 'What they sometimes call pseudocide?'

'I don't know if it should be treated as that. I'm sure there'd have been a fake suicide note if that had been the plan, but no note's been found. I think that was intentional. I believe it was planned with his sister so they could make a life insurance claim. In a single action, he escapes his debts and sets himself up with a small fortune in insurance money. If there was any hint of suicide, that might have affected the chances of a successful claim.'

'That's a good point,' said Roscoe. 'But do we even know whether his life was insured?'

'Tom and I are on our way to meet up with the DCI who was in charge of the case. We'll know more later today.'

'Good,' he said. 'By the way, Tiffany Edwards has called several times. She needs to speak to you urgently. Have you got her number?'

'Yes, it's all right, sir. I'll catch up with her later.'

While eating her salmon salad in the sun, Sunita told Vickers she wanted to show Geoff Harrison a photograph of Kirk Blackhurst when they met him.

'We need to be absolutely certain we're dealing with the right person,' she explained.

'I'm not sure that's necessary,' he replied between mouthfuls of beef lasagne.

'Listen, Tom, this case has become so complicated, and this business of whether Blackhurst went overboard or not is so mysterious, we need confirmation at every stage that we're on the right track.'

Vickers shrugged his shoulders.

'I suppose it won't do any harm to get him to confirm it's a picture of the missing man,' he said. 'So, what are your current thoughts?'

'I'm more inclined than ever to think there's something suspicious about his trip on the night ferry,' she said.

'So, you think he was never on the boat in the first place? He somehow made his way south and reappeared in the Midlands under a new identity?' he said.

'Looks like it.'

'And left his car worth a few hundred quid behind in a car park to help make it all look authentic?'

'Yes.'

'But wouldn't he need money for travelling, accommodation and food?' said Vickers.

'He must have saved up a pool of money in preparation for his new life,' she said.

'I suppose so. So, shouldn't we be considering the various suspects we've got and see if one of them could actually be Kirk Blackhurst? He could be living and working in our patch in front of our very eyes. Is he a teacher, a barman, someone working at the hotel?'

'I've already considered all the options,' she said. 'Not one of our main suspects, as far as I can tell, resembles the man in the picture. Craig Goodhope and Jack Bayliss are about the right age, but there are no facial similarities. Kevin Leggett is too old.'

'Well, the boss has got the top team working on it.'

She nodded and smiled.

'The thing is I'm annoyed with myself, Tom,' she said. 'I've got a nagging suspicion I've seen Kirk somewhere before, and I can't remember where.'

After continuing their journey past the tranquil waters of lakes Windermere and Thirlmere, Sunita drove them through the town of Keswick until they reached Harrison's hillside home, Burnside Villa, in the hamlet of Carnthwaite.

Harrison, a burly man with sparse grey hair and twinkling brown eyes, was sitting on a bench outside his semi-detached cottage, gazing out towards Skiddaw mountain, when they drew up. He greeted them warmly and invited them into a small but comfortable living room with Cumbrian landscapes on the walls.

'You're Tom Vickers, aren't you?' he asked the inspector in a Liverpool accent, shaking his hand. 'One of my CID friends tipped me off you were making inquiries. So, when you called me this morning, I'd been half-expecting to hear from you.'

'Pleased to meet you, sir. Yes, that's right, I did have a few words with an inspector in your old CID office yesterday. This is my colleague, DS Roy.'

Sunita smiled and shook the retired DCI's hand.

'Nice one. So you want to hear about Kirk Blackhurst, do you?' asked Harrison.

'Yes,' said Vickers as he and the sergeant sat down on a grey sofa. 'We've brought a photograph.'

Sunita passed their host the colour image of Kirk. Harrison nodded at once.

'Yes, that's him,' he said. 'That's Kirk.'

'You were obviously the SIO in the case?' said Vickers.

'That's right, fella. It took up several months of my life, and I'm afraid to say I never quite got to the bottom of it.'

He sat down at a dining table in his bay window after handing the photograph back to the sergeant.

'Tell me again what prompted all this?' he asked them.

Vickers exchanged glances with Sunita.

'It's quite straightforward,' said Vickers. 'We're dealing with the murder of a woman who's been described as a rising star of the beauty business, Candy Goodhope.'

'I remember seeing something about that on the news,' Harrison muttered.

'Traces of Kirk's DNA were picked up on a soft drink can near the body.'

'Very interesting,' said Harrison, stroking his chin. 'I bet that got you lot puzzled, didn't it?' He roared with laughter before adding, 'Looks as though that little scally might be alive after all, don't you think?'

'We think there's a strong possibility, sir,' said Sunita.

'I'll be straight with you,' he said. 'From very early on in the case, I became convinced Kirk Blackhurst hatched a plot with his sister to falsify his own death. He'd a bad criminal record, partly fuelled by his demand for class A drugs. He was proper skint. But we couldn't prove there'd been a plot to fake his death, could we? And we couldn't find any evidence of how he came to disappear either. We checked the footage of as many CCTV cameras around the docks as we could. We interviewed Kirk's sister several times. We questioned the captain, the crew, the port staff. We issued appeals in the media. Even sent a team of officers to Belfast.'

'But it was all in vain?' said Sunita.

'Yes. At one point, we received an anonymous tip-off that he was in hiding at a friend's house. I had a whole team of people working on that for two weeks. In the end, it was too much of a drag on personnel and resources. We just had to let it drop.'

'Had Kirk taken out life insurance?' asked Sunita.

'I wondered how long it would be before it came round to that,' said Harrison with a broad smile. 'Yes, Blackhurst was heavily in debt at the time he was last seen alive. But just three months before his disappearance, he'd taken the step of insuring his life with the British & Colonial Life Insurance Company.'

'Presumably, no payout was ever made?' said Vickers. 'With all these questions about what happened, surely the insurance company would have smelt a rat, wouldn't they?'

'I'm afraid you're wrong. I got to know the man from the insurance firm quite well. Ronan Sedgwick, his name is. Of course, they made their own rigorous inquiries, as you'd expect. But they were forced to conclude in the end that there was no reason to withhold payment. There was no real evidence of suicide, was there? Once Hannah, Kirk's sister, had gained a presumption-of-death certificate, there was no barrier to releasing the money.'

'So the money was paid to Hannah Griffin?' said Sunita.

Harrison nodded.

'That's right,' he said. 'Four hundred and fifty thousand pounds.'

* * *

As soon as the pair had returned to Sunita's house after their four-hour journey, she tried to call Tiffany Edwards. But, as had twice happened during the afternoon, the videographer's phone went straight to voicemail. This time, Sunita left a message, asking Tiffany to call her.

Half an hour later, at half past seven, as she was drinking a cup of lemon tea in their living room, her mobile began ringing, and she was relieved to find it was Tiffany responding.

'You're hard to get hold of,' Sunita complained as she answered and leaned back on the cream leather settee.

'I could say the same about you,' said Tiffany. 'Listen, I've got a confession to make. I've got some pictures on my phone that you might be interested in. I took them in the Courtyard Bar shortly before Candy was killed.'

Sunita sat up sharply as though she'd been struck by a thunderbolt. Tom Vickers, who was pouring himself a lager across the room, noticed her surprised reaction and glanced across in concern.

'What?' she exclaimed indignantly. 'You're telling me this now?'

'Yes. I'm sorry I didn't say anything earlier,' said Tiffany. The atmosphere between them had become frostier than a Siberian Christmas.

'I'm annoyed with you,' said Sunita with the face of a grumpy child.

'I was grieving for Candy and I wasn't thinking properly,' Tiffany explained. 'Not only that. My baby hadn't been sleeping. But then the other day, I remembered taking the photos. There are ten altogether. Would you like me to send them over?'

'I suppose you'd better,' Sunita hissed. 'You've got my email address, haven't you?'

'Yes,' said Tiffany. 'I'll do it now and, while I've got you, I thought I'd mention the podcast.'

'Podcast?' said Sunita. 'What podcast?'

'It was something Candy had been working on in secret,' said Tiffany. 'It was meant to be a surprise for her fans – an account of her early life. I was thinking you might find it useful – you know, for your research. We only made a draft version of the first episode, but I think you'll find it fascinating to listen to.'

'All right. Send that over as well,' said Sunita before she hung up.

'Who on earth was that, Sunita?' asked her partner, taking a seat beside her.

'That was that muddle-headed Tiffany Edwards, who ran Candy Goodhope's social media campaigns,' she replied. 'She's just remembered she took some pictures in the Courtyard Bar on the day of the murder.'

'Blimey. Is that the first time she's mentioned it? She's a bit of a dozy cow. Didn't she realise the importance of something like that?'

'She says she was upset over the death and then her baby's been keeping her up. Never mind,' said Sunita. 'We'll have a look at the pictures and see where it takes us, if anywhere.'

A few minutes later, they discovered Tiffany had emailed over ten photographs together with the Candy Goodhope podcast. Sunita downloaded them onto her personal computer while Vickers looked over her shoulder.

'I'll have a listen to the podcast later,' she said. 'The most important thing is to examine these pictures. There's six of Candy, Roxanne and Tiffany in various poses. There's two of Roxanne with Mark Tanner; and there's one of Tiffany with her arms round the barman. Oh, there's also a picture of somebody's dog. Look.'

'I don't know why she sent us the photo of the dog,' muttered Vickers.

'Hold on, Tom. Let's have another peek at that photo of Tiffany hugging the barman.'

She scrolled back to the picture she wanted.

'Do you see those two men at the fruit machines in the background?' she asked.

'Yes.'

'That bald man in the red shirt is Kevin Leggett, the guy from the bail hostel. But can we get a better look at the second man – the guy in the check shirt?'

Vickers helped her to zoom in on the second man, who was tall and slim with short hair. The left side of his face was showing.

'Could be anybody,' said Vickers.

He noticed a smile creeping onto Sunita's face like a shaft of sunlight streaming through a blanket of cloud.

'You recognise this second guy, don't you?' he said.

'Yes,' she said. 'I think I do.'

Chapter 43

Sunita Roy rose early on Saturday, leaving her partner sleeping peacefully. Despite it being the middle of May, it was a cold morning. She slipped on a white dressing gown before tiptoeing downstairs to the living room. After carrying out some online research, she called a colleague from the force drugs team. Then, without stopping for breakfast, she set off for the CID office.

'It's all starting to fall into place now,' she informed the chief inspector as soon as she reached his room.

Roscoe was eagerly scrolling through reports on his desktop computer after arriving just a few minutes before her. He glanced up from his desk with a genial expression as she came in.

'That's good,' he said, 'because while you've been gallivanting round the Lake District, we poor mortals have failed to make any progress at all in tracing this guy Kirk Blackhurst down here.'

Sunita placed a photograph of blonde-haired Tiffany Edwards hugging the barman in front of him.

'Who's that lucky fellow with the glamorous Tiffany?' he asked.

'That's Ellis Buckley, head barman,' she replied. 'But that's not the reason I'm showing you this. Can you see the two men behind the couple? The bald guy in the red shirt is Kevin Leggett, but until last night, the other man – the tall guy holding a whisky glass – was a mystery. But I now know who he is. If you look carefully at the structure of his face with his high cheeks and slightly pointed chin, you'll see there's more than a passing resemblance to our friend Kirk Blackhurst.'

'Good God,' said Roscoe. 'I think you're right, Sergeant.'

'And if I'm not mistaken,' she said, 'he's now calling himself Brendon Blake.'

'How do you make that out?'

'While in the Lake District at the sister's house, we saw some photographs of Kirk Blackhurst before he disappeared, and his features reminded me of a face I'd seen recently. I couldn't place it at the time, but when I saw this photograph taken with Tiffany's camera, I realised where I'd seen the man before. Do you remember our visit to the school a few days ago?'

'Yes, of course. We went to question Wimbush.'

'Yes. Do you remember the caretaker, a man with crooked teeth?' she asked. 'I'm pretty certain that's him.'

Roscoe took another look at the photograph.

'The man in the blue boiler suit? You're absolutely right, Sergeant,' he said as a smile crept across his face. 'That's excellent work. So you believe he could be the guy that killed Candy Goodhope?'

'I'd say he's definitely a person of interest,' she said, taking a seat in front of his desk.

'It's interesting you should find this out at this stage. The crime scene manager from Myrtle Cottage handed me this sheet of paper while you were away.'

He picked up a document from his in-tray and passed it to her.

'It's a list of names and payments,' she said with a blank expression.

'That's right,' he said. 'We weren't sure what it was to begin with. It was found in Miranda Higley's writing bureau. Then we realised the list gave details of deposit payments made by her lodgers. And that name, Brendon Blake, is on the list.'

'So at some point, Blake was lodging at Myrtle Cottage?' she said.

'Looks that way. The date suggests he moved in four years ago.'

'At some point, he moved out because he's now living at the school in tied accommodation,' she said, thinking out loud.

'So, could we be looking here at the man responsible for both murders?' asked Roscoe, leaning back on his chair.

'I'm not sure, sir,' she said. 'I've spoken to the drugs team, and they've confirmed Blake was on their radar over possible drug offences.'

'So what's your thinking? You seem hesitant now.'

'I'm a little hesitant,' she said. 'If Brendon Blake killed both women, the motive was undoubtedly money for drugs. The theory would be that he murdered Candy when she refused to let him have her cash. He might have seen her make the withdrawal from the bank and pursued her to the hotel. He might have then followed her up to her room, strangled her, seized the money and taken a sip from the can before going.'

'It's a good working hypothesis,' said Roscoe, 'and, if that's what happened, it would explain his DNA being on the can of drink. But can we also tie him in with the murder at Myrtle Cottage five days later?'

Sunita shrugged her shoulders.

'It follows the same pattern, preying on lone women. He calls into see his former landlady. He needs money. She refuses to give it to him so he kills her before stealing the cash she'd withdrawn earlier. The trouble is we've got no tangible evidence. Brendon Blake wasn't caught on any cameras, and there's no forensics from Myrtle Cottage to place him there.'

'Anyway,' said Roscoe, 'he certainly looks like a candidate for the Goodhope murder. I'll put in a quick call to Merseyside Police. Then we'd better head over to the school and see what he's got to say for himself.'

* * *

After Tom Vickers had arrived at police headquarters half an hour later and he had been fully briefed, all three set off towards the public school in the chief inspector's car.

'There's a lot at stake here,' said Roscoe as they headed onto the M42 motorway. 'If this man Brendon's real identity is Kirk Blackhurst, he's not going to be too pleased at his new life coming under the microscope.'

'Not to mention the fraud charges, guv, which he and his sister are likely to face,' said Vickers, who was sitting in the back.

'We'll have to keep our wits about us,' said Roscoe. 'How much was it you said the sister has received from the insurance company, Sergeant? Four hundred and fifty thousand pounds?'

Sunita glanced across from the front passenger seat.

'That's right, sir. Harrison was so helpful. We've promised to keep him updated on the case.'

Once they had arrived in the school car park and met up with PC Derek Underhill and another constable from Queensbridge, they all set off towards the main entrance. They were buffeted by a strong breeze sweeping across the grounds as they approached the doors. Then a middle-aged man strode out of the building.

'I'm one of the teachers. Can I help?' he asked Roscoe.

'We're looking for Mr Blake,' said the chief inspector with a frown.

'He's probably in his flat at the end of the building,' said the teacher. 'But he could be in the boiler house. Is everything all right?'

'Just need a few words with him.'

'Has Mr Wimbush been informed you're here?' asked the teacher.

'Not yet,' said Roscoe. 'To be honest, we don't need to trouble the head. It's Brendon we need to see.'

'Mr Wimbush always has to know if strangers come onto the school premises,' the teacher insisted. 'He's very particular about it.'

'Well, we're not strangers. We're the police, as I'm sure you can see,' said Roscoe, pointing to the two uniformed officers accompanying them.

While the teacher hurried off in the direction of the headmaster's study, Roscoe led the team along the path that skirted the front of the building. They had nearly reached the flat mentioned by the teacher when Blake himself emerged from a stout wooden door marked 'Caretaker'. He was carrying a bucket.

'Mr Blake,' yelled Roscoe. 'We need to have a word with you.'

'What about?' Blake asked cagily.

'A number of things,' Roscoe replied.

Blake dropped the bucket and sprinted away, past the flower border beside his flat and disappeared round the corner.

'After him!' shouted Roscoe as Vickers and the two constables set off in pursuit.

Chapter 44

After chasing Brendon Blake round the building, the three policemen were in time to see him dart back inside through a rear entrance.

Vickers led the constables through the door and into a huge cloakroom full of blazers and straw boaters. At this point, they seemed to lose track of him. Leaving the cloakroom, the three men found themselves in the middle of a long corridor without knowing in which direction Blake had gone.

'We'd better split up,' said the inspector. 'You two go back towards the main doors where we met that teacher. I'll try this direction.'

Vickers turned left and had only taken a few steps along the corridor when he met one of the teenage boarders in school uniform. He was emerging from a door on the right, which was marked 'Chapel', with a guilty expression.

'Sorry, sir. Mr Simpson asked me to tidy the hymn books,' said the boy, no doubt assuming the detective was a teacher.

'No problem,' said Vickers. 'You haven't seen Mr Blake, the caretaker, have you?'

'You've just missed him, sir. He's in the chapel. I saw him going up the clocktower stairs,' said the boy.

Vickers made his way along the aisle of the small chapel and found a door at the far end which led to a spiral staircase. He set off up the stone steps at a steady pace, but he had paid less heed than he should in recent times to his physical fitness. He began puffing and panting as he reached the third floor and could tell there were dozens more steps to climb.

Every now and then, he would stop and listen. Twice he thought he heard the sound of footsteps from higher up, but he couldn't be sure. Perhaps he was wasting his time. Blake obviously knew the building well. He could be anywhere.

When he reached the top step, he came to a door bearing a wooden sign saying 'Danger – Keep out'. This would surely have suggested itself to the caretaker as an ideal place to hide, Vickers told himself.

Disregarding any concerns for his personal safety, the inspector drew back the door to reveal a set of small wooden circular steps leading upwards towards a shaft of daylight above. As he climbed, he could hear a rush of footsteps. He looked up to see a pair of feet disappearing into a void above him.

'Not far now,' a voice in a northern accent called out from overhead.

'We need to talk,' shouted Vickers, stopping for a moment to catch his breath. 'Why don't you come back down and hear what we've got to say?'

There was no reply. Seconds later, Vickers opened a small door, clambered up a few final steps and found himself on the roof of the tower. The bellcote, topped by a ball finial and weathervane, rose from the centre of the leaded ogee roof, surrounded by a low, crenelated stone wall. Sitting in a gulley a few feet away was the sinister figure of Brendon Blake, who was leaning his lower back against the south wall of the tower, scowling.

'So, you finally made it to the top,' sneered Blake as he folded his arms and stared across at the inspector. 'There's a wonderful view from up here, don't you think?'

Vickers glanced around at the spectacular rural views displayed before him. He could see playing fields, farmland and, in the distance, the church spire of St John the Martyr in Norton Prior. He could make out the figures of Sunita and the chief inspector standing down below, staring up at them. He glanced away. He'd never had much of a head for heights.

'You should watch your step,' warned Blake. 'Some of the stones up here are loose. Look.'

He brushed his hand against some stonework. A few pieces of stone cascaded to the ground. 'Who are you, anyway?'

'My name's Vickers. Tom Vickers. I'm a detective inspector with Heart of England Police.'

'Are you now? So, why are you here?' asked the caretaker.

'We'll tell you all about it, if you just come back downstairs,' said Vickers. A wind whipping across the roof was making it hard for him to hear the caretaker clearly, and he was concerned that the man was too close to the edge.

'You'll have to give me at least an idea what it's about first.'

'Well, we believe your real name is Kirk Blackhurst.'

'Really? And what gives you that idea?'

'You look like him, for one thing.'

'Come on. You'll have to do better than that.'

'Well, do you remember when you were younger and you broke the law a few times in Kendal? The police took a sample of your DNA and now traces of the same DNA have just turned up at a crime scene in Queensbridge. We've got you on camera nearby at around the time.'

'Smart-asses, aren't you?' he smirked.

Then, unexpectedly, Blake stood up and gazed out across the fields.

'Don't be a fool, man,' shouted Vickers. 'We're something like a hundred feet from the ground.' He darted across, attempting to grab hold of Blake's arm. The caretaker struggled free and wildly struck out.

The inspector was concerned that Blake – or Blackhurst – had already been involved in one episode with suicidal traits. He shuddered at the thought of him featuring in a second.

Pieces of stone broke loose as Blake struggled to maintain his footing. Vickers then succeeded in grabbing the caretaker's arm and made several attempts to haul him back towards the door.

But Blake resisted. 'Let me go, you bastard,' he cried out.

For several seconds, they rocked to and fro, tussling together before they fell down onto the curved, steel roof. Vickers was left dazed by the force of the tumble, allowing his opponent the chance to grab his hair and strike his head repeatedly against the silver-coloured metal.

Flashes of light briefly afflicted the inspector's vision. He then felt Blake attempting to lift his whole frame and drag him towards the parapet. There was a rush of air round him as his head and upper torso were pushed over the edge of the roof. He was suddenly gazing down at the gravel path below, where his colleagues were standing.

'Get ready to meet your maker,' Blake announced.

After that strenuous climb up the tower, the inspector seemed devoid of energy, almost bereft of hope. Is this how his nineteen-year career in the force was to end, with him hurtling from this lofty steeple to his certain death on the gravel path below?

Somehow, he recovered his senses. He could not let this humble school caretaker overcome him. He was the police officer here. He was the one entrusted to protect the public and uphold the law. Come on, he told himself. You've triumphed over tougher opponents than this.

Gradually, he found a new determination not to let this man gain the upper hand. He grabbed hold of the crumbling wall and prevented himself slipping any further out. Then, while Blake seized the inspector's right leg in a desperate attempt to propel his whole body from the tower, Vickers kicked out wildly. This forced his opponent to release him and provided the right moment for him to haul himself back to safety.

Blake was not done yet. He launched himself at Vickers in a ferocious new attack which left the detective sprawling in the gulley. The caretaker leaped onto him, grabbed his hair and began thumping his head down against the roof again. But Vickers summoned up all his strength, swung round sharply and knocked his assailant away with a yell of triumph. The caretaker toppled onto the roof with a thud.

'Have some of that!' Vickers announced gleefully.

Blake attempted to heave himself up and face his adversary again. But within seconds came the distant sound of friendly voices and of footsteps tramping up the nearby steps.

The strident tones of PC Underhill could be heard saying, 'Stand away from the officer, or you'll be tasered.'

Blake glanced round in annoyance, but he could see no point in continuing his onslaught. Begrudgingly, he stepped back towards the doorway where Underhill was waiting. He raised his hands in a gesture of surrender.

'I've done nothing wrong,' Blake shouted. 'This is police brutality.'

Underhill ignored him.

'Put your hands behind your back,' the constable ordered before a colleague handcuffed the caretaker.

Underhill helped Vickers to his feet.

'Are you all right, Tom?' he asked the inspector.

'I've had better afternoons,' said Vickers, who then turned towards the suspect. 'Brendon Blake, you're under arrest on suspicion of the murder of Candy Goodhope at the Queensbridge Arms Hotel on Saturday, 6 May and for assaulting a police officer.' He then recited the standard caution before they accompanied the caretaker back to the ground floor.

* * *

Sunita ran towards her partner and threw her arms around him when he emerged from the chapel.

'Are you all right?' she asked.

'Yes. I'm fine,' Vickers insisted while Roscoe patted him on the back.

'I was so worried when I saw you and Blake on the roof,' she added.

After Blake had been escorted away, Roscoe turned to Vickers. 'Are you sure you're all right, Tom?' he asked.

'Well,' said Vickers, 'apart from having dust all over my clothes, what feels like a cracked skull, a thumping headache, an aching back and bruised legs, I suppose I'm not too bad.'

'I'm sure the school nurse will be able to sort you out with an aspirin,' said Roscoe.

'An aspirin?' he replied. 'After what I've just been through? I'll settle for nothing less than a couple of pints in The Fleece.'

Chapter 45

'Have you had enough time with your client?' the chief inspector asked the middle-aged lawyer who was sitting beside Brendon Blake.

'I think we're just about ready,' replied Roger Sims, a duty solicitor who had been invited to represent Blake after his arrest.

The interview room on the ground floor at St James Street was a cold, depressing place. The plain cream walls needed redecorating. The only natural light filtered in through a solitary window overlooking the car park.

Sunita Roy was the last person to arrive. She sat down opposite the bespectacled lawyer and placed a manila envelope on the table in front of her. Roscoe was switching on the digital recording equipment at the back.

'Before we go any further, thank you for providing us today with your fingerprints and DNA, which we're sending for analysis,' said Roscoe, taking a seat beside his sergeant. 'First of all, why did you run away when we came to arrest you?'

'I've been caught for a couple of driving offences,' Blake replied. 'Thought it was something to do with that.'

Roscoe sneered.

'I hope you're not trying to take us for fools,' he said.

'No, honestly, I thought it was the traffic offences.'

'We'll let that lie for the present,' said Roscoe. 'Could you give us your full name?'

Blake folded his arms and stared into the chief inspector's eyes.

'Brendon Blake,' he said.

'Date of birth?'

'Second of February 1990.'

'And where were you born?'

'In this town, Queensbridge.'

Roscoe frowned.

'We know none of that's true, don't we?' he said. 'For one thing, we can detect a slight northern accent.'

'My parents were northerners.'

'I'd like to see your birth certificate or some form of ID,' said Roscoe. 'But I have my doubts about whether you would be able to provide anything like that.'

The solicitor interrupted.

'Chief Inspector, before the interview, I had a long discussion with my client,' said Sims. 'He's explained that police believe he's given himself a new identity. He denies this and insists his real name is Brendon Blake.'

'We understand he previously used the name Kirk Blackhurst with a different date of birth,' said Roscoe. 'For the purposes of this interview, I'm going to proceed on the basis that, like many people, he uses a different name from the one given at birth.'

'Brendon Blake's the only name I've ever had,' said the suspect.

'All right. I'm not going to argue,' said Roscoe. 'We'll assume for current purposes that your name is Brendon Blake. Now the reason we've brought you in for questioning is that we're investigating the murder of a woman called Candy Goodhope at the Queensbridge Arms Hotel, and you were one of the last people with her before her death.'

'Is this the beauty video girl who's been on the TV news?' asked Blake. 'The blonde woman on TikTok?'

Sunita interrupted. 'And other social media.'

'You don't deny that you were at the hotel on Saturday, 6 May?' said Roscoe.

'I don't remember being there,' said Blake. He smiled, exposing his crooked teeth.

Roscoe turned to Sunita. 'Show him the photograph.'

Sunita took out the image showing Blake and Leggett playing on the fruit machines and placed it in front of the suspect.

'Do you agree that that's you in the background?' said Roscoe.

Blake bent forward and spent a few seconds studying the image.

'Looks a bit like me,' he admitted.

'Come on,' said Roscoe. You must remember whether you were at the hotel or not. That's only two weeks ago.'

'I *have* been to the hotel,' said Blake. 'It's just that I don't remember when. All right. Let's say I was there.'

'Candy Goodhope's face has been on TV for the past fortnight and all over the press,' said Roscoe. 'You clearly know the woman we're referring to. What did you talk to her about?'

Blake glanced at his solicitor before conceding, 'All right. I called into the hotel for a couple of Lemmys and got playing on the fruit machines. I just fancied my luck.'

'I'm sorry. What's a Lemmy exactly?' asked Sunita.

'I can answer that,' said Sims with a smile. 'It's whisky and Coke, named after the singer of the rock group Motörhead, who was partial to them.'

'Thank you,' said Roscoe. 'Mr Blake, what time did you get there?'

'About a quarter past five.'

'How did you get into conversation with Candy?' asked Sunita.

'She was a little the worse for wear,' said Blake. 'She was moaning about her boyfriend failing to turn up and that his phone was on voicemail. I didn't take much notice. I was on a winning streak and got about twenty-five pounds out of the machine while she was rabbiting away.'

'What time did you leave?'

'After I'd finished my drinks, which must have been just before six.'

'Was she still in the bar at that time?' asked Roscoe.

'If I remember rightly, she left around the same time. I didn't see where she went.'

Sunita had been watching Blake gesticulating over the table.

'Mr Blake, I've been watching your hands,' she said. 'Do you ever wear a ring?'

'I did at one time,' he said. 'I haven't done for a while. Why is that relevant?'

She didn't reply. Instead, she turned her attention towards Roscoe, who had folded his arms and was leaning back on his chair.

'Mr Blake, you followed Candy Goodhope out of the bar and up to her room, didn't you?' he said.

Blake shook his head.

'No. I left the building,' he said. 'I went back to my flat at the school.'

Sims interrupted to say, 'Surely, Chief Inspector, the hotel has cameras installed and my client would have been filmed leaving. Can you not find the footage? I'm sure it would clear my client.'

'Which exit did you use?' the chief inspector asked Blake.

'I went out through the back door into the car park,' he replied.

'The answer to your question, Mr Sims, is that we are still in the process of studying the camera footage from the hotel. I have to say that I'm not happy with your client's response. We believe he went up to Candy Goodhope's bedroom. Your client was wearing a check shirt and, at around a quarter past six, a guest in another room glanced out from her nearby balcony and spotted through the window a man with just that kind of shirt strangling poor Mrs Goodhope to death. Not only that, we have DNA evidence linking Mr Blake to the murder scene.'

'That can't be right. I was never there,' said Blake, shaking his head. 'You're trying to fit me up.'

'Give me a moment to explain,' Roscoe continued. 'Mrs Goodhope was found dead at approximately twenty-five minutes past six in the evening in her hotel room, Room 224. We believe the time of death to be around 6.15 p.m. When police entered the room, they found a Coca-Cola can on the sideboard and this was sent away for analysis. When checks were carried out on the National DNA Database, a match for this genetic material was found to a man named Kirk Blackhurst, who disappeared from the Birkenhead to Belfast ferry on 23 April 2015.'

'Excuse me, Chief Inspector,' said Sims. 'What evidence have you got to support these assertions?'

'We've got a fair amount of evidence,' replied Roscoe. 'There's the photographic evidence, for one thing.'

Sunita took the police profile picture of Blackhurst from her envelope and placed it on the table beside the hotel bar picture so both men could see them.

'We also have the DNA evidence from the drink can indicating Mr Blake was in the victim's room.'

Sims shook his head and seemed lost for words.

Blake shrugged his shoulders and gesticulated wildly with his hands. 'Why are you saying all this?' asked Blake. 'I had nothing to do with the woman's death. And who's this Kirk fellow you keep going on about?'

'I'm saying all this because we believe that you and Kirk Blackhurst are one and the same person,' said Roscoe. 'We believe that, under your previous identity as Blackhurst, you needed to make a fresh start because of mounting debts. You faked your own death, travelled to the

Queensbridge area and began living under the new name of Brendon Blake.'

'Chief Inspector,' said Sims, 'this claim about my client's identity seems crucial to the case against him. My client and I clearly need more time to discuss this. Could we have a break for half an hour?'

'I suggest we adjourn until two o'clock,' said Roscoe. 'That'll give us a chance to have a light lunch.'

He added, 'I haven't even mentioned yet that we've been in touch with Merseyside Police – who've been leading the search for Kirk Blackhurst. They've raided the home of Blackhurst's sister, Hannah Griffin. They've seized her computer and an initial search has found an interesting email, asking her to pay some money into a bank account in the name of Brendon Blake.'

Chapter 46

Solicitor Roger Sims glanced up with a solemn expression when the two detectives returned to the interview room.

'My client realises now it's in his own interests to come clean and tell you honestly what he knows,' said Sims. 'He had nothing to do with this woman's death and feels that, if he cooperates, you'll realise that fact.'

Roscoe nodded as he sat down beside Sunita.

'All right,' he said. 'Let's see what he's got to say. Mr Blake, you accept that your real name is Kirk Blackhurst?'

Blake, who until that point had been staring down at the floor, raised his head and gazed into the chief inspector's eyes.

'Yes,' he said. 'I was named Kirk Brendon Blackhurst at birth. I moved to the Midlands in 2015 and began using the name Brendon Blake.'

'For the tape,' said Roscoe, 'you now accept that, on the night of 23 April 2015, you made it appear you'd vanished from the Belfast ferry when, in reality, you left Merseyside and moved to the Midlands?'

'Yes. And before you and your police mates make trouble for my sister, I want it made clear that this was all my idea. Hannah had nothing to do with it.'

Roscoe leaned forward and placed his arms on the table.

'There are two officers on their way here from Merseyside who'll be questioning you about that, and I'm sure they'll also be asking your sister some tough questions as well,' said Roscoe. 'But our team here aren't concerned with your faked disappearance. We're solely concerned at this point with the deaths of Candy Goodhope and Miranda Higley.'

'I'll tell you what I think happened,' said Blake, sitting back in his chair. 'When you're playing the machines, you usually put your drinks down on top. Both of us must have had a glass and a can of Coke and put them down on top of the machine I was playing. When she left, she must have taken the wrong can. That's all I can think.'

Roscoe glanced at Sunita.

'I don't believe that for a minute,' he said. 'She might have been the worse for wear, but I don't believe *you* were after just two shorts. You knew exactly where your glass and can were, and you'd have noticed straight away if she'd taken yours in error.'

Blake shook his head.

'You must believe me. I didn't go up to anyone's room in that hotel. I was gone from the hotel by six and caught the bus back to the school.'

'Anyone vouch for that?' asked Sunita.

'Well, I suppose the driver and the other passengers, if you could trace them.'

Roscoe shrugged.

'Leaving all that aside for the moment, we also need to talk to you about your relationship with a woman called Miranda Higley,' said the chief inspector. 'How did you know her?'

'This is the lady attacked in Abbots Green last week?' asked Sims.

Roscoe turned his head towards Sims and nodded. 'Yes, nine days ago.'

'And you believe my client may be involved in that in some way?' said the lawyer, peering at Roscoe over his glasses.

'We're only asking questions at this stage,' the detective replied. 'There are certain signs that the two deaths may be linked.'

He turned back to face Blake.

'So, I repeat, how did you know Mrs Higley?' he asked.

'She was my landlady,' said Blake. 'I took a room with her four years ago. Then last year, I lost my job as a maintenance man and wasn't able to pay the rent. She knew the head of Biddington Hall School was looking for a caretaker so she had a word with Mr Wimbush, and that was it. Job done.'

'Did you keep in touch with her after you took up your new post?' asked Sunita.

'Yeah. I'd go round there every now and then.'

'Mr Blake, you've had a drug problem for a while, haven't you?' said Roscoe. 'And you're also fond of gambling. We've had a team round at your flat where we've picked up traces of class A drugs and seen evidence on your computer of extensive visits to gambling sites.'

'I gave up drugs, and I only have a flutter on the horses now and again. Surely I can spend my leisure time how I like, can't I?'

'The point is eight hundred pounds went missing from her cottage the day Mrs Higley died,' said Roscoe. 'Since buying drugs and gambling cost quite a bit, it's crossed our minds you might have taken that money.'

Blake shook his head. 'No. I didn't go over there on the Thursday she died.'

'So, where did you go that day?' asked Roscoe. 'We've spoken to one of the school secretaries and she said you weren't at work.'

'I've got a girlfriend in Queensbridge. I was with her.'

'We'd need her name address and also details of your bus journey,' said Roscoe. 'I'm minded to leave matters there for the moment, but I'm afraid you'll be remaining in custody until you've been interviewed by our colleagues from Merseyside.'

* * *

After two uniformed constables had escorted Brendon Blake away to the custody suite, the two detectives made their way back to the CID office.

'I'm fairly certain Blake is behind the two murders,' said Roscoe while they climbed the stairs. 'He was wearing a check shirt as shown by your photograph. His drugs craving and gambling meant he needed money. His DNA was in her room. He certainly had the motive and the opportunity, coupled with a criminal background which involved burglary and theft offences.'

'I know all that, sir,' said his sergeant as her brow wrinkled in deep thought. 'But I'm inclined to believe his explanation that it really is possible Candy might have taken the wrong can up to her room along with her Bacardi.'

'Are you?'

'Yes. She was in such a state, wasn't she? She even left her laptop behind. Don't you remember? Tasha Garvey, the barmaid, had to run after her, and she told me Candy was on her own.'

'That doesn't mean anything,' Roscoe insisted. 'Blake could have waited until Tasha had returned to the bar and then gone after her. Or maybe he followed her when she visited her room with the money earlier in the afternoon, so he knew her door number. Anyway I'll get George and Dawson to delve into his alibi and the bus journey. I'm sure we're close to cracking the case.'

But Sunita was far from convinced of Blake's culpability for the murders. Despite her earlier notion that Blake might be responsible, her mind was beset by doubt. 'We must be missing something,' she told herself. 'I'm sure we must be missing something.'

Chapter 47

Tom Vickers was roused from his bed by the spicy aroma of Indian food cooking in the kitchen on Sunday morning. He slipped on his black dressing gown and crept downstairs.

While Sunita was tending to a saucepan on the Aga, he sneaked up behind and threw his arms around her.

'Tom, you idiot!' she exclaimed. 'I nearly tipped this over.'

'What are you cooking?'

'It's a traditional Bengali breakfast,' she said. 'If you remember, I've made it before. Deep-fried luchis, which is flatbread, dipped in chickpea curry along with some eggs for you.'

'Smells delicious.'

She turned round and kissed him.

'Could you set the table? This won't take long,' she said.

After their meal, they sat at the dining table, discussing the two murders.

'Have I told you the latest? The boss now firmly believes Brendon Blake carried out both murders,' she said. 'He reckons getting money for drugs was the motive. But he can't prepare charges until we've made a few more checks. Meanwhile, he's in a huge row with Merseyside, who are desperate to take Blake to Liverpool for questioning.'

'Whatever happens, it's going to be a while before Blake's back cleaning boilers and changing light bulbs,' said Vickers.

'I keep thinking we have overlooked something,' she said. 'When the boss and I first went to Myrtle Cottage, we were so preoccupied with the state of the body and interviewing Daniel Higley that I don't think we had a proper look over the place. I think I'll give Barry Teague a call and see if he's around.'

'As it's Sunday, he might well be,' said Vickers.

'It's only a twenty-minute drive from here,' she said. 'Do you fancy going over there with me?'

'No. As I told you, I need to go back to my place in Halesowen and check how things are over there.'

'All right. I'll see you later,' she said, bending down for him to kiss her before she left the room.

* * *

Less than a week had passed since Sunita had visited Myrtle Cottage, but a lot had happened since she had last been there. Although the roses in the front garden were now fading and the box hedge needed another trim, she was reminded of how charmingly the cottages presented themselves in the May sunshine.

Barry Teague had been looking out for her and opened the front door while she was approaching along the path.

'Are you making any progress?' he asked.

'Yes, some,' she said. 'We've interviewed a lot of people and even been up to the north of England regarding one person who might be involved.'

'Oh really? Well, I hope you catch the bastard quickly. We don't want anyone else's lives ruined like ours have been. My wife's around this weekend. She's gone up to the village shop. Did you want more information about Mum?'

Sunita shook her head.

'Not really. But I'd like another chat with you,' she said after following Teague into the sitting room. 'I'd also like to look round. I just feel that we might be overlooking something. Oh, this room looks different.'

The settee had changed places with the dining table and chairs.

'Yes. The old set-up reminded me too much of Mum,' he said.

The parrot immediately sprang into life. 'Come in, dear,' he squawked. 'Where's Dan?' Then he cackled and whooped on his perch, nodding his head.

Teague laughed. 'I'm afraid Gabriel is still making a lot of noise,' he said.

'The last time I was here, he was calling out, "Where's the money?"' she said. 'Is he still doing that?'

Teague smiled. He stepped across to the cage and clicked his fingers along the bars of the cage while pulling faces at the parrot.

'Yes, I don't know why. He's got a set of phrases he brings up from time to time. Sometimes he surprises you with something different he's picked up.'

'I did wonder at one stage if the person who killed your mother might have demanded money from her and that the parrot might have picked up the phrase "Where's the money?" from the attacker,' said Sunita.

'No. You must have heard it wrongly. He's actually saying, "Where's Mummy?" It's been part of his repertoire for a while.'

Sunita shrugged her shoulders.

'We'd never have been able to use it as evidence in a court of law anyway,' she said with a laugh. 'Couldn't really call a parrot as a witness. The judge would never accept it.'

Teague laughed. 'No, although Gabriel probably wouldn't have a problem being sworn in. Do you know when we might be able to hold a funeral?'

'It's down to the coroner, I'm afraid. I suggest you have a word with the coroner's officer in Queensbridge.'

Sunita walked slowly round the room, looking for anything she might have missed before. Finally, her eyes rested on the Welsh dresser.

'What's that speaker on the end of the sideboard?' she asked.

'It's Mum's Echo speaker – which she uses with her smartphone to run her Alexa device.'

'Oh, her voice-activated assistant,' said Sunita, stroking her chin. 'What did she use it for?'

'All manner of things. I set it up for her so she could turn on lights in different rooms, read emails, check the weather and for home security. She wasn't sure about it at first, but she got used to it.'

'I've got a feeling no one from our scenes-of-crime team picked up on her Alexa device when they were here. Have you got all the information about your mother's phone and Amazon accounts?'

'Yes.'

'Could you let me have the details, including passwords? I'll get our digital forensic analyst to look into it. We haven't got her phone – looks like it was stolen by the killer – but he might still be able to do something. You never know.'

* * *

When she got home from Abbots Green, Sunita logged onto her computer and sent digital specialist John Hepworth an email containing all the information about Miranda Higley's use of virtual assistant technology. Then she spent several hours delving into Candy Goodhope's social media accounts.

At five o'clock, she heard Tom Vickers' Audi roaring up Old School Lane and driving through the gates of her home. She stood up and ran to the front door to greet him.

'How's your house?' she asked him with a broad smile.

'Everything's fine,' he said, kissing her on the cheek. 'I've aired the place out a bit and had a word with the neighbours. I still can't make up my mind whether to sell it or rent it out. How were things in Abbots Green?'

'Fine. I've discovered Miranda Higley had an Alexa device,' she replied, 'so, although we can't find her phone, I'm wondering if Hepworth can get information from her Amazon account that might help us.'

'Great idea,' he said.

'I've also been looking into Candy Goodhope's Facebook and Instagram accounts,' she said. 'Come and look at this.'

He followed her into the living room. Candy's public Facebook page was open on Sunita's desktop. She sat down in front of it.

'What am I meant to be looking at?' he asked, placing a hand on her shoulder.

'Have a look halfway down,' she said. 'It says, "Coming soon: Pioneering podcast from top British beauty guru Candy Goodhope. My early life. My parents' struggle. The laughter and tears. And the man who nearly wrecked my life."'

Chapter 48

The chief inspector heard footsteps approaching from behind as he climbed the stairs to the CID department on Tuesday.

'Good morning, sir,' said Sunita Roy, who caught up by the time he reached the landing.

'You're looking like a ray of sunshine this morning, Sergeant,' he remarked. 'Looks like that day off yesterday's done you a power of good.'

'Thank you, sir, but it wasn't a day of leisure. I was working hard all day on the case with John Hepworth, and I'm pleased to say my gut instincts seem to have been proved right.'

'Excellent, Sergeant. Please come and see me in my office in a minute, and you can tell me all about these instincts of yours.'

Twenty minutes later, Sunita tapped on Roscoe's door.'

'Are you free now, sir?' she asked.

'Yes. I was just going to get a sandwich from the canteen, but that can wait. Come in and tell me what you've found out.'

'Well, I believe I've cracked the case by focussing on two aspects of modern life,' she said. 'Podcasts and the use of a virtual assistant.'

'Sounds intriguing,' said Roscoe. 'So, who've you got in your sights – the headmaster or the caretaker?'

'No, sir,' she said, taking a seat near his desk. 'It's not the men from Biddington Hall.'

'I think you're probably mistaken, Sergeant. Brendon Blake stands out a mile as the killer in my book. All that nonsense about Candy taking his can by mistake is just a smokescreen.'

'With respect, I believe the suspect I have in mind had the motive, the means and the opportunity. Not to mention the resolve. Let me explain. Because Candy Goodhope built her career on social media, it's occurred to me for some time that that's where we might find the explanation for her murder. I was intrigued when Tiffany Edwards told me on Friday that Candy had been involved in a secret project to make a podcast about her early life.

'So, I spent Sunday afternoon looking for any mention of the podcast on Candy's social media sites. There wasn't very much, except an advert which alluded to a man that almost wrecked her life.'

'Interesting,' said Roscoe, who was following every word. 'But I still think Blake makes a better fit. He's been a maintenance man all his life and must have knowledge of nail guns.'

'If you'll allow me a few minutes more, sir,' said Sunita.

He nodded and she continued, 'Since Friday, John Hepworth's been focussing on Candy's Facebook page and found a post that she quickly deleted. He managed to retrieve it, and it said the first episode of her podcast would contain details about a teacher in Gloucester who took advantage of her, groomed her and raped her. She described the teacher, who was never reported to police, as now a grey-haired man with dark-framed glasses who stank of cigarettes.'

'Good God!' said Roscoe. 'That sounds like Dan Higley. Have you and John heard the podcast?'

She nodded. 'Yes, and it's grim listening, sir. Candy reveals her abuser had a gold band on the ring finger of his right hand and gives enough information for some listeners to be able to identify him – without actually naming him. Tiffany had been making the podcast with Candy and had been sworn to secrecy about it. But, fortunately, Tiffany realised its significance to our investigation and alerted us. Hepworth reckons that, by chance, Higley must be one of the few people to have read this deleted post about the podcast.'

'A very clear motive for murder,' said Roscoe. 'So we think Higley got in through the hotel's rear door, followed her up to her room and confronted her?'

'Yes, sir. It looks as if they argued and he strangled her.'

'Poor woman must have been terrified in those final moments,' said Roscoe. 'Of course, we also know Higley had a strong motive for killing his wife because of his money worries.'

She nodded.

'That wasn't all we unearthed,' Sunita continued. 'We also took a look at Miranda Higley's virtual assistant – you know, her Alexa device. Hepworth's got a contact who works at Amazon, and early yesterday, he put in a request for her latest data. Since her son, Barry, was jointly responsible for the account, we had all the passwords and permissions needed. Hepworth's contact came up trumps. He found a recording that proved Dan Higley visited Myrtle Cottage at around eleven o'clock in the morning on the day of the murder.'

'That's not what he told us,' said Roscoe. 'He only mentioned coming in the afternoon.'

'I know.'

'Why do you think the camera at the village shop didn't pick up his morning visit?'

'He probably knew about the CCTV, parked some distance away and walked up from the bottom of the lane to dodge the camera. Anyway, this recording, amazingly, shows Miranda was actually talking to Alexa when her husband showed up.'

'Can we hear that recording?' he asked.

'Yes,' she said, slipping her mobile phone from her pocket. 'I've got a copy of it here because I knew you'd want to listen to it. Miranda had asked Alexa to read her an email her son had sent regarding his weekend plans. She was in the throes of sending him a reply when she was disturbed by a knock on the door.'

The pair listened in silence after Sunita pressed the play-back button on her phone and the gentle tones of Miranda Higley echoed chillingly round the room.

> Alexa: *What would you like to do?*
> Miranda: *Reply.*
> Alexa: *What's your reply to Barry?*
> Miranda: *Hi Baz, What time on Saturday were you… Come in. I'm in the middle of something … What do you mean the divorce isn't happening? Have you been drinking? … Don't you dare … Take your hands off me. … Dan, you're hurting me–*
> Alexa: *Here is your reply.*

For a brief moment, Roscoe sat stunned in his office chair, gazing at his sergeant and shaking his head.

'So the recording ends there?' he asked.

'Yes, sir. Alexa didn't receive a response so the last words of Miranda Higley were kept in draft form in her email account. What appears to have happened is Dan snatched her mobile off the dresser in a rage and turned Alexa off.'

'He probably took the phone away after killing her,' Roscoe muttered. 'Sergeant, we need to get a warrant for his place in Evesham and get over there. I'll get Dawson to go to the court for one straight away. He can join us over there.'

He stood up from his desk.

'Well done, Sergeant,' he said. 'You've triumphed again.'

'Thank you, sir, but I was only following my intuition,' she replied modestly.

'I'm so glad you did. If only we had more detectives like you, Sergeant. After all our efforts interviewing countless suspects, it finally appears we're on top of things.'

Chapter 49

Daniel Higley was in a furious temper as he sat in the interview room at police headquarters after his arrest. He kept drumming his fingers on the table and staring out of the window morosely.

'I don't suppose the chief inspector will keep us too long,' said his solicitor, Dipak Sharma, a stout middle-aged man, who like Higley, wore glasses.

'They'd better not,' said Higley. 'They've got absolutely nothing on me. They treated me like dirt when they turned up at my flat this morning. I've got a good mind to write to the police complaints people.'

Sharma shook his head. 'They cautioned you about both murders?' he asked.

'Yes,' said Higley. 'As I told that woman DS Roy before lunch, there's no way I could have carried out either of them.'

'That sounds like them coming now,' said Sharma on hearing footsteps approaching outside.

'Sorry to keep you waiting,' said the chief inspector, stepping through the door with his sergeant, who was carrying a tablet computer. 'Just had a few loose ends to tie up. Sergeant, you know Mr Sharma, don't you?'

'Yes,' she said with a smile. 'We've met several times, haven't we?'

Sharma nodded. 'Mostly in here,' he muttered.

'I want to start by talking to you about Candy Goodhope – known in her school days as Candice Cosgrove,' said Roscoe. 'She had a problem with you, Mr Higley, didn't she?'

'No. Not to my knowledge. I taught her maths. End of story,' said Higley with a scowl.

'She was in the process of making a podcast about her early life,' said Sunita, 'and you came to know about it, didn't you?'

'No.'

'You knew more about Candy than most of the teachers because she nearly drowned on a school trip, and you were tasked with helping her and her family,' said Sunita. 'You found out at the start of May that she was making a podcast that would have proved extremely awkward for you. It accused you of sexual grooming and rape.'

'Don't be absurd,' Higley snapped back. 'I never behaved inappropriately to her in any way.'

'It just so happens we've got the full recording Candy made with her friend Tiffany. Here is part of it.'

She pressed a key on the tablet's keyboard. Suddenly Candy's velvety tones filled the room like a ghostly message from beyond.

> *I want to tell you about the lowest point in my life which happened when I was just a few weeks short of my seventeenth birthday. I had nearly drowned on a school trip abroad the year before. One of my teachers befriended me, along with my parents, over several months, and I felt he was someone I could trust. My life was at a low point, but he took advantage of me and had unprotected sex with me in his car against my will. I was too ashamed to say anything before.*

Now I'm planning to reveal some of the details. I'll tell you all about it in the second episode of this podcast.

'Mr Higley,' Sunita said, 'you found out on Facebook that Candy had made this recording because, for two days, she publicised it on her page.'

'Don't know anything about it,' he said.

Roscoe intervened. 'Your former teaching colleague, Steven Wimbush, told us how you spent a lot of time with Candy after she nearly died. It's obviously you she's talking about.'

'The girl was messed up in the head.'

'We believe you're the one who's messed up in the head,' said Roscoe. 'We believe you found out somehow – probably through social media – that she was staying at the Queensbridge Arms Hotel. You went over there on the evening of 6 May and strangled Candy to death to prevent her making these allegations against you public.'

'I was visiting my friends the Montgomerys in Abbots Green that Saturday afternoon.'

'That's funny,' said Roscoe. 'CCTV camera from a shop picked up your grey Volvo entering the hotel car park around six o'clock. Then we assume you did what a number of other members of the public have done – you waited for someone to use the back entrance with a keycard and closely followed them.'

Higley appeared shaken but said nothing in response. He placed his hands on the table in front of him. Then he noticed Sunita was staring at his hands.

'What's the matter?' he asked.

'Candy also says on her podcast that her abuser had a gold band on the ring finger of his right hand. You're wearing a gold ring,' said Sunita.

'What of it? It's my wedding ring,' he retorted.

'Why don't you wear it on your left hand like most people in the UK?' asked Roscoe.

'Just personal preference. I'm left-handed,' said Higley.

'We've got a witness who saw Candy being strangled by a man wearing just such a ring,' Sunita continued.

'Well, it bloody well wasn't me,' Higley fumed.

'I'd like to turn to the murder of your wife,' said Roscoe. 'You're probably aware that she had recently invested in an Amazon Echo device and that your stepson, Barry, had helped her set it up in Myrtle Cottage?'

'Yes, vaguely,' said Higley.

'Your wife was actually in the throes of asking Alexa to send Barry a message when you arrived at the cottage at around eleven o'clock on 11 May.'

'No. I told you before. I phoned in the morning and only went round in the afternoon, when I found the body.'

'You told us that before. But we've got evidence you were there in the morning at around eleven. And confirmation of this comes from your wife's own lips. Listen to this.'

For the second time in a matter of minutes, a softly spoken woman's voice filled the room in a poignant reminder of their passing.

> *What do you mean the divorce isn't happening? Have you been drinking? … Don't you dare … Take your hands off me … Dan, you're hurting me–*

'These words, which we've recovered from the Alexa device,' said Roscoe, 'were timed at around eleven o'clock – the time when we believe the attack was committed. What was it, Mr Higley, that made you murder your estranged wife in such a barbaric manner?'

'I wasn't there then,' said Higley. 'There must be some kind of mistake. These gadgets are notorious for getting things wrong.'

Roscoe stared across the table at the suspect.

'Mr Higley, I'm afraid the game's up. As you know, we searched your flat this morning. We've found a trace of blood on one of your shirts and on the steering wheel of your car. We're confident that, on testing, the samples will prove to come from your wife. We've also found the money you stole from Candy Goodhope and Miranda Higley was paid into your bank account in two separate payments.'

Higley stared at the detectives for a moment, then he sighed and dragged a hand over his eyes. 'Looks like you've got me all stitched up, then,' he said.

He gazed down at the beige lino on the floor, shaking his head.

'The other thing we haven't mentioned,' said Sunita, 'is that you don't have an alibi for the time of your wife's murder. Gill Montgomery says you simply dropped her off at the hospital, and you didn't stay. She had to get a taxi home.'

'You guys are very different from those kids I used to teach – Mark, Candy, Denise,' said Higley, in an unexpected change of tone.

'How do you mean?' asked Roscoe.

'They never did their homework,' said Higley. 'But it looks like you guys have. I'm very sad about Candy. We had a good thing going at one time, you know, and we loved each other.'

'Good God, man,' said Roscoe. 'She was more than twenty years younger.'

'I just went to her room to talk to her,' said Higley. Sharma tapped him on the shoulder, but Higley continued, 'I just want to say this. I saw her getting in the lift and watched it rise to the second floor. I got in the next lift and just arrived in time to see her fumbling for her keys and entering the room. I banged on the door and forced my way in to question her about the podcast. She said she wasn't going to mention me by name, but I couldn't take that chance.'

Sharma tapped Higley on the shoulder again and whispered in his left ear.

'I've just been advised to make no further comment,' said Higley, 'before I make matters any worse for myself.'

'You behaved with ruthless savagery towards both women,' said Roscoe. 'Candy Goodhope was a young woman in the prime of her life who was carving out a successful career for herself in the beauty business. Your wife was still in her late forties and, by all accounts, a talented home tutor besides being a pillar of the local community. Their horrified families will learn shortly that their lives were destroyed by you in a selfish display of barbarity.'

Roscoe then warned him he would be charged with both murders. Higley sneered but gave no reply.

Once the accused man had been taken down to the custody suite and Sharma had left, Roscoe sat in quiet contemplation in the interview room beside his sergeant.

'Amazing, isn't it, Sergeant?' he said. 'We had the guy under our noses all the time. Of course, I was always highly suspicious that he'd killed his own wife, as you know, but I'd never have ranked him as a suspect for the first murder. Thanks to you, we've got all the evidence we need to put before the CPS.'

'I must admit I had a few doubts at one stage about Higley's involvement in his wife's death,' she said.

'We're all entitled to have doubts, Sergeant,' he said. 'The fact is you've brought forward the crucial evidence so he can be charged with both murders. You've surpassed yourself this time, Sergeant.'

'It's kind of you to say that, but it was mainly a team effort, and I also had a bit of luck towards the end.'

'I've told you this before,' said Roscoe. 'You make your own luck in this game.'

Chapter 50

The chief inspector raised his glass to his lips after work on Friday evening. He took a sip of his favourite beer, QB Bitter, a medium-strength beer produced by the Queensbridge Brewery Company.

'Looking forward to the weekend, guv?' asked Tom Vickers as he joined him at the table in the Golden Fleece, the CID's regular pub which was close to their office in St James Street.

'Yes. I'm taking Helen away for a few days.'

'That'll be great,' said Vickers, taking a swig of his lager.

'Early tomorrow morning, we're setting off for that hotel in Bournemouth where we stayed before. It's taken a bit of arranging, but I'm in Norris's good books after we cracked three cases simultaneously.'

The inspector frowned.

'How do you make it three, guv?' he asked.

'The two murders and the insurance plot,' said Roscoe.

'Of course. Have you heard any more from Merseyside?'

'Yes. They called me this afternoon. Brendon Blake and Hannah Griffin are due in court next week on fraud charges. There's been a lot of excitement about the case in the press, of course, which has caused no end of problems up there. Griffin's ex-husband has sold his exclusive story to one of the Sunday papers about his own take on his ex-brother-in-law's return from the dead.'

'It strikes me Blake and his sister both deserve to be sent down for a long time,' said Vickers. 'And what about Dan Higley?'

'Did you hear about the blood on Higley's khaki shirt and on his Volvo's steering wheel?'

'No, guv.'

'They were proved positive for Miranda Higley's DNA. We also found Dan's DNA among scrapings from his wife's fingernails.'

'Brilliant.'

'He's been remanded to appear at the Crown Court in August.'

'So I heard, guv.'

'Where's the sergeant got to?' asked Roscoe, gazing around the busy, open-plan pub. 'She told me earlier she'd be coming over.'

'Sunita called me a few minutes ago,' Vickers replied. 'She'll be here any time now.'

Roscoe leaned back in his seat. He glanced around at the noisy horde of early evening customers gathering in front of them. Four women from the headquarters' civil staff arrived, gossiping and giggling, and commandeered the table next to them.

He had long regarded Vickers as a close confidant, and he was impressed by the positive effect his sergeant had had upon him. He once wore crumpled clothes while going through marriage turmoil. But, in recent times, Sunita had had a calming influence, encouraging him to dress more smartly.

'All right, guv?' asked the inspector. 'You seemed a million miles away then.'

Roscoe laughed.

'Sorry, Tom, I was. I was just thinking what a great influence the sergeant's had on you. I remember those days when you slept in the office sometimes and looked like your shirt had had an argument with your trousers.'

Now, it was Vickers' turn to laugh.

'Yes. Fortunately for me, I met Sunita and, although we had a couple of false starts, we're now happily together.'

'I was also wondering if we'd see George and Brett Dawson,' muttered Roscoe.

'I thought they might be joining us. Ah, this looks like someone now.'

Sunita Roy's puzzled face appeared in the doorway. Then, on recognising her colleagues at the corner table, her eyes lit up, and she made her way towards them.

'Let me get this,' said Roscoe, standing up and searching for his wallet in his trouser pocket.

'Thank you very much, sir. Just an orange juice, please,' she said with a beaming smile.

She bent down to kiss Vickers as she joined him on the bench seat while the chief inspector crossed the modern pub and joined a queue at the bar.

Once Roscoe had returned with two freshly filled pint glasses and Sunita's juice, her boss asked about the two constables.

'They won't be coming,' she said, taking a sip of her drink.

'Oh, what's happened?' asked Roscoe.

'They've both gone to a snooker club,' she explained.

'A snooker club?'

'Yes, Brett's only just joined, and George showed interest in going along.'

'I thought they weren't on speaking terms,' said Roscoe.

She nodded.

'Apparently, they've made it up. Brett was impressed by the way George caught Mark Tanner, and they're suddenly big pals.'

Roscoe took a sip from his second pint and shook his head.

'Well, I'm not often stuck for words, but this looks like one of those occasions,' he said. 'Before you came in, Sergeant, we were talking about Dan Higley.'

'I've just been working on the finances of the case,' Sunita admitted. 'That's why I've been a little late getting over here. Higley's reason for taking money from both women is clearer to understand now. There's been cash-flow problems at the charity where he works, and this has cut his personal income. There were lots of bills among the unopened post at his home, and he had an overdraft at the bank.'

'You can see why he was fighting the divorce.'

'Yes,' said Sunita. 'His wife was apparently demanding that she should retain the cottage and was being extremely difficult towards him in the divorce proceedings. He's been moaning to the custody sergeant about having to go cap in hand to his estranged wife and begging to be allowed to renovate their garden room so he could earn a little money.'

'Taking all that into account,' said Roscoe, 'you can begin to understand how Higley was becoming a desperate man, worried about his future. But thousands of men in Britain find themselves, from time to time, in similar tough financial straits, Sergeant. And they don't all go out and murder their wife in a search for a solution. Equally, if events in your past catch up with you – something which happened to both Higley and Brendon Blake – you face up to them. You don't feign death or commit murder.'

He took a sip from his beer. 'Higley was a highly dangerous, selfish man who posed a significant risk to women. There's no excuse for what he did.'

Sunita nodded in agreement before speaking out with her own thoughts.

'The way I'd like to remember this case,' she said, 'is that the killer's been brought to justice thanks to testimony left behind by the victims themselves.'

'Voices from the dead, you mean?'

'Yes, sir. Voices from the dead.'

THE END

The Book Folks & Joffe Books Story

The Book Folks began in 2013, founded by Erik Empson with a simple but powerful goal — to publish highly readable, compelling fiction that readers would love. With a focus on crime fiction, thrillers and gripping mysteries, The Book Folks quickly built a loyal audience and became known for championing talented authors from the UK, Ireland, the US and beyond.

From gritty police procedurals and psychological thrillers to fast-paced action and suspense, The Book Folks earned a reputation for curating addictive stories at affordable prices — often introducing readers to hidden gems and breakout talent.

In 2025, The Book Folks proudly became part of Joffe Books, the UK's largest independent publisher. Joffe Books started in 2014 when Jasper Joffe published his mum's long-rejected romance novel — which unexpectedly became a bestseller. That spirit of risk-taking and reader-first publishing has defined Joffe Books ever since.

Together, Joffe Books and The Book Folks are united by a passion for page-turning fiction and a deep respect for the authors who create it. We're proud to publish some of the best-loved names in fiction — including Joy Ellis, Faith Martin, Caro Ramsay, Simon Brett, Helen Forrester, and Robert Goddard — as well as fresh voices bringing new energy to the genre.

We never forget that everything begins with the author's story — and that continues with you, the reader.

We love hearing from you, so get in touch any time at feedback@joffebooks.com.

And if you'd like to receive free books and hear about our latest releases, sign up to our newsletter:
www.joffebooks.com/freebooks

Thanks for reading — and for being part of our story.

www.thebookfolks.com

Printed in Dunstable, United Kingdom

73046245R00163